JOCELYNE SOTO

Posting "certain types" of pictures online is never a good idea. Especially when you're the star player of your college football team.

But I did it anyway.

Never did I think that by posting my pictures online that I would find someone that I would actually be interested in.

But I did.

I saw her pictures, she commented on mine and the conversations were nonstop. She was the girl of my dreams and I wanted to meet her. Who knew that the girl of my dreams was the shy girl that sat next to me all semester?

Now that I know who she is, I want my shot. Only if she would give it to me. Every chance she gets, I get turned down, but I'm not giving up.

I will show her that she is worth it, even if she may not think so.

Para Mi Madre
Mis Hermanas
Mis Sobrinas
Y para yo misma.

AUTHOR NOTE

This book touches upon the subject of childhood sexual abuse. Some scenes are explained in detail.
If that is something that you are not comfortable with, please do not read.
If you would like more information, please follow the QR code below. Thank you.

PROLOGUE
TWELVE YEARS EARLIER

THERE IS a coldness in the air that I don't like.

I feel it every time I set foot in this house. Sure, at times love fills it, but the love is always overpowered by the cold.

Cold that I feel down to my bones.

Even when I feel the ice against my skin, I act as if I'm happy to be here. I act as if what happens in other parts of this house doesn't terrify me.

As long as I act like everything is okay and I'm here, playing, everything will be.

Right?

No, but I will keep telling myself that until I believe it.

I hear my mom's voice in the other room as she talks to my grandma and my aunt. She had sent my dad to the store, so he will be back soon. The sooner he comes back, the closer we are to driving home.

The closer I am to no longer being in this cold house. Feeling the coldness against me.

I continue to move the cars against the cement floor. Even

if I'm ten years old, the cars are the only thing grabbing my attention right now.

Anything is better than sitting around and just waiting for the terrifying parts to come out.

Even with the sound of my mother's laughter and the little car's wheels sliding against the floor, I hear the footsteps.

Footsteps that sound light. Footsteps that should sound heavy, especially with all the weight that comes with it.

I don't look up. I just keep my eyes on the movements of the car. Then the footsteps come closer and stop a few inches away from where my leg sits. When I see the boots, the car rolling on the floor no longer has my attention, even if I wanted it to. No, my eyes may be on the car, but my attention is fully on the pair of boots that have arrived.

Swallowing down the urge to cry out for my mother, I look up and see a pair of brown eyes. A pair of eyes that weren't the same ones that terrified me, but they still looked the same.

Does this set of brown eyes know what the other pair does?

By the way the owner of the pair of boots crouches down to my eye level and the way the smile on his face forms, I know the answer.

He knows.

But is he going to stop it?

"I have a new video game upstairs. Do you want to see it? Play with it if you want?"

I like video games.

My sister has one at her house and whenever I spend the night, she lets me play.

But he said upstairs.

That's not where the bad stuff happens, but it's still a place I don't spend a whole lot of time in when I'm here. My dad always said to stay on the main floor since the room we always slept in was down here.

I should listen to him.

I should stay down here.

But I don't want to continue playing with the little car and besides the video game could be fun.

So I nod. I nod and push myself off the floor and follow him upstairs.

I walk behind him, the stairs creaking along the way.

The whole house creaks and the sound just adds to the coldness of it. It's so unwelcoming, I hate it.

But I still walk through the house like I love every single second of it.

As we reach the second floor and he guides me to the closed door at the end of the hall, I hear my mother's voice. My grandmother's.

The closer I get to the door, the more their voices grow distant.

It's the creaking of the door opening that takes my attention away from the voices and back to why I'm up here in the first place.

The video game.

He gives me a smile when he opens the door and waves me in.

I give him a small one back as I walk into the room, feeling uncomfortable the second that I do.

He walks in behind me, closing the door.

My eyes wander around the room, seeing the mess that it

5

is. There are clothes everywhere, boxes on top of more boxes. The room looks like it should belong on that show I see on TV all the time about people that don't throw away their trash.

I stay standing by the door as he walks deeper into the room and goes to stand by the bed.

He waves for me to come closer, and I do.

As I walk over to him, I see that there isn't a TV in here. Nothing to play the video game on.

"Do you want to sit?"

No, but I sit anyway.

He stays standing, coming closer to me, making me want to be downstairs with my mom.

"He told me what he did to you."

I look up at him when he says those words, but still, I don't say anything.

I saw on his face earlier that he knew, but is he going to stop it? Is that why he brought me up here?

"He told me you liked it, so I thought I would see how true that was."

No, he isn't going to stop it. I should have known that. I shouldn't have believed him when he told me that there was a video game.

I want to cry.

I want to scream.

I want my dad to come back so that we can leave.

"Lie back. Unbutton your pants."

As much as I don't want to listen, I do exactly what he says.

He watches my movements and once I'm lying on my

back with the button on my jeans popped, he comes even closer.

My eyes stay on his hands and follow all his motions. I watch as he takes off my pants and then when he moves to lower his.

I watch as he reaches into his underwear and takes out the thing that all boys have.

I watch until he leans forward, and I feel his skin against mine. When he touches me, that's when I close my eyes.

I close my eyes and do not move.

Maybe if I don't move, he will stop.

Maybe if I don't scream out for my mom, I won't get in trouble for coming upstairs.

Maybe if I think about the daisy I saw on the wall before I closed my eyes, all the fear I have will go away.

So that's what I do.

I continue to stay still, with my eyes closed and not say a word. Not even when it's over.

I hate this house and all the terrifying things that come with it.

CHAPTER ONE

HUNTER

Present Day

THE MUSIC IS POUNDING, vibrating through the whole house. The floorboards are shaking from all the sound, the same sound that isn't letting my ears register any of the conversations that are happening around me.

Not that I care what the people surrounding me are saying. I don't give a flying fuck about them and their stupid conversations.

No, my attention isn't on what is being spoken, it's on the couple that is currently making out in the corner of the room.

Usually, things like this don't capture my attention, but this time it did.

The couple may think that being surrounded by darkness nobody will notice who they are. Or maybe they think that people will just look the other way and pay them no regard.

But I paid them regard.

I noticed.

I noticed and saw red.

Of course I fucking noticed. How could I not? Especially when the female in the couple is my goddamn girlfriend, Jenna.

Yes, girlfriend. Who I haven't seen in weeks, but just because I haven't seen her since July, doesn't mean that I forgot what she looked like.

How she styles her hair.

Or better yet, the way the set of stackable rings I gave her for her birthday in June shined in the light.

I know every fucking inch of her, of her body, and I have for three years, of course I'm going to goddamn notice her making out with someone that isn't me.

Especially when it's someone that is supposed to have my back on the football field. Someone that is supposed to be my best friend. My fucking teammate. A brother off and on the field.

I don't know what pisses me off more, the fact that Jenna is cheating on me, or the fact that she is cheating with someone I thought I was close to.

At this very moment, I can't think of an answer. I can't think about anything.

The only thing I can concentrate on is the two of them swallowing each other's tongues, and trying my damned hardest not to beat the shit out of something.

I shouldn't have come to this stupid party.

The only reason that I'm here, at a party celebrating the end of summer before school starts back up again on Monday, was to see her.

I had missed her.

I missed my fucking girlfriend and it had come to the

point that phone calls weren't enough anymore. I needed to lay eyes on her, feel her in my hands.

So when Jenna had told me that she was coming to a party at the Alpha Rho house tonight, I thought I would surprise her.

Training camp had ended a day earlier, and since she knew I was supposed to arrive back on campus tomorrow, I thought it would be the perfect surprise.

I pictured her smile. I pictured the way her eyes would brighten up when she laid eyes on me after weeks apart.

But I guess I'm the one getting the fucking surprise tonight. Just my fucked-up luck.

Shaking my head, I finally abandoned my spot by the door, finishing the beer that was handed to me by one of my teammates, and head over to the happy couple.

A few people stand in the way, but after shoving the drunk ones to the side and walking around the sober ones, I make it to them.

The second I see where Jaxton's my good for nothing best friend hand is, I see the darkest red possible. The fucking bastard has one hand in Jenna's hair and the other under her skirt and by the way it's moving I can only guess what the fuck he is doing.

And in front of the whole fucking frat house.

How nobody is seeing what is happening is beyond me. I'm getting humiliated and no one gives a shit.

If I wasn't boiling already, I would be now.

"You know, Jenna, I never thought that you were one to be open to voyeurism," I throw out there, completely surprised at the calmness that laces my voice.

I'm anything but calm.

At my words, Jenna's eyes pop open and as soon as she sees me standing right next to them, she pulls away from Jaxton.

Surprise coats her face, but that's it. There isn't an ounce of remorse for her actions anywhere in her facial expression or even in her eyes. There is a hint of fear though, so that's something.

"Hunter, what are you doing here?" Seriously? "You're not supposed to be here until tomorrow." There is a shakiness to her voice, most likely the fear, but still no remorse anywhere in her expression for getting caught.

I resist the urge to roll my eyes at the girl that I thought was my everything for the past three years.

I can't help but wonder if she has been faithful at all during that time.

"Yeah, well the camp ended early and I thought I would surprise my girlfriend," I say through gritted teeth. If we weren't in public right now, I would be going ballistic on her, but I'm trying hard to rein it in.

"Jacobi, it's not what it looks like," Jaxton throws out, getting between me and Jenna.

From the looks of it, he's a lot more remorseful about me finding them in a compromising situation than Jenna is. Go fucking figure.

I move slightly closer to Jaxton, coming toe-to-toe with him, only an inch in height separating us. "So it didn't look like you had your tongue down my girlfriend's throat and your hand on her pussy? During a fucking frat party?"

His face becomes a shade of red that resembles a tomato with a hint of nervousness, like he's afraid I'm about to beat the shit out of him. You would think the asshole would have some balls and instead of standing there scared, he would be defending their actions.

But looking directly into his eyes, I can see that he feels bad about what they were doing.

"I'm sorry, man. This isn't how I wanted to tell you."

Wanted to tell me?

Is he shitting me right now?

He wanted to tell me that he was fucking my girlfriend? Was he going to do it over dinner or something?

"You wanted to tell me? You wanted to sit me down and tell me that you were screwing my girl behind my back and have me be okay with it?" I watch as he swallows, but his eyes never waver from me. "How fucking long has this been going on?" I growl through my teeth, feeling my hands form into fists and getting ready to punch something.

"It doesn't matter," Jenna mutters from behind Jaxton, flipping her dirty-blonde hair back.

"Like fuck it doesn't. How fucking long Jenna?!" I'm yelling. I'm yelling at the one person that I thought I would never raise my voice at but yet here I am. I'm yelling at her and she is looking at me like I'm wasting her time.

"Since you left," Jenna answers, stepping around Jaxton and coming to stand right in front of me.

Her lipstick is messed up and her hair is a bit of a mess, but she doesn't care. She stands only a few inches

from me with her shoulders pushed back and the same indifference from earlier coating her face.

"You left me. I had to find someone to keep me warm at night," she purrs, coming close enough that I can feel the whisper of the words against my skin.

"Jenna," Jaxton warns, trying to pull her back. Like I

13

would do something stupid like lay a finger on her. I wouldn't. Him on the other hand, that's a different story.

"I went to training camp, not break up with you. It wasn't even my choice, and you knew I was going to come back."

It was my dad's "suggestion" for me to spend my summer in an elite football camp. Because according to him, that's what's needed to get NFL scouts to notice me, for NFL teams to draft me. I couldn't care less about either of those possibilities.

"And you know I have needs." She shrugs.

So much for being loyal to each other.

Has she always been this bitchy? Has she never really cared about me and what we had? The more I stand here looking at her, the more I think that I was just her meal ticket.

Un-fucking-believable.

I nod at her statement, and I try to collect myself as best as I can before I say anything.

Never taking my glare off the girl that I thought I was going to have at my side through it all, I say exactly what I know I want to say.

"Fuck you." I point at Jenna and then I turn to her little fuck buddy, or whatever the fuck he is to her. Jaxton still looks like he is trying not to shit his pants. "And fuck you. You both can burn in hell."

Turning, ignoring the people around us that have now figured out something was going on, I head straight to the door and beeline out of this hellhole.

I really shouldn't have come to this fucked-up party in this shithole they call a house.

"Hunt, hold up!" I hear Jaxton's voice behind me, through the music.

Of course, it's him following me out and not Jenna.

I ignore my so-called friend and continue to walk straight to my truck.

"Jacobi, you got to listen to me. Please," Jax begs as I reach the driver's side door.

With one hand on the handle and my keys digging their way into the other, I take as much of a deep breath as I can before turning to face him.

His facial expression is similar to the one that he wore inside, except this time it's filled with a lot more remorse than it was before. I just don't know if that remorse is because he got caught or because he feels bad for what he did.

We stand there for a good second just staring at each other, before he speaks. "Jenna told me you guys were done. If I had known that you two were still together, I wouldn't have done anything."

I guess that's my confirmation that Jenna Bryan doesn't give a shit and a half about me or what I thought we had.

I face my "friend" head-on. "A text. A fucking text message would have given you the answer you needed. A single fucking text to me and I would have told you we were still together. But no, you decided to go behind my back and fuck her. Some friend you are."

My fist is wrapped around my keys so hard that I'm sure that there will be blood when I release the tension.

Jax continues to look at me until he finally nods his head and drops it between his shoulder blades.

"I should have done that. I just didn't think. I'm sorry you had to find out this way."

I guess the friendship we've built these last few years wasn't as strong as I thought.

Just like my relationship.

"Like I said inside." I opened the car door a little too aggressively. "Fuck you and fuck her. I don't want shit to do with either of you."

I slam the door shut and Jax is left there dumbfounded as I pull out of the parking spot I was somehow able to find in front of the house.

I guess being the star quarterback of a division one school has its perks.

People leave parking spaces for you to take and your girlfriend decides that your dick isn't enough for her and goes after your teammates.

Yeah, being the star player is fucking peachy.

All I demand is respect and if I can't get that from the people that are closest to me, then who?

Shaking my head, I try to throw the last half hour out of my mind, at least until I get to my place and put all my anger into a punching bag.

The twenty-minute drive from the Alpha Rho house to my apartment goes by in a blur. I don't even remember crossing into this side of campus.

I pull into my parking space and slam my head against the headrest as soon as I turn off the engine.

How the fuck did I not see this coming?

They've been seeing each other since I left and I'm just now finding out about it? Nobody on this huge ass campus thought that I should know that this was going on? Because I'm sure someone has seen them together a time or two.

The thing that throws me off the most is that Jenna and I would talk almost every night, and not once did I think that she was capable of something like this. Of cheating on me and still acting like she missed me and loved me whenever we talked.

In the three years that we have been together, has she always been like this?

No, she was sweet and caring, but what if that was just an act?

This whole situation is frustrating the hell out of me.

I wonder how many other women are out there that are just like her. Conniving and feeling no remorse at all.

I slam my head a few more times against the seat before finally deciding to head inside.

But once I'm inside my apartment, it's no better. There are signs of Jenna everywhere.

Her blanket.

Her pictures.

The sweater that she left back in June before I left.

Things I was perfectly fine with being here this morning, but now I want to burn everything to a crisp.

Ignoring everything, I head to my room and throw myself on the bed.

After a few minutes of wallowing in self-pity, I roll over and slide my phone out of my pocket.

Look at that, a few calls and texts from some of my teammates. I guess news has already started to spread.

You know what's not on the screen?

A call from Jenna. Or even a message.

Go figure. I guess I shouldn't have been so blind to the evil bitch that she really is.

Ignoring the calls and texts, I open my web browser and type a question into the search engine.

How to get over a bitch that cheated on you?

It's stupid, I know but hey, I need a distraction. I need something to take my mind off going back to the party and beating the shit out of Jax. What better way to do that than to look through sob stories of guys that have gone through the same thing?

No way is any answer that I find going to be helpful.

Within seconds, there are thousands of results on my screen.

I click on one of the first links that takes me to a forum on a site called HEX, where someone asked my exact question.

Perfect.

Reading through the post, I cringe a little at the pain that this guy exudes as he talks about what the girl did to him.

Damn. Dude was not only cheated on, but it was with his own cousin. That has to be rough.

I continue to scroll until I reach the comment section. Scrolling through the hundreds of comments this post has, I don't find anything helpful. All I read are comments from people that say things like fuck the girl's friend, or her sister. I wouldn't do either.

One person even suggested public humiliation, and since that's what got me here, I scroll past that suggestion. And I continue to scroll past everything else until one comment captures my attention.

StevStev0064 told the original poster that he should do something to boost his confidence. To look past all the shit that the girl put him through and to find a community that will hype him up and can give him the confidence he lost when the girl left him, back.

That's not bad advice at all. I would have told someone the same thing.

One thing that throws me off about StevStevoo64's comment is the suggestion that the poster become part of a community on the platform that people go to share pictures. Show people what this girl messed with.

My curiosity gets the best of me, and I click on the page the person linked and I'm directly taken to a page called *Confidence NSFW*. Right away I see so many posts of strangers posting pictures of their bodies.

Very naked bodies.

I shouldn't be surprised by all the nudity I'm seeing, especially with NSFW in the name.

But fuck, there's a guy's dick staring back at me. A fucking warning would have been good.

I won't lie though, the dude has a nice dong and I'm sure he doesn't have his girl looking in other places for pleasure.

Fuck.

What the fuck am I doing?

Why am I currently scrolling through pictures of naked women and men?

I don't have confidence issues.

I'm Hunter fucking Jacobi for crying out loud. The star quarterback for California University, one of the top division one schools in the Western Conference. Girls fawn over me and guys wish they were me every time they walk past me.

I never once doubted myself before, no way am I going to be doing that shit now

My thumb is about to press down on the lock button when one of the captions on a post stops me.

Of course the caption is attached to a picture of a guy with his dick in his hand, but I ignore that and concentrate on the caption.

You're confident on the outside, but how is that working for you on the inside?

Well, shit.

It only took fifteen words on a random stranger's post to make me realize that everything that happened with Jenna and Jaxton, not only filled me with rage but made me lose a bit of self-assurance.

Why cheat?

And why with my best friend? Out of all the people on this campus, hell in this city, why my fucking friend that has been in my life just as long as she has?

The more I think about it, the more I see that Stev-Stevoo64 is right. The confidence I have has been shot and I need to boost myself up.

Is putting a nude online the way to go, though?

I mull it over for a few seconds and before I know it, I'm pushing myself off the bed and discarding my clothes.

What better way of getting your confidence up than by posting a picture a bunch of people are going to fawn over? Because they will fawn over it, I know they will.

I go to my bathroom and snap the picture and the whole time I'm thinking only one thing.

Fuck you, Jenna.

CHAPTER TWO

SELENA

JUST SEND IT.

Just send the stupid text message.

Hit send and do your part.

If he doesn't respond, he doesn't respond. You would have done your part by reaching out and him not texting back is on him and not you.

Just send the damn message!

Stop being a chickenshit, Selena!

I close my eyes, hover my thumb over the blue arrow and press down. When I hear the swish sound that signifies the message has left my phone, my eyes finally pop open.

It's sent. I sent the overly long, and stupid message.

Holy crap.

My heart is pounding as I throw my phone on my bed, not wanting anything to do with it.

I don't know why I do this to myself. I don't know why when it comes to situations like this with guys, I overthink every little thing.

For example, if he doesn't text me for four days straight? I automatically think he's ghosting me.

He doesn't want to go to the beach with me and play arcade games when I suggest it? I think he's overly busy with work and we will go next time I bring it up.

He only wants to see me when it's convenient for him? I think there is someone else and he's just using me.

It's the last one that triggered where I am right now, chewing on my nails, looking at my phone sitting on my bed as if it were a bomb, waiting for it to ding.

Here's a little backstory about my current situation. About three months ago, I matched with this guy on a dating app. We hit it off from the very beginning. He was funny and cute and after a few nights of talking through texts, we went out on our first date.

It was my first real date and at the end of it I had this huge smile on my face. Happy that I had finally gotten the courage to put myself out there, especially after everything this life has decided to throw at me.

After that first date, me and this guy continued talking and hanging out, and after a month, I thought that we were progressing in a certain direction. In the direction of *more*. Relationship and sex, type of more.

A girl has needs, okay?

We continued to see each other, and by see each other, I mean I would head over to his place late at night and we'd fool around. And that's it.

We'd go to his room, watch TV, make out and go to second base, but nothing more. I asked one night if he was comfortable going further and he told me yes, but that at the time he couldn't see us doing much other than what we were currently doing. To give him time.

I didn't know exactly what he meant about the whole not seeing us doing much and I didn't have the guts to ask. So I dropped it and gave him time.

That should have been my first red flag.

The second red flag should have popped up when our communication started to dwindle.

After two months, I started to question everything.

I started to question it more when my text would go unanswered for days or when my invitations to hang out outside of his apartment were turned down.

That's when my emotions started to go haywire and my mind went to overthinking overload. The current state it's in.

I had never been in this position with a guy before, and it pissed me off.

Was he not answering my text because he was busy? Or was I being overly annoying? Was I forcing whatever was happening between us and now he was ghosting me for real? Or the biggest question of them all, was I being too clingy? Was sending a text message to check in once a week too much? Or worse yet, did he not find me attractive anymore after he spent time with me?

I shake my head at the last one.

I did ask if I was being clingy, because that's something I don't want to be, and you want to know what happened? The text went unanswered.

That's when the crying started.

I was being ghosted after two months. Two months filled with planning future dates, excitement and possibilities and bam ghosted.

Look, I understand ghosting after two days or even two weeks.

But after two months? After you develop some sort of connection? Now that's just bullshit.

If a guy no longer wants to see me, just fucking tell me. Tell me how you feel, have a conversation with me and then maybe I wouldn't want to sneak into your apartment and Lorena Bobbitt, you because you fucking made me feel worthless of even a text.

If a man wants to be a coward and ghost someone that has been in his life for more than two months, then that's what he deserves.

Geez, Selena. Bring it down a notch or two.

I close my eyes and take a deep breath, trying to calm myself down as much as possible.

Once I'm calm, I sit on my bed, grabbing my phone in the process.

Being ghosted like this fucking sucks, and I'm starting to get angry at him for making me feel like I'm a piece of shit and angry at myself for caring so much.

I got my feelings involved and my hopes up, okay? But I deserve fucking better.

I've spent all week planning out a text to send him. A week filled with so many thoughts about me not being worthy.

I even wrote out texts in my notes until I was finally happy with one that I could send.

The text I was finally happy with...

. . .

ME: **It's okay, you know... If you aren't feeling this anymore, it's okay to call it. There won't be any hard feelings. Just tell me so I don't keep trying to take up your time.**

Nice and straightforward.

Now that I've sent it, all there is to do is wait and see if he texts back.

He most likely won't, given that he hasn't answered anything from me in the last two weeks.

I think a part of me is okay with the fact that he won't text back. I did my part, now I have to see if he's man enough to do his.

And if he's not then fuck him. I don't need that shit in my life.

Fuck, why is dating so damn frustrating? Why can't it be all hunky-dory like it is in the movies and in romance books? Why does it have to be so damn emotionally draining?

I hate putting myself out there.

As an introverted person, I hate starting a conversation with someone in fear that they may consider me annoying, or worse, too needy. Case in point, this.

You would think that coming from a big Mexican family that is filled with social butterflies, that I would be able to not only start a conversation with someone, but to also date.

Maybe the reason I can't figure out dating is because I scare men away.

Is it possible for a twenty-two-year-old undergraduate student in her fifth year of college to scare men away?

Yes, yes, it is. I'm most likely going to die alone with fifty billion cats.

I throw myself back onto the bed, throw my phone back down before grabbing a pillow and letting out a scream.

Can't have my mom barging in while I'm having an emotional meltdown about a boy.

Am I really not worth a simple text? Just a few words that say, "hey, I don't see this going anywhere, let's end it." would suffice.

The more I think about it, the more I feel the burning at the back of my eyes.

I know I am worth more than this, I have to be but this whole thing is making me doubt every little thing about myself and I hate it.

I hate this.

I hate men.

Well, I hate some men. The ones that are assholes and make you feel unworthy.

Throwing the pillow on the floor, I reach for my phone again when my hand freezes.

Ding.

Ding.

I look at the device, waiting to hear any more dings. After about a minute, no more sounds come from the rectangular object.

But yet I don't move to grab it.

It has to be him, right?

Who else would text me close to midnight?

It's definitely not my sisters.

It has to be him.

Letting out a breath that I didn't know I was holding, I finally move my hand and grab my phone, keeping the screen facing down.

There are so many scenarios running through my head right now, and as much as I want to cry, I don't.

"You can do it, Selena. Turn the phone over and be done with all the crying."

Taking a deep breath, I flip the phone over in my hand and with my eyes closed, I tap on the screen.

One deep breath.

Two.

I open my eyes and there staring back at me, mocking me is two texts from *him*.

Of course he would answer this text and not the others.

Rolling my eyes, I unlock the screen and read the messages.

Scott: **Sorry.**

Scott: **Yeah, let's call it. You live a little far from me to make anything work.**

What in the actual fuck?

Live a little far? Dude, I'm a thirty-minute drive away from your apartment, and that's on a bad day. And I'm the one that drove to him all the time! That's a shit-ass excuse.

Live a little too far my fucking ass. This is what I get for swiping on someone that's two years older and wasn't a college student.

I should tell him to go fuck himself but I don't. Instead I answer with something generic and block the fucker's number and delete the text thread.

I don't need this type of shit in my life and I cried over the fuckhole.

If I told my dad about this bastard that I actually considered going into a relationship with, he would call me a *pendeja*. Honestly, I would have agreed with him.

Uh, I seriously can't believe I spent days crying over this *pendejo*. Now I'm more pissed off and over it than I am sad.

It fucking hurts, don't get me wrong, but I'm over it and it hasn't even been a full five minutes.

Men seriously suck.

I think I'm going to quit dating and dating apps for a while. I don't need a man. Although, it would be nice to not do things by myself all the time but seriously, I don't need a man at this point.

What I need is a book, Netflix playing in the background and a warm *concha* to take the pain away.

As I push myself off my bed, ready to do just that, another notification comes in but this time it isn't a text message.

Looking at the screen, I see that it's a notification from HEX, an app that I haven't used in months.

Sometime last year, I was looking for pictures for an inspiration board for a book that I was reading. I wasn't finding what I was looking for so I decided to randomly type the word DILF into Google and well, I was met with DILFS alright, naked ones. I should have expected that but it never crossed my mind. One of the pictures caught my attention because I had seen the same one, only cropped, on a dating app a few weeks back. So what did I do? I click on the damn picture of course and got taken to a site known as HEX.

It's like a version of Reddit but this one is geared more toward eighteen-to-forty-year-olds. Anyway, somehow with one click I went down the rabbit hole of groups, communities, and pages of nakedness. After about an hour or so, I closed it down because it somehow felt wrong.

Yet the next morning, I couldn't stop thinking about it.

I went back and started to look at the post that people were putting out there a little differently. I wasn't seeing them as invading people's privacy or as porn. It was more like awe and admiration. People that were comfortable with their bodies and confident with themselves had balls to put it all out there.

So I made an account and I started interacting with people. At first it was just commenting on random pictures of women, hyping them up and complimenting them on their appearance. Even telling a few that I wanted to have their confidence one day.

Look, just because I'm straight doesn't mean that I can't appreciate a woman's body. Some of the women that post on this app are hot as fuck and I'm confident enough in my own sexuality to be able to admit that.

After a while, I started to comment on the men's posts as well. These people didn't know me, so a guy with a six-pack wouldn't care that a girl like me was complimenting his body or his forearm porn.

Somehow through all the interactions, I made a few

29

friends along the way. Friends that I would just talk to about the most random shit. Sure, it was just through messaging but in that moment, that was enough, and it felt good. It was these friends that encouraged me to finally post a picture of myself.

It scared me.

I'm not a small girl, not big either, but somewhere in the middle. With clothes, my body looks like just the average body of a woman that possibly has a small tummy, but without clothes is a different story. My stomach hangs and there are stretch marks in a few places.

I have always been insecure about my body and how it looks when naked. Sure there have been times, like when I was fooling around with Scott that I was okay with my naked body.

But those moments have been far and few.

Of course I was scared about sharing it.

With my body insecurities, it freaked me out that I was actually considering posting a picture of myself, a nude picture at that, online for everyone to see.

But I pushed that feeling to the side and took a picture of just my breasts pushed together. Once I edited out any identifying features, I liked the picture that was staring back at me.

I posted it.

Within an hour, it had hundreds of comments and likes from both women and men. To say that wasn't a confidence booster, I would be lying.

I liked it, so I kept taking pictures of myself and posting them. I liked the feeling that it gave me. It was like a form of liberation.

With each passing post, I would reveal more, until I was showing everything, and I mean everything. Ass, tits, pussy. Everything was out for random people on the internet to see.

But of course, with posting those types of pictures, comes the unwanted messages. The people telling you that you should show more or the ones telling you what they would like to do to you.

Did I engage in those conversations? Sometimes. But I always stopped it when it became uncomfortable for me.

I did this for a few weeks and in that time, I was able to see myself differently and I liked it. But it started to become boring and too repetitive, so I stopped posting. Stopped engaging. Stopped the sexual conversations I was having with strangers.

I never deleted the account even though I took the pictures down. It's still there and occasionally I will get the random notification.

But the notification that I just got is one I haven't seen in a while.

It's a message.

Nobody messages me here anymore, especially since I have no pictures up.

My curiosity gets the best of me and when I open the app, I see that it's a message from one of the girls that I would always talk to.

She was my main hype woman when it came to my pictures, always commenting about how good I looked. Since I stopped posting, I hear from her occasionally.

I open her message and I see that it's a link to someone's post on *Confidence NSFW*.

The community I always frequented.

. . .

EVERLIES99: I thought you would like this one. Reminds me of those book boyfriends of yours ;)

I shouldn't have told her I like reading romance books.

Sighing, I click on the picture to see exactly why she thought I would "like" it.

The second the picture pops up, I can see why.

Holy abs Batman.

This man is fucking ripped, and the longer I stare at him the more I wonder if this man is even real.

No way a man in real life actually looks like this. No wonder the girl that sent me the picture said it would remind me of a book boyfriend.

I wouldn't mind for this book boyfriend to jump out of the pages, that's for sure.

He's definitely a man made for fiction.

There are so many pieces to the picture that I can't concentrate on just one.

There are abs, there's that V that I'm sure most men wish that they had, and oh my god the veins popping from his forearms. His body looks young, like the guy is in his twenties. There is no face and yet I have an online crush on this man already.

Because *damn*.

But seriously, is this guy real?

I don't know but this picture is enough to bring out the account I created all those months ago out of retirement.

One little comment won't hurt.

It's not like a guy that looks like he belongs on book covers would even notice someone like me, even if it is online.

Maybe he would if things worked out like they did in the fictional world.

But as I push post on the comment, I know for a fact that it never would.

CHAPTER THREE

HUNTER

YOU WOULD THINK that the world is ending by the way my phone is vibrating on my nightstand.

It stops for a few minutes and then it picks up again. I have no idea how I slept through it but somehow I did and now I'm afraid to even pick up the device.

A part of me wonders if it's Jenna finally feeling remorse for the shit that went down last night and is apologizing.

Given everything though, I highly doubt it.

After a few more minutes of buzzing, the noise finally gets to me, so I give up on going back to sleep and see what the hell is going on.

The second my thumb meets the screen, I feel my eyes go wide when I see the thousands of notifications pop up. Some from my teammates, some from Jaxton, none from Jenna and almost all of them from the app HEX.

Last night after I took the picture, I found out that I had to download the app, create an account and agree to so many privacy agreements to even post. I was going to give up after the fifth agreement but I didn't and ended up posting the picture right before midnight.

It was a simple picture, just of my chest and some of that happy trail that ladies love so much. I may have also added some arm porn to it as well. But somehow that picture popped off because now I have more comments and messages than I know what to do with.

Definitely not what I thought would happen after not getting any type of notifications last night.

I don't even get this much interaction when I post a shirtless picture to my Instagram account and NFL teams follow me on there.

Treading carefully, I open the app and start reading the comments. Most are from women, I'm guessing, commenting fire emojis, eggplants and the tongue emoji.

I don't even have to Google what that means.

There are also comments from men, again I'm guessing. Some are giving me compliments as if we are friends and others are telling me what they would do to me.

Okay, so that's enough of that.

There are also messages, let's see if those are any different.

Clicking on the little envelope icon in the corner, I'm met with an endless stream of messages exactly like the comments, but with more detail.

The first message I click asks if I could send a picture of what's below the waist to hang on their wall.

Ignore.

There's another that is asking me for an ASL? What does that even mean? Are they asking if I know ASL?

So many messages and most of them are creepy. I guess

that's what you should expect when you post a picture like this online.

There are a few normal messages. For example, one person is just complimenting my body and then peaced out.

Another is a woman, I know because she said so in her message, and she is asking me for my workout regimen to give to her husband.

That's sweet, I guess.

I ignore the rest of the messaging and head back to the comments. I don't reply to any of them, just scroll past all the compliments and the advances as if they weren't there.

As I'm scrolling, one comment gets my attention because it's the most normal one. It sticks out from all the raunchy ones that flood the post.

SENFULL94: I mean... I think I've seen better.

I cackle at the words.

This random stranger just looked at my picture and just said meh. I fucking love it. Never in my life has anyone said I was just meh.

Makes me want to prove something to this SENFULL94 person.

Tapping on the comment, I type out my reply.

HUN4ALL: That sounds like a challenge to me ;)

. . .

The comment is posted and given how early it is, I don't expect a reply, so I close out the app and go about my morning.

It being Sunday there isn't much planned for today, even if our first game of the season is in two weeks. Coach Young likes to give the team Sundays off because he likes to watch Sunday football. I'm not going to complain about it.

But given that I've been gone from the team for the majority of summer workouts and practices, I would have appreciated the extra field time.

My father's words of how an NFL training camp would be beneficial to me floats through my head as I get everything out to make myself an omelet.

Roy Jacobi cares about one thing and one thing only and that is money. He is always thinking up ways on how to make more money and one of those ways is through me.

What better way to become the epitome of rich than to have a son that's a professional athlete?

My father has always and will always see me as his next paycheck. From the second he realized that I could throw a football he has had me in every Pop Warner and club team he could find.

In the beginning, I didn't mind it. I liked waking up early in the morning, getting all my football gear and hopping into the car with my dad. I loved playing football. So I continued into middle school and then when high school came, I treated it as if it were my main stage.

I embodied everything that my father wanted me to be. I became the star football player of my little high school in the middle of nowhere Montana and was treated like a rock star everywhere I went.

And because of that, my father had high hopes when it came to the college that I would go to. There wasn't a weekend during my senior year where I wasn't touring a college or talking to recruiters or coaches. Some of the top schools in the country were at my disposal.

Some of that had to do with my football skills but I'm not stupid to know that it also had to do with the money my father promised to donate in our name.

Schools like LSU and Alabama wanted me on their team, and I had every intention to sign my letter with one of those schools but ultimately decided on Cal U.

Was my father pissed? Yeah, but it was still a D1 school, and I was still playing at the top, so eventually he dropped it.

As I've gotten older and spent the last three years, almost four, playing college ball, I've realized that I don't love it as much as I used to. Having the pigskin in my hand day in and day out doesn't have the same effect it once did.

I keep telling myself that it's just a phase and I will get out of it but a part of me is afraid that I won't.

Because football is who I am, it's what people know me as, what happens when that's gone? Who am I then?

That is a question that I don't want the answer to.

The buzzing of my phone takes my attention away from the mental football crisis.

Making sure the omelet is flipped so that it doesn't burn, I grab my phone out of my shorts pocket and see another notification from HEX.

I wonder if it's SENFULL94 commenting back.

Opening the notification, I'm taken directly to the comment section and to the new comment that was just posted from SENFULL94 themselves.

I don't know why but for some reason seeing that they replied makes me smirk.

What smart-ass shit did they say this time?

SENFULL94: It wasn't but maybe it should… I'm just trying to figure out if you're real… For all I know you can be a catfish.

If I'm real? My reply is instant.

HUN4ALL: Oh I'm real, I can prove it to you that I'm definitely not a catfish, if you want…

I wait for a reply to come through. They just posted the comment less than a minute ago, so they have to be still around.

Sure enough, the reply comes through seconds later.

SENFULL94: go for it.

Why the fuck am I smiling at a random stranger's comment on my half nude?

No idea, but because I find this person interesting, I check out their profile. I need to know at least something about this person. Maybe they have something on there that tells me who they are.

I plate my omelet, momentarily forgetting about it as I click on the name and head to their profile. A profile that has a hand-drawn daisy as their main picture and a bio that reads "the stuff you read about in those spicy books." That's it, there is nothing posted.

Because curiosity gets the best of me, I click on the likes and comments section of the profile and see that their last interaction they had with a post before mine was last year.

Interesting.

I wonder what it was about my picture that made them start commenting once again.

One thing I do notice about this person's comments is that they probably posted explicit pictures too. There are so many comments that they liked from people commenting on how good they looked.

They even liked a comment from one person asking if they can lick their tits.

There are so many comments like that and some that are worse than mine.

I guess I can say this person is a woman with amazing tits.

Damn, if only I could see them myself.

Focus, Jacobi, don't be a fucking pervert.

Ignoring the profile, I go back to the comment and think of a reply, but instead of typing out words, I open the profile again and send a message.

HUN4ALL: I'll show you I'm real on 1 condition.

. . .

Within seconds, I get a response. I guess this girl is an early riser.

Why I'm getting joy from this, is beyond me. This definitely not a normal way to communicate with people.

But I'm doing it anyway. Anything to make me forget about Jenna and all that fucked-up shit.

SENFULL94: And what would that be?

I smirk at the reply, so many things popping into my head. One of them is asking for a picture, you know tit for tat, but asking a stranger for a nude seems wrong. So fucking wrong. I go with something easy.

HUN4ALL: What the hell does ASL mean?

I've gotten so many messages with those three letters and each time they confuse the hell out of me. Might as well get the meaning from someone that has been a part of this community longer than I have.

SENFULL94: LOL and here I thought that you were going to ask for a nude

· · ·

I wanted to. Fuck, what is wrong with me?

SENFULL94: ASL = Age, Sex, Location

HUN4ALL: Sex as in sexual orientation?

SENFULL94: lol no. As in your gender, what you identify as. Male, female, nonbinary.

Okay, now the three letters make a lot more sense. I feel like a total noob for even asking.

HUN4ALL: So what's your asl?

SENFULL94: 22, F, California.

California? I wonder if there's a possibility that she's somewhere near me. And given that she's twenty-two it's likely. College town and all that, but California is fucking huge. There can be a ten-hour drive between us.

I think I need to get my head checked if I'm thinking of meeting a person that I met online in real life.

My phone buzzes as another message comes in.

. . .

SENFULL94: What's yours?

Smirking, I type out my response.

HUN4ALL: 21, M, and also California.

SENFULL94: Huh, small world.

Very small world. I'm in the middle of typing out a message asking where in California she's located when another message from her comes through.

SENFULL94: So how are you going to prove that you're real?

As soon as I read the message, I disregard all the words typed out and start typing new ones. It's a witty response but as I finish up the sentence, I realize I can do better.

I close the app and open my camera.

She wants to know I'm real, I'll show her. Forgetting about my breakfast even further, I head to the bathroom, where I take off my shirt and lower my joggers even more than what I did last night, and flex.

Snap.

Snap.

Snap.

Three pictures to get the perfect one. After editing and cropping out my face, I open the app again. I go back to where I posted my picture last night.

The difference between then and now is that this time I am putting a caption and tagging a certain twenty-two-year-old female from somewhere in California.

Here you go SENFULL94. Now do you believe I'm real?

I think I'm liking this app. It's definitely a good way to forget about Jenna and Jaxton.

If SENFULL94 isn't a total bitch too, that is.

CHAPTER FOUR

SELENA

NO.

No, I still don't believe that this man is real, because no man outside of fiction looks like that.

Sure, I've been around some very hot guys in my life and living close to the coast and spending most of my time on a college campus, there's the benefit of seeing guys shirtless all the time, but this is nowhere near that.

This guy is on a whole different level and I'm sure he knows it too.

I'm surprised that he responded to my comment and messaged me. I, for sure thought that he was just going to scroll past it, but I guess not.

Pretty sure if he had seen a picture of me, he wouldn't have initiated contact.

This guy may be a real-life book boyfriend but I'm nowhere near that level.

I'm the side character that has a stomach with the stretch marks, wears size-twelve jeans and has split ends up the fucking wazoo.

I'm not the overly gorgeous girl that has the body of a model and I will never get a man like the one currently staring back at me on my phone. I'm what I would call average. Am I beautiful? Yes, I think I am. No actually, I know I am. I have full lips, dark and long lashes that make my eyes pop, and let's be honest tits that most girls would love to have. But there are things about myself that I would love to change, just like any other person on this earth.

As much as I'm excited that this guy is talking to me, I know that all these pictures and conversations are just a fantasy. I know that they are nowhere near what real life is like.

Ignoring the post, I close my phone and concentrate on what I woke up so early to do, get shit ready for the first day of school tomorrow.

First last day of undergrad, I guess you can say.

After five long years, I'm finally finishing up my undergraduate program at California University. It took me so long to get to this point because I didn't know how to do the whole class-registration thing my first year. After a major change, an added minor, and failed class or two, here I am. Ready to finish and move my life forward, maybe even travel a little once I'm done.

Even though it's only the first day, I make sure that I have everything for tomorrow's classes ready to go in my backpack. Syllabi, a charged laptop and iPad and any other material that my professors have said we needed. Thank God all my textbooks this semester are e-books because otherwise my back would be hurting.

I'm adding a few miscellaneous things when I hear my mom calling my name.

"Lena! ¡*Ven a comer!*"

Did I mention that I live with my parents?

I'm what people would call a college townie. When it came to going away for school, I decided to stay close. So, I applied to Cal U, which is in the same city I grew up in and a thirty-minute drive from my parents'. It's one of the top schools in the state, and when I got in, I decided to not use student housing or get an apartment, it just didn't make sense.

So here I am, twenty-two years old and still living with my parents.

There's nothing wrong with living with them. I still have my independence but living under their roof, I have to respect some rules they have in place.

Like coming home every night and no boys in my room.

But living here helps me save and adds unlimited access to my mom's cooking, so I'm golden.

"¡*Ay voy!*" I yell toward the closed door. Abandoning what I was doing, I head to the kitchen.

Walking into the kitchen, I see my mom at the stove and since the house is an open concept, I also see my dad in the living room watching a baseball game.

Why there's a baseball game at nine in the morning, I have no idea. I shouldn't be critical. I'm sure in a few minutes I will be sitting next to him watching the same game.

The second my mom sees me, she hands me two plates of food, silently telling me to put them on the table.

I place the plates on the table as she makes three mugs of coffee and once that is all settled and she's sitting at the table with me, we start eating.

"*¿Ya estás lista para la escuela?*" she asks me before taking a bite of her food.

I take a bite of my chilaquiles before answering her. I would say I'm overly prepared for school. "*Si*. I just need to put gas in the car."

She nods at my statement. "Do you need any money? For food or books?"

I'm already shaking my head before she even finishes her sentence. "*Estoy bien*. I got paid on Friday."

"*Y para el semestre?*" And for the semester? Is her question.

When it comes to my family, we aren't rich, but we aren't poor either. I would say we're somewhere between lower and upper middle class.

My parents tried their hardest to provide the best life they could for their four daughters and along the way, they were able to take part in some profitable investments.

They are able to live comfortably but are were still things that they worry about, like paying for college for whoever wanted to go. Because given my parents' income, we didn't qualify for a whole lot of financial aid.

Somehow, I became the only one out of four daughters that decided to go to a four-year university. And every time a new semester starts, Mom and I have this conversation.

And every time I give her the same answer. "My grant came in, so it's covered."

It's not a lie, it is covered but not by a grant, but by a loan.

I've gotten grants and scholarships throughout the years but it's never enough to cover everything, even with my part-time job. So instead of burdening my parents with the bill, I took out a few student loans.

Sure, I will be stuck with paying them back once I graduate, but like I said, living with my parents helps me save.

"If you need any money, tell me." She gives me those eyes of hers that tell me she means business.

I nod. "I will."

We finish breakfast and after helping my mom clean up, I watch the game with my dad for a little bit before heading to the store and running a few errands with my mom.

It's not until almost ten at night that I realize that I never responded to the post I was tagged in.

Opening the app, I see that not only didn't I respond, but I also have an unread message from him.

HUN4ALL: Let me guess... not real enough for you?

I let out a small snort when I read the message. I guess he read my mind when I saw his post.

SENFULL94: I see it, and I like it, but I have still seen better and not very convinced that's really you. Lol

I go back to picking out my clothes for tomorrow when a notification comes through. Another message from Mr. HUN4ALL.

I wonder what his name is.
Picking up the phone I read his message.

HUN4ALL: You're back! and here I thought that my post scared you away.

HUN4ALL: Two things. 1 you have def have not seen anything better than me and 2 what more do I have to do to show you that I'm in fact real?

I think I might like this guy. The fact that he is going along with this says something. Most people would just ignore me and move on with their lives and go interact with someone else.

SENFULL94: 1. you think a little highly of yourself, don't you?

HUN4ALL: If you looked like me, wouldn't you?

SENFULL94: Maybe a little, Mr. Arrogant.

HUN4ALL: Not arrogant, just very self-aware

. . .

SENFULL94: Basically, the same thing lol but you are right, I will admit. I haven't seen anything better than you.

HUN4ALL: Hell yeah! That's what I like to hear. Now can I get an answer for number 2?

SENFULL94: Why is me knowing you're real so important??

HUN4ALL: IDK. I guess I've never had anyone doubt my good looks before.

SENFULL94: I'm sure someone has brought you down from the body of a god pedestal that you think you're on.

HUN4ALL: You think I have a body of a god?

SENFULL94: I didn't say that and of course that's what you would hold on to.

. . .

HUN4ALL: Yeah, you did. Now are you going to answer my question?

SENFULL94: I don't know lol a picture of you doing a funny gesture?

I don't know what is happening here.

There was no lie in my statement. The only reason I put it out there is because I thought he was a catfish and he could still very much be. Photos can be stolen and manipulated. I know I manipulated pictures when I put my stuff out there.

Of course, I did. I don't need people from my real-world finding the nudes I've put on the internet. Even if they are deleted.

HUN4ALL: I can do that, with a condition of course.

I roll my eyes. This guy and his condition**s.**

SENFULL94: What's the condition this time? *Eye roll emoji*

. . .

HUN4ALL: I love it when girls roll their eyes at me! Prove to me that YOU are real. For all I know, you could have lied with your sex and age and you're really a guy. Which I would be okay with, but why lie?

SENFULL94: lol I'm not lying but okay and how exactly do you want me to prove it to you?

HUN4ALL: same way I am? Picture of you doing a gesture? You posted pics on here before, right?

He must have looked at my profile and seen all the comments and replies that are still attached to it. I don't blame him for wanting to know exactly what I'm asking of him.

But do I want to post a picture here again?

It's not that I hated posting my pictures, the opposite, I just didn't care for all the messages I got because of them.

I guess I took too long to answer him because within a few minutes, my new pen pal is sending another message.

HUN4ALL: If you want of course, I'm not trying to force you to do anything.

.   .   .

HUN4ALL: Actually no, forget it. I reread the message and realized it sounds really creepy and pushy AF! A day on this app and I've turned into a pervert. I'm sorry!!!!!!!!

I can't help but laugh at his message. There have definitely been times where I felt like I was too forward with things pertaining to this app. Especially since nobody knows who you are, you get a certain level of confidence that you normally don't have.

SENFULL94: Don't apologize! Not pushy at all lol I'll prove I'm real.

HUN4ALL: really?

SENFULL94: really. Now pick a gesture before I change my mind!

HUN4ALL: Peace sign?

SENFULL94: So generic, but it works.

. . .

HUN4ALL: Want to do it tomorrow?

SENFULL94: I have a few things to do but I can make it work

HUN4ALL: Yes! I look forward to it!

SENFULL94: See you tomorrow hun4all.

I close the app, not even waiting for a reply and head to my closet to take out the tripod I haven't used in months. Without thinking, I get ready and within minutes I'm standing in front of my phone with the camera wide open.

There is a tinge of excitement as I stand here, with the camera pointed in my direction. It reminds me of the confidence that exuded out of me when I first started to do this. I liked it then and I like it now.

Sliding off my sweats, I get into position.

I set the timer, slide my shirt off and place it in front of me only showing a portion of my chest. As the timer gets closer to being up, I form a peace sign with my visible hand.

Tick.

Tick.

Click.

I go and grab the phone and instantly like the picture that is staring back at me. It's sexy and I kind of want to show it off. All I have to do is edit my tattoo that is showing and then I can post it.

Hopefully HUN4ALL likes the picture.

I don't know why I care what a virtual stranger thinks of me, but I do.

But at least I'll have a distraction from the first day of school.

CHAPTER FIVE

HUNTER

A PART of me hates the fact that it's Monday and a part of me is elated.

I hate it because of the shit show that went down with Jenna. Given the number of texts and Instagram DMs I'm ignoring, the whole team and half the athletic department knows she cheated on me with Jaxton. It's only been thirty-six hours and everyone on this fucking campus knows that my girl stepped out on me.

I hate it more because I have a class with Jaxton and a few teammates, and I know I'm going to get hounded.

Without a doubt, Jax will stop me and try to apologize another million times.

Even with the distraction I've had with HEX, I'm still not at the stage to forgive and forget.

The elation comes from a strange woman that said she would send me a picture.

Is it weird that a stranger I just started talking to yesterday is possibly sending me a nude? Yeah, a bit, but for some reason, it doesn't feel weird to me when it should.

I don't know why, but every time I saw her username come across my screen yesterday, a small bit of excitement rolled through me.

Am I only excited because the banter with this person serves as a distraction? Honestly, that is probably the answer, but it feels nice and after a few messages I realized that that type of conversation wasn't something I had with Jenna. So as long as the excitement is there, I will keep the distraction close.

It's just that at this very moment that said distraction has been absent for most of the day. So I'm currently hating this lovely Monday.

The day started out fine, just like any other first day of a school year. Since the football season is already in full force, my morning consisted of two hours of fieldwork and then an hour of weight lifting. The whole time I avoided all the questions that consisted of Jenna, Jaxton or what the fuck happened at the Alpha Rho house. After a good five minutes, people knew to avoid me.

The day continued exactly how the day started. Like shit.

After practice, I felt like deadweight and almost fell asleep during my first class while the professor was explaining the syllabus. It's a writing course that I have to take in order to graduate but I still felt bad when the professor cleared his throat and my eyes shot open.

I grabbed food after that, and it seemed to help to keep me energized until the second practice of the day hit.

Now it's time for my night class and thankfully the last class of the day. My plan is to get through this hour and forty-five-minute class, grab some food and head home to knock out.

Right before I get into the designated classroom, I check my phone for any notifications for what feels like the first time.

There's a message from my dad, one from my mom, but none from the HEX app.

I turned off all notifications except the ones that have to do with SENFULL94.

Did I have to do that? No, but I wanted to. Like I said before, I get excited whenever I see her name across my screen. If she really is a she.

Pocketing my phone, I shake off the slight disappointment and prepare myself for what's about to come of this class.

The one class I share with Jaxton, my ex-bastard-of-a-fucked-up friend.

I pull the door open to the auditorium-style room and I see that nearly all the seats are taken. I guess I was running a little late and I didn't notice.

Looking around, I see that there are two seats that are open. One in the back next to Jaxton and a few of our teammates, and the second one in the third row from the bottom next to a girl with dark hair.

Jaxton sees me and tries to get my attention, calling my name and waving me over.

This isn't shit I want to deal with. I'm dealing with enough at practice.

Shaking my head and letting out a sigh, I walk down to the third row pulling out the chair next to the brown-haired girl.

I feel everyone's eyes on me as I take a seat, but I ignore every single one of them as I situate myself.

The girl next to me must have sensed movement because she lifts up her head from the scrolling she was doing on her phone and looks up.

In a slight glance in her direction, I notice that her eyes that are surrounded by full, long eyelashes are the same shade of her hair. Her eyes are a dark chocolate brown and for some reason, as she stares at me, I can't seem to look away from them.

I've never seen this girl before, I'm sure of it. If I had, I for sure would have remembered those eyes. They're pretty.

They're pretty?

What the fuck? Did I actually think that about a random girl's eyes?

As I shake my head, it seems the girl finally registers who is sitting next to her because her pretty eyes go wide. Not only do her eyes go wide but her face fills with surprise.

I watch as she looks from me and then turns back slightly to where my teammates sit and then turns back to me with a confused look.

Like she's silently asking me why I'm sitting next to her when I should be sitting with the athletes of the class.

If only I could explain it to you, girl with pretty eyes, if only.

I ignore her confused look and start taking out my laptop and opening it to the syllabus. The whole time I can feel her stare on me.

Thankfully the professor walks in and starts class and her stare is turned elsewhere.

"Welcome to Biology 440: Anatomy and Physiology!" The professor waves her hands up in the air as if sitting in one of the hardest courses at this school is the best thing ever.

It's not.

There are so many horror stories from this course and if it wasn't a damn requirement for me to graduate, I wouldn't have taken it.

"Before we start, let me take attendance to make sure that everyone is here!" She literally claps her hands. I'm calling it right now. This professor was a cheerleader back in her day. There is no reason to be that peppy this late in the day.

She goes through the whole damn roll sheet and since there are over fifty students in this class, it takes a while.

"Hunter Jacobi?" She looks around like she expects me to jump up and match her peppiness.

"Here." I raise my hand slightly and she throws me a nod.

"Selena Montez?" she calls out and the girl with the pretty eyes raises her hand.

"Here."

Selena. A pretty name to go with the pretty eyes. It fits her, well, I think it fits her. I know nothing about her. But she looks like a Selena.

I wonder why I don't ever remember seeing this girl before. Yet again, it is a big school, so we might have crossed paths before and I just don't have any recollection of it.

Turning my attention away from my neighbor, I try to grasp everything that Professor Peppy explains about what to expect from the course.

Just her explanation alone is already giving me a headache and did I mention that this course is a year long? Yeah, at the end of the semester we all have to sign up for the next course and hope we get in.

Thank god for athlete and fourth-year class registration priority because otherwise I would be screwed.

Peppy doesn't grasp my attention the whole time though. I check my phone every five minutes to make sure I didn't miss a notification from HEX.

Nothing.

Maybe SENFULL94 got bored and decided she no longer wanted to talk to me.

If that's the case, I guess I have to say goodbye to my distraction and find a new one to take its place.

Maybe I can talk to someone else on the app.

Who? The man that wanted me to send him pictures of my dick so that he could stare at it before he goes to bed?

Yeah, I'm not going to do that, but maybe there's another community that I can find. Maybe one related to those that play football and hate it because of their father's. That's a thing, so there must be, right?

"Okay before we leave, I want you to turn to your neighbors and exchange numbers. You know, just in case you miss a day, and you can grab their notes," Peppy announces and I swear she does jazz hands.

I turn to my left and remember that I'm the last person in the row. That means that I will be getting Selena's number.

I'm cool with it.

I turn to my neighbor and see that she's already looking at me.

"If you don't want to give me your number, that's completely fine, I could ask the girl on the other side when she's done," she says, giving me a sheepish smile.

Her voice.

It wasn't what I was expecting.

I was expecting something soft and sweet but that's not it at all.

It has a roughness to it, like it wants to have a rasp but it doesn't. Like her eyes, I like it.

"Okay then," Selena says, turning away, taking my mind out of the stupor her voice put it in.

"No, wait, sorry." I shake my head to remove the cloudiness. "Yeah, let me get your number. I'm sure with football, I might need to grab your notes once in a while."

I reach forward and place a hand on her shoulder to turn her back to me.

Again, her eyes go wide with the motion.

"Sorry." I hold my hands up as soon as I release her.

I shouldn't really be touching people that don't want to be touched.

"Here." I pull out my phone, opening up the phone app and handing it to her. "Put your number in and call yourself that way you have mine."

She takes it and starts typing.

"I'm Hunter, by the way," I say and she looks up at me through her lashes like I'm stupid.

"I know," she says before going back to typing her number in.

Of course, she knows who I am. Everyone at this school knows who I am.

Selena hands me back my phone and within a second her phone dings.

"Well, that's taken care of, see you later, Hunter," she says, grabbing her bag and starting to make her way out of the classroom.

As I turn to leave myself, I see Jaxton looking at me and I just know that he's going to corner me the second we step out into the hallway.

Something that I clearly don't want.

"Selena, wait," I call out, stuffing my laptop into my backpack haphazardly and going after her.

She stops in her tracks, almost to the door, waiting to see why I'm stopping her.

I'm starting to think that this girl only has one facial expression and that's confusion.

"Let me walk you to your car, or dorm or whatever," I throw out there.

Selena does that thing that she did at the beginning of class. She looks around like she is expecting someone to jump out of nowhere and tell her it's a joke.

Finally, she turns back to me. "Why?"

At least her expression changed slightly. Instead of being confused, her eyebrows are bunched up together and her lips are in a pout. A sexy pout.

You just broke up with your girlfriend, Jacobi. Stop finding things you find attractive about this girl.

I give her a shrug. "It's late and dark outside and my mom raised me to be a gentleman."

She is still giving me the same expression when she speaks. "I'm fine, and I'm sure your friends are waiting for you."

I look over to where her eyes go, and I see that a few of the guys are hanging back, indeed waiting for me. I ignore them.

"Yeah, I don't want to hang out with my friends right now."

"But you want to walk *me* to my car?"

"Like I said, I'm trying to be the gentleman that my mom

raised me to be." I give her a smile and she throws an eye roll back.

She stares at me for another minute before she sighs. "You're not going to drop this, are you?"

I shake my head. "I'm afraid not. So you can let me walk you to your car or I follow you. Either way, I will be there, might as well let me walk next to you."

Why am I pushing this? Never, and I mean never, have I volunteered to walk one of my classmates to their car. This is new even to me.

She gives me another eye roll. "Fine. Walk me to my damn car."

This girl doesn't take my shit. I kind of like it.

Selena turns to leave before I can even comprehend her answer. Before I know it, she's already out of the room and I'm playing catch up with her.

I'm at her side when she steps through the doors and walks in the direction of the library parking lot.

As we walk together in silence, I notice a few things about the girl.

One of them being her height. She has to be around five-six or five-seven because her head passes my shoulder and I stand at six foot one. Jenna always stood at chest level. Not this girl.

If I had to guess, I would also say this girl was an athlete in the past. She definitely looks like one.

From what I can see, and that isn't much, I notice that she has a natural tan to her skin. Selena is wearing a long-sleeve school shirt that definitely has have me noticing how it accentuates her chest.

It looks like a glorious one.

Fuck, what is wrong with me? I need to stop thinking about her in that way. She's not a piece of meat.

I also notice that the girl doesn't say much. She just walks across the parking lot with her arms crossed as if she were cold, looking straight ahead.

This girl is an enigma and I think I like it.

"Are you a transfer?" I ask when I can't take more of the silence.

She shakes her head. "Nope, this is my fifth year here."

Fifth?

"Are you a biology major?"

Again, she shakes her head. "An exercise science major."

Same as me.

How is this the first time I've crossed paths with her?

"You look confused." Selena throws out as we approach a dark-blue Civic.

"Sorry," I say as she unlocks the car and throws her bag in the back. "I'm just trying to remember if we have ever crossed paths before."

She nods, taking her lower lip between her teeth. "We've had a few classes together, but never had a conversation. You've always stayed in your corner and me in mine."

"Interesting," I say, totally blown away by this whole thing.

"Yep. Well, thanks for walking me to my car. I'll see you Wednesday." Selena throws me a small smile before climbing into her car.

Instead of walking away, I wait for her to pull out and she gives me a small wave before making her way out of the parking lot.

Once her car is outta sight, I make my way to my own car.

As I'm getting comfortable in the driver's seat, my phone vibrates in my back pocket.

Sliding it out, I check the screen and see a notification from HEX. Someone tagged me in a post.

Could it be?

Who else would tag me in a post? I've only talked to one person.

There is excitement flowing through my blood right now, telling me there is no way in hell I'm waiting until I get home to open the app.

Lowering my phone, I open the app and go to the notification center and see that I was in fact tagged in a post by SENFULL94.

My excitement grows even more.

I click the notification and I'm taken directly to a post of a woman that has beautiful curves all over, a shirt covering half her body and a hand holding up a peace sign. My eyes don't know what to concentrate on. Her curves, the tops of her breast peeking out, the way her shirt hides a part of her but still shows everything.

She's not showing her face, but what she is showing is absolutely fucking beautiful. A mouthwateringly beautiful woman.

SENFULL94 is a very beautiful woman and I have the pleasure of witnessing it.

Holy fuck.

CHAPTER SIX

SELENA

THE SECOND I GET HOME, my shoes come off, followed by my jeans, and then I just throw myself onto my bed.

Whoever told me that stacking four classes back-to-back all in one day was a good idea, deserves a good kick in the ass.

Oh right, that person was me. Because I wanted to just be on campus for three days out of the week instead of five.

It's day one and I'm already regretting every bit of it.

My classes aren't hard, well apart from anatomy, but they are mentally draining. It's a lot of thinking and by the end of the day, it feels as if my brain has melted completely.

I ate three meals at least and had plenty of water, so that's a plus. But I'm still mentally drained and I can already guess as to how this semester will go.

On the bright side, the guy that I've had a secret crush on for the last, oh I don't know three years, finally talked to me.

Hunter Jacobi.

Star quarterback for Cal U, talked to me, of all people. He sat next to me, talked to me, has my number and walked me to my car. Those are things that I never thought would happen. I was a little shell shocked when he sat in the open chair next to me and the shock continued until I was halfway home.

I've had a crush on the guy since we shared a class together my second year and his first. It was a statistics class and for some reason, my eyes always found him and watched his every movement. I wasn't lying when I told him that we never had a conversation, but that doesn't mean I didn't try. I did once but of course the other girls in that class were always all over him. That was also the class where he met his girl-friend, Jenna.

So, nothing came from that little crush and for the next three years whenever he was in the room, my eyes always found him. When I was around him, butterflies would fly in my belly.

The butterflies would weaken at times when I would hear people talking about how big of a prick he was, but they were always there. I think because I always thought that he was nothing like what people described him to be. Trust me, from what I've witnessed, Hunter Jacobi is everything that people described and at times I wonder why the hell I ever had a crush on him in the first place. The guy is an egotistical prick that always gets what he wants.

His jersey number is one for crying out loud.

Yet butterflies were in full force today and I need to get them in check before I do something to embarrass myself the next time I see him.

Can't have that.

Forgetting about Hunter Jacobi at least for tonight, I close my eyes waiting for sleep to take over. It doesn't, especially when my phone dings and my eyes fly open.

It's the HEX ping. I know it by heart.

I completely forgot that I posted a picture as I was driving off the library parking lot. I was going to post it as soon as I woke up but I completely forgot and then the day got crazy and it went over my head. For some reason, I remembered when Hunter was walking me to the car, so as soon as I hit the stop sign, I hit post.

Patting the bed for my phone, I find it and check the notifications right away.

Like I suspected, there are over fifty messages and over one hundred comments on the picture. I tackle the comments first. Some are hyping me up, others thanking me for posting again and of course, the ones that are just a little creepy.

The very top comment is the one that has me smiling.

It's from HUN4ALL and it's just a bunch of heart eyes emojis.

I guess he liked the picture.

A smile doesn't leave my face as I click on his profile and see that he also posted a picture less than fifteen minutes ago. The caption, though, has my smile growing even more.

I'm real but SENFULL94 is REALly beautiful.

His picture is like mine, but instead of holding his shirt over his chest, he is holding it over his crotch, and of course with his visible hand holding up a peace sign. This picture leaves absolutely zero to the imagination.

Holy shit balls.

This guy's body really is insane.

I know I swore off dating men for a while but damn, I wouldn't mind exploring this man, with my tongue.

And no, that isn't a joke.

This man is something else and I can't believe he goes about everyday life with this body hidden behind clothes, it's just mind blowing.

Bypassing the comment section, I head straight to the messages and type something out before hitting send.

SENFULL94: Okay, no man has a right to look like that. *Wide eyed emoji*

If this guy was standing in front of me right now, would I have the courage to say those words to his face? Probably not. Introvert and all that, but I would want to.

HUN4ALL: The way I see it, a woman that looks like you shouldn't be wasting her time with a fucker like me.

SENFULL94: And why is that?

. . .

There's a pause in the messages, but soon he is replying, and his message is everything that I wish a guy in the real world would tell me.

HUN4ALL: Because that body deserves to be cherished and handled with care

Well then, I was not expecting him to say that. I feel like I need to clear my throat and drink some water after that. I should have also expected for this conversation to go from somewhat normal to flirty, they always do even when it wasn't your intention.

A thing about me, I can't flirt for the life of me in person, but through a screen when the other person doesn't know me? Absolutely.

SENFULL94: What if I don't want it to be cherished or handled with care?

Typing out those words isn't a problem, saying them will most likely cause me to break out in hives.

A reply is instant.

HUN4ALL: then how exactly do you want that body of yours to be treated?

. . .

If he's the one doing the treating, I can think of a few ways. But I don't type that out.

SENFULL94: getting manhandled would be nice…

Look, I may not have a whole lot of experience when it comes to some sexual activities, but just because I lack the experience doesn't mean I don't know what I like. Posting on here, reading romance books, exploring my own body and even those few times that me and Scott fooled around, has taught me that.

HUN4ALL: FUCK! Don't say things like that!

SENFULL94: And why is that?

HUN4ALL: Because I now have images in my head that involve my hands and your body and I shouldn't be thinking about that!

SENFULL94: I mean you could if you wanted to…

. . .

HUN4ALL: Do you want me to?

SENFULL94: Do I want you to manhandle me or do I want you to picture me in your head?

HUN4ALL: Both.

I don't even think about a response before I start typing and hit send.

SENFULL94: Yes.

———

Hunter

Fuck.

I don't even know what this girl's face looks like and with just her words, she has me as hard as a steel rod.

Is this what people come to this app for? Why they use communities like this one? To get off?

I just thought it was to get a confidence booster but I'm not going to lie, interacting with a girl like SENFULL94is a confidence booster in and of itself.

And from what I've seen, she's exactly my type. Her curves are just an added bonus. Add the fact that she wants to be manhandled into the mix, this girl is fucking perfect.

HUN4ALL: If I ever get the chance to meet you in person, I will do all the manhandling you want. But since there is a screen between us, I guess I will have to use my mind.

I wait for a response to come in right away, but it doesn't. Maybe I scared her off with the whole meeting- in-person thing.

Do I want to meet her in person?

I don't know. It's been like two days and it's not like we've been talking to each other every waking minute.

It's just that for some reason I feel a pull to this person, and I've felt it from the very start. So maybe I want to see if that feeling would translate to real life.

The phone dings.

SENFULL94: I guess you and your mind are going to have your work cut out. What with picturing scenarios and all.

I read the words and instantly forget where the conversation was a few minutes ago.

. . .

HUN4ALL: Do you not want to meet in person if the chance comes up? We do live in the same state.

SENFULL94: Do you really want to meet a stranger off the internet? I could be a scorned woman looking for her next kill, for all you know.

HUN4ALL: Are you?

SENFULL94: No lol but you don't even know my name or what my face looks like or the rest of my body. It might not be appealing to you in person.

Not appealing? Is she serious? I've been at full mast ever since I saw her picture. Everything about this girl is appealing. Just the thought of her has my dick twitching.

HUN4ALL: Is there a way to send pictures through these messages?

. . .

SENFULL94: yeah, the three dots next to the typing area…Why?

HUN4ALL: I want to show you something.

I click on the three dots and just like she said, I have the option to take a picture or to use one from my camera roll. I choose the take a picture option.

Not moving from my position on my bed, I snap a picture of my shorts tenting, showing just how appealing I find her.

HUN4ALL: This is just from seeing your picture, now imagine what it would be like if I see you in person. *picture attached*

It takes a few minutes but eventually a reply comes through.

SENFULL94: you're…

HUN4ALL: hard. Your picture made me hard at first glance. So, trust me when I say I will find you fucking appealing in person.

· · ·

She goes silent once again and after a few minutes, I send another message

HUN4ALL: Did I scare you away?

Reply is instant.

SENFULL94: Not only are you hard, but also big *wide eye emoji * but no you didn't scare me away, I'm just wondering something.

HUN4ALL: What are you wondering about?

SENFULL94: If you're planning on taking care of your... situation.

She's not suggesting what I think she is, is she?

HUN4ALL: I don't know, do you want to help?

Another instant reply.

. . .

SENFULL94: Yes, yes, I do.

CHAPTER SEVEN

HUNTER

I'M PRETTY sure that even if I tried, I wouldn't be able to close my mouth from the shock that the last message elicited.

I see the words, I've read them over a hundred times in a span of two minutes but yet they haven't registered just yet.

She wants to help me.

She wants to *help* me with the current situation happening in my shorts.

Holy shit.

This girl is forward as fuck. I like it. First it was the manhandling comment and now this. I think I've found my dream girl. Not what I expected from this interaction.

I clear my throat a few times before I'm able to type out a response.

HUN4ALL: And how do you plan on helping? Since you're there and I'm here.

. . .

Is this a phone sex type of situation? Oh shit, will I be able to see this girl? Hear her voice? Fuck, just thinking about it is getting me more worked up.

SENFULL94: I was thinking....

HUN4ALL: Yes?

SENFULL94: I could send you a few pictures myself and possibly describe what we could be doing if we were together?

My fingers don't type fast enough.

HUN4ALL: yes, yes, YES!

I was going to take care of the situation myself, but if she wants to be helpful by sharing a few more pictures of herself with me, I will take anything I can get.

SENFULL94: You sound all too eager for that lol

· · ·

HUN4ALL: If I get to see more of you, I will always be eager.

She goes silent for a few minutes, so I send another message for good measure.

HUN4ALL: You know I'm not talking to you just for sex, right? I only started the conversation because I found your comment intriguing, and I've continued it for that same reason. I don't want to make this all about sex.

SENFULL94: You do realize we haven't had an actual conversation yet, right?

HUN4ALL: I do but that still doesn't mean I'm not interested in getting to know more about you. I'm for having all the conversations.

It's not a lie.

For the first time in a very long time, I feel like I have a connection with someone that might go deeper than just surface level. I know now that what I had with Jenna was exactly that, and it was that way for three years. The fact that a random woman online is getting me excited about having a conversation, tells me that I should have left my relationship a long time ago.

These conversations may have only started two days ago but it's serving its purpose. It's distracting me from the shit with Jenna. It's distracting me from the love I'm losing for my sport. The anger I hold for my father. And it's making me realize that the person that I show while I'm on campus isn't the real me. I just pretend to be that person because that is what is expected of me.

People on campus expect me to be the rich prick with the god complex. To be the cocky asshole that they expect the star quarterback to be.

I may be rich, and I may be good at throwing a ball but I'm nothing like they think of me.

Now that I think about it, it may be why Selena was so shocked by how I was acting around her. She was probably expecting the cocky, arrogant asshole she has heard around school that I am. Her confused expressions now make sense.

The pinging of my phone brings me back to the present.

SENFULL94: I wouldn't mind getting to know you either.

HUN4ALL: You wouldn't?

SENFULL94: No, I also find you intriguing.

I don't know why but that last part makes me grin and

want to pound at my chest. Reining in my excitement, I reply.

HUN4ALL: so we drop the sexual stuff and get to know each other as friends?

SENFULL94: I mean... I don't mind the sexual aspect that is going on here. If you are willing, we can continue that and still get to know each other along the way. That is if you want to of course, no pressure or anything on doing something you are not comfortable with.

It's like dating through an app, without the names, faces and hearing each other's voices.

HUN4ALL: Faces?

SENFULL94: How about later down the road?

I can respect the fact that she isn't comfortable with sharing her face with me just yet. We're strangers. She may have shared a picture of her body but sharing your face with someone is completely different.

. . .

HUN4ALL: I'm okay with that.

SENFULL94: cool. No sharing these messages outside the two of us?

HUN4ALL: I'm not into sharing either way. What's mine is mine.

I just wish that certain people would respect that, then maybe I wouldn't be in this fucked up situation where I'm avoiding a friend. But then I would still be with Jenna and completely blind to her extracurricular activities that didn't include me. And I wouldn't be talking to SENFULL94.

SENFULL94: Possessive, I like it…. So, do you still need help with your situation below the belt?

So, we are jumping straight into things. Have I mentioned that I like this girl?

HUN4ALL: a helpful hand is always appreciated ;) A mouth would also work.

. . .

SENFULL94: Well, I can't use my mouth, but I can send something else that is helpful. *Picture attached*

Because of the shift in conversation, my dick is currently at half chub, but the second that the picture comes through, that changes to the point of pain.

Holy. Fuck.

It's a picture of her tits. Full on and small peek that I got earlier pales in comparison. Her chest is fucking mouthwatering, and I wish I could reach through the screen and take them in my mouth. They look like they would not only be a handful but a mouthful as well.

They are fucking amazing.

HUN4ALL: FUCK. Yeah, that is extremely helpful. They look fucking perfect. Do you like when they are played with?

Not taking my eyes off the screen, I stroke my dick through my shorts, trying to relieve some tension. I picture her chest in front of me and playing with them every way I can think how. I wonder if her dark pink nipples form the perfect peak when a hint of coldness hits them. Maybe she likes them nibbled on, sucked on, bitten into.

Because if I could, I would do just that. I would worship

her chest right before I situated myself right between the two and fucked them.

Fuck, that is certainly a glorious image. And her reply just adds fuel to the fire.

SENFULL94: I'm glad you think so. And yes, I do like when they are played with. The grabbing, the nibbling the pulling, all my favorites.

Fuck. I grab at my cock and give myself a few good strokes trying to relieve some of the pressure.

HUN4ALL: You don't mind if I stroke myself to them, do you?

I have to ask, because trust me I know how wrong this may seem to someone outside the two of us.

SENFULL94: I don't mind… If I get to see…

Fuck. This girl is perfect.

Without thinking, I take myself out of my shorts before turning on the camera and taking a picture of my hand wrapped around my cock and send it right away without a second thought. I continue to stroke myself to her picture until she replies.

This time her reply doesn't consist of any words. This time is just another picture of her breast but now she has her hand gripping the mound and her nails are digging into the skin. I can see her skin turning red from her grip.

I guess she does really like it a little rough.

Fuck, I wish it was my hand instead of hers right now.

HUN4ALL: Does that feel good?

SENFULL94: It does... Are you wishing it was your hand instead of mine?

HUN4ALL: A fucking mind reader, because yes, without a fucking doubt. Want to know what I would do to them?

SENFULL94: Tell me.

My breath is starting to get labored, and I try my hardest to type out the words I want to say while giving my cock all the attention it needs.

HUN4ALL: If you were in bed next to me, I would get rid of your shirt completely and I would dive

into your perfect tits without any hesitation. I would suck on them, bite on them, mark them so that you would know I was there.

Shit, that image has me sliding off my basketball shorts completely. I don't know how much longer I'm going to last, it feels like I'm close to the edge and we just started.

SENFULL94: What else do you want to do to them?

HUN4ALL: I want to straddle your body while you hold them together as tightly as you can so that I can slide my cock between them. You don't know how badly I want to fuck them right now.

SENFULL94: Probably not as bad as I want you to...

I don't hesitate to take another picture and send it her way as my reply. This time there is nothing but my hand just wrapped around my cock. If she uses her mind, she can see exactly what I'm doing. I hope she doesn't mind a second dick pic. Another picture comes through from her but this time it's not of her chest. No, this time I'm gifted something else.

At first, the only thing I can concentrate on from the picture is her bare legs; long and with a caramel tint to them. Then I move my eyes and see the rest of what she sent. No longer am I solely concentrating on her legs, now it's where her hand is.

How I didn't notice this first is completely beyond me.

In the picture, not only is she showing me her legs, she is also showing me her panties. They are lacy, see-through and green and under those panties is her hand.

She's playing with herself.

HUN4ALL: Did my fun make you want to play along?

SENFULL94: Yes!

HUN4ALL: How close are you? Do you have any toys? Because that last picture might be my undoing and I don't know how much longer I can go.

SENFULL94: I think one more picture might send me over the edge and yes, I have a few toys. Some that vibrate, maybe even a glass dildo...

. . .

Fuck, a glass dildo?

That is something that I will have to ask to see later on, but for now, her wish is my command. I take another picture, one of my hands cupping my balls and my shaft standing at full mast, showing her just how much she would take if she were here with me.

SENFULL94: If only I could wrap my mouth around it. Not only have you in my mouth but fucking my tits like you described, coating them with everything you have.

Jesus fuck. She has a way with words, doesn't she? They perfectly paint a picture and I'm near exploding.

HUN4ALL: Can I get your name?

SENFULL94: What? Why?

HUN4ALL: So I have something to say when I release my load.

. . .

I'm so fucking close I don't know how much longer I can hold off, I feel the precum leaking from the head and coating my hand and shaft. I don't think she is going to respond until a ping comes in.

SENFULL94: Len

Len. Lennie. I like it.

Going back to the pictures she sent my way and her post, I continue to stroke myself as I picture everything that we described. I picture her in my hands, picture tasting every inch of her and devouring her body the way it deserves. It's fucking glorious and after one stroke, two, I can't hold off any longer. Grabbing my discarded boxers, I shoot my load into them.

Her name slips through my lips, followed by a moan.

"Shit," I pant out.

It's been a while since I've come that hard and that fast.

HUN4ALL: fuck. Can we do that again?

SENFULL94: yes please

HUN4ALL: whenever you want, just say the word

. . .

SENFULL94: :) one thing though

HUN4ALL: What is that?

SENFULL94: You got a name, do I get one too?

I start typing out my name in response before stopping myself. I shouldn't give her my real name, should I? What if I do and she is able to figure out who I am or worse yet, she knows me in real life? She did say no face and now that I think of it, that might be a good plan. Len might not even be her real name.

So, I erase the message and type out another response.

HUN4ALL: Chase.

SENFULL94: Nice to meet you, Chase.

HUN4ALL: Nice to meet you too, Len.

CHAPTER EIGHT

SELENA

"OKAY, that is all for today's lab. Have a good weekend and if you are on the football team, good luck tomorrow. Go Sea Lions!" Professor Leininger says to dismiss our Friday night anatomy lab.

If you ever wondered what a mascot is for a college that is close to the ocean, just think sea animals. Out of all the sea animals in the world, Cal U decided to go with sea lions. They could have chosen otters or sharks, but nope they chose sea lions.

They're cute and everything and at times can be deadly but they don't really fit into the whole school spirit thing.

At least the mascot is slightly better than the damn school colors. Ocean blue and sunshine yellow. Blue for, you guessed it, the ocean and sunshine yellow for the sand and sun combined. Seriously, who comes up with this stuff?

"Walk you to your car?" Hunter's voice interrupts my whole school spirit mindset.

It's been two weeks since the first day of the semester.

Two weeks since he sat next to me and two weeks since he walked me to my car for the first time.

After every class, which is three times a week, he has asked me the same question. And every time I give a small smile and nod. Might as well go along with it than fight him on it. We don't say much to each other, just the occasional comment about our one shared class or the food at the dining hall. But that's mostly it.

Him walking me to my car has become some sort of habit and I won't admit it to him, but I actually like it and I find it thoughtful. He is still a cocky bastard after all.

"Not tonight," I say, pushing out of my seat and slipping on my backpack. "I have a test in two weeks, so I thought I would get some studying done up on the third floor."

I don't mention the fact that I suck at taking tests and that is why I'm starting the study sessions two weeks early.

"You can't do that at home?" he asks, following me out of the room.

"I can, but according to the hundred texts I received during class, my sisters are home, which means noise. Which also means I won't get anything done," I say as I walk out of class. I can feel him following right behind me.

I turn to wave bye when I notice that he is looking at me funny. "What?"

He blinks and shakes his head a bit before he answers. "Nothing, sorry, um, how long are you staying?"

I look at the time on my phone and see it's close to nine. I can get a good two hours of studying done before my eyes give out.

"Like two hours."

He nods. "It will be late then and even darker."

"Yes, it will be."

"You'll have to walk to your car by yourself. In the dark."

"I'm a big girl, Jacobi. I can handle it." I give him a small wave and start making my way to the third floor of the library.

I hear footsteps behind me. Great, he's following me again.

"Did you just call me Jacobi?" he asks the second he comes to my side, matching my strides.

"That's what people call you, right? Jacobi? Even professors call you that," I state, turning to head to the elevator. If he's going to follow me, I rather not take the stairs and be out of breath before I get to the third floor.

"Yeah, but you have never called me that." He sounds a little sad when he says that.

"I can call you Hunter if that's what you prefer." I push the elevator button, begging it to arrive quickly.

"No, Jacobi is fine," he says just as the elevator doors open. I step in and I can't help but to raise my eyebrows at him when he does the same.

"What are you doing?" I ask as the doors close.

"Going up to the third floor with you," he says matter-of-factly.

"Why?"

He shrugs, keeping his eyes looking straight ahead. "I should study too. With football in full swing, I don't get a whole lot of time."

I narrow my eyes at him. "Your girlfriend doesn't mind that you are going to be studying with someone who isn't her the night before a game? Speaking of the game, don't you have a team dinner or something to attend?"

But seriously, does Jenna know he's been walking me to my car three times a week? Does she care?

"Team dinner was last night, and I don't have a girl-friend," he mutters out.

Huh. That's news to me.

The butterflies start to flutter in my stomach knowing that piece of information, but I hunker them down before they turn into something more. Like my hope being up.

"Sorry, I didn't know," I say as the elevator dings and the doors slide open.

"Really? And here I thought everyone on campus knew."

I just shrug, not saying anything. What is there to say? From just a few words, I can tell it's a sore subject. No need to torture him with it.

We walk out of the elevator together and he follows me around the third floor until I find a table that I'm happy with. Surprisingly, he doesn't say anything or complain, he just follows.

Pulling out a chair and get comfortable to study for a few hours, I become slightly surprised when Hunter pulls out the chair across from mine and gets situated.

I guess he's really staying. Why though, I have no idea?

Once we are all squared away, we don't talk, we just do our own thing on our laptops. I'm halfway through the fifth question of my child development study guide when Hunter breaks the silence.

"So you have sisters?" he whispers, not looking up from his laptop.

"Yeah, three. I'm the youngest," I answer.

"Damn, four girls. That must have been a loud childhood," he mutters, still not looking up. Whatever he's doing, must be very interesting.

"It was, especially when you add being Mexican into the mix."

That small snippet gets his attention, and he finally looks up.

"You're Mexican?"

I nod. "Yeah," I give him a small smile. "I would have thought that my name would have given it away."

"Your name?"

"Selena? Like the singer?"

"Gomez?"

I shake my head. "Quintanilla. She was big in the nineties?"

Hunter just shakes his head, silently telling me that he doesn't know who I'm talking about.

I can't help but smile a bit and feel a little surprised. "Seriously? You don't know who she is?"

He gives me a small smile in return. "No idea, but maybe if I hear one of her songs, I will."

Shaking my head, still with a smile on my face, I pull out my earbuds and hand one of them to him, which he takes.

Once the earbud is in his ear, I pull up my music app on my phone and find the song that I'm looking for. As soon as I have it, I press play and watch him as he listens to it.

I see when recognition finally registers and the butterflies I felt a little bit ago return when I hear his laugh.

"Okay, I've heard this song once or twice," he says with a bright smile before handing me back my earbud.

"Once or twice," I huff jokingly. "I heard it my whole damn childhood, I know every one of her songs."

"Your parents must have really liked her if they named you after her," he says, closing his laptop and giving me his full attention.

I shake my head. "Not my parents, my sisters. Like I said, I'm the youngest and when my mom became pregnant with me they all wanted to name me. Selena was the only one that they agreed on."

"That's awesome," he says, his smile never leaving his face. Why am I just noticing that Hunter Jacobi has a beautiful smile?

"Do you have any siblings?" I ask before I get lost in his smile.

He nods. "A younger brother and sister. They're fourteen and ten."

"They must really like having you as a big brother."

At my comment, his smile disappears and instantly I regret saying the words. I hit another sore subject.

"We aren't that close," he says with a shrug, opening up his laptop again, ultimately ending the conversation.

I want to ask, but I don't. I just go back to studying.

I don't want to insert myself in something I don't belong with, no matter how much I was liking the conversation going on.

At some point, I end up on the HEX website to check my messages, and sure enough, there is a message waiting for me from a certain someone.

There have only been messages from him since I posted my picture, since I haven't posted anything else.

Making sure Hunter isn't paying attention, I open the thread.

. . .

HUN4ALL: How was your day today?

A simple question that brings a small smile to my face. This is how our conversations have been going for the last couple of weeks. We actually have conversations about mundane things, with the occasional sexual activity. We've been getting to know each other and it feels nice to have someone to talk to.

Someone that is there when I'm having a rough day.

SENFULL94: It was okay, nothing special, just like any other day. How was yours?

I get a reply instantly.

HUN4ALL: Uneventful and tiring.

SENFULL94: Well at least tomorrow is Saturday so you could sleep in a little.

HUN4ALL: I wish, I have to be up at 5 am to head to the field. It's going to be a long day.

. . .

He says "field" a lot and it makes me wonder if he's an athlete. Given that he's twenty-one, I'm going to guess yes and that he might be in college. I should ask but that goes against all the rules of anonymity.

SENFULL94: Well if you need a nightcap after your long day tomorrow, you know where to find me ;)

HUN4ALL: I certainly do and I will take you up on that. The only thing that will make tomorrow worth it is if I get to see that gorgeous body of yours.

I like that he likes my body. Growing up, it has always been something that I've been self-conscious about, always felt the need to change. Having someone like Chase tell me that I'm gorgeous and that he likes the way my body looks, gives me a boost to my confidence. But having that boost can be dangerous because I might never want to get rid of it. For now, though, I'm going to grasp at anything that I can.

SENFULL94: Well let me know when you become free and I will make it happen!

. . .

HUN4ALL: YOU'RE THE BEST!

SENFULL94: Night Chase. <3

HUN4ALL: Night Len. <3

I close out of the browser and try to go back to studying but my brain isn't registering anything that's on the screen in front of me.

Looking at the time, I see that we've already been here for an hour. I guess an hour of studying is better than nothing.

"I'm going to head out," I whisper to Hunter as I pack my stuff up.

He nods, following suit. "I'll head out with you."

There is no point in arguing at this point, he's going to walk out with me regardless of what I say.

Once we are all packed up, we make our way out of the building, and like other walks to my car, we do it in silence.

It's during these walks that I sometimes wonder if he enjoys the silence as much as I do, or he is only silent because I am.

Not a word is spoken until we reach my car.

"Are you going to the game tomorrow?" he asks when I open the driver's side door.

I shake my head. "I don't really care for football."

"Who doesn't like football?" he says, the smile from earlier popping out a bit.

I match it and give him a shrug. "Grew up in a house that only watched baseball. A baseball game I would attend."

"Unbelievable. I can't have my seat neighbor not liking football, I'm the star quarterback after all," he says as if he's really offended by the topic

"Sorry to disappoint, Jacobi. It just doesn't do it for me." I shrug, throwing him a smile.

"I'm manifesting this, I will have you attending football games before the season is over. Guaranteed." He points at me and the boyish grin that he is sporting might be my absolute favorite that I've seen come from him.

"We'll see," I say, getting into the car. I'm about to close the door when he stops it.

"Text me when you get home, okay? It's late and all." Why can't this version of Hunter be around a lot more instead of the arrogant one?

I give him a nod. "I will."

One more smile is thrown in my direction before he pulls away. "Night, Selena."

"Night, Hunter." That smile of his grows more when I use his first name instead of the moniker everyone on campus uses.

He lets me close the door and I pull away and when I get home thirty minutes later, I text Hunter Jacobi for the first time telling him that I'm home. The whole time butterflies are fluttering.

My crush on the star quarterback is back and in full force.

And he will never notice.

CHAPTER NINE

HUNTER

EVERY INCH of my body hurts. The slightest movement has me cringing on the outside and silently crying on the inside.

Playing the position I play should come with a few aches and pains but nothing like this. This isn't normal.

No, this is what happens when your coach makes you play every play you have as punishment for losing the first two games of the season.

According to him, it's my fault that we lost because I've decided not to communicate with any of my teammates and it's ruining our dynamic.

He's partly right.

I have stopped communicating but it isn't with the whole team, it's just one person and maybe anyone that took his side in things and said I was overreacting for shutting him out.

A few of the older guys and some rookies are on mine, but even an outsider can tell that the team is divided. And it's all because of a damn girl.

And being one of the captains, I have to fix shit before

they get even more out of hand and we end up losing the whole season.

Can't be having that, because then Roy Jacobi will have a disappointment of a son and ruin all his chances of being an NFL dad.

Putting the thoughts of my dad on the back burner, I grab my stuff from my locker and head over to where Jaxton is sitting putting on his shoes.

Coach went hard on all of us today and as I get closer to my teammate, I see that he is still coated in sweat.

"Think we can talk?" I say, not even throwing out a greeting.

Jax looks up, his eyebrows bunching up in confusion and for a second I think he's going to fight me for approaching him but eventually he gives a nod.

"Yeah," he says through a sigh.

I nod toward the door and as we walk out of the locker room, I can feel all of our teammates' eyes on us as we head for the door.

Pretty sure they are going to gossip like little girls the second we're no longer in sight. They're worse than high school girls, I swear.

I walk through the tunnel until we reach the field. At one point, standing right in the middle of the fifty-yard line was my sanctuary. It was the only place where I knew who I was, now I'm not even sure who that is.

"So, what's up?" Jaxton throws out, coming to a stop a few feet away from me.

I face my one-time friend, the one that I was close to and could depend on. I let out a sigh. "Look, I've been an ass these last couple of weeks. I'm not going to apologize for the reason behind it, but I will apologize for shutting you out and not letting you tell me your side of things, to hear your apology that I know was sincere. I just grouped you together with Jenna and I wanted no part of it. I was pissed, pretty sure I still am, but the more I think about it the more I realize something."

"And what is that?" Jax's stance is defensive, like he's waiting for me to punch him. I should, and trust me, I wanted to, but I won't do it now. He doesn't deserve it. Well, he does, but my fist isn't going to meet an inch of him when Coach Young is anywhere near the field.

"That I can't hold on to Jenna's actions forever. I need to move on and put her and her shit behind me and I shouldn't take my anger for her out on you or the team. Even though you were part of the equation."

He looks at me, not saying a word. A few minutes pass by and I think he's going to punch *me* when he shifts but he holds out his hand.

"I am sorry for the shit that I caused even if it wasn't all on me. I still made that choice to sleep with your girl and for that, I am sorry. If it makes it any better, I broke it off with her that night."

"I wish I could say I'm sorry about that." I shake the hand he is offering.

He shrugs. "We didn't have anything real, it was just fucking and her way of playing you."

I just nod.

"So we're good?" he asks.

"We're not back to being best friends, don't know if we will ever get back to that, but yeah. We're good."

"You think Coach will stop kicking our asses now?" He gives me a smirk.

I snort. "I sure fucking hope so. I don't know if my body can take another beating."

———

HUN4ALL: What is your ideal date?

SENFULL94: My ideal date? That's what you are using for one of your ten questions?

We are currently playing ten questions. I wanted to know more about her so I came up with the game, with a few rules of course. Nothing too personal, and nothing that reveals who we really are.

As for the date question, I have no idea why I asked it. I guess a part of me wants to know just in case these conversations move from taking place through a screen to in person. It probably will never happen, but stranger things have gone down.

HUN4ALL: Yes, I'm using this as one of my questions.

SENFULL94: Why?

.   .   .

HUN4ALL: just tell me

SENFULL94: You really want to know?

Oh my god, this girl. Even though I'm slightly annoyed, I still find myself smiling. I picture her sitting in front of me giving a smirk, egging me on and trying to annoy me to the best of her ability. That image dies down a bit when I don't have a face to picture.

I really wish I knew what she looked like.

HUN4ALL: If I didn't, I wouldn't have asked.

SENFULL94: *eye rolling emoji* A spontaneous trip to a bookstore.

HUN4ALL: THAT'S your ideal date??? A trip to a bookstore???

My mind right away starts to think of every bookstore I know of to take her to.

Calm down, Jacobi. You don't even know what her real name is.

· · ·

SENFULL94: Don't judge. I'm a book nerd, going to a bookstore is like heaven. I can be there for hours if I wanted.

HUN4ALL: So you read?

SENFULL94: I do. Almost every day.

HUN4ALL: What kind of books do you read??

SENFULL94: The ones you find at a bookstore

Witty. I like it and add that on top of the eye rolls she continues to throw my way, this girl is a handful. I like that even more, especially when I add her body to the mix.

HUN4ALL: such a nerd

SENFULL94: A BOOK NERD, thank you very much and yet you are still here talking to me.

. . .

HUN4ALL: Okay a book nerd, and that's because I have a sweet spot for you and your conversations.

SENFULL94: And here I thought it was for my body.

HUN4ALL: Oh, your body is definitely an added bonus ;)

I wait for her reply to show up on the screen when I take a peek at the time.

One in the morning.

After my conversation with Jax, I went to talk to Coach and tell him that Jax and I were cool on the field and we were going to start working as a team.

The man looked at me as if I had three heads and just said "we'll see," and told me to leave.

Given the pain my body was in, I came home right after that and took a scorching hot shower to help with the muscle soreness. After I ate dinner, I checked HEX and there was a message from Len asking me how my day was going.

That was five hours ago and the conversation is still going strong.

I've come to really like our conversations. We talk about anything that is on our minds without giving away too much.

But the more that we talk, the more I want to know her in

real life.

It's been a little over a month since she commented on my picture, and yet I have no idea what her voice sounds like, or even what her face looks like. It's like a weird version of a dating app and I'm starting to dislike not really knowing her.

SENFULL94: you haven't even seen all of it

HUN4ALL: And I'm sure I would like every single inch of it when I do

SENFULL94: Maybe one day.

Yeah, maybe one day indeed.

HUN4ALL: Maybe one day soon ;)

SENFULL94: Maybe...

I should change the subject, but honestly, I don't want to.

. . .

HUN4ALL: You never told me where in California you lived. Maybe we might be close enough to meet and make that maybe actually a possibility.

I wait for her to respond right away, but after a solid two minutes, I conclude that I scared her off. I guess she really wants to keep who she is a secret. It was a simple comment, it's not like I'm going to ask for an address and show up at her door. I'm not that creepy, though I have gone up a few notches on that scale since I started using this app.

Closing out of the app, knowing Len will message back when she wants to, I open up Instagram and get lost in the scroll of pictures.

I start getting bored when I come across one picture posted by the psychology department and right in the middle is Selena Montez with a wide smile and bright-brown eyes.

There is a natural beauty about the girl. Her hair has a wave to it and it looks like it would be soft to touch.

I tried to touch it once but she pulled away before I could feel it. I was reaching for a piece that was framing her face so her pulling away made sense. She called me a weirdo and went back to listening to the professor.

Like I said, I've become more of a creep.

Tapping on the picture, I see that the page tagged her and I can't tap on her username fast enough.

"Who is Selena Montez?" I say out loud.

The second her profile loads, I'm a little shocked by what I see.

Since I've met her, Selena has been an anomaly to me. Like there is something about her that I can't quite pinpoint. She's a quiet person, doesn't really talk unless someone speaks to her first and she's always on her phone or laptop with her headphones in.

There have been times when it's just been me and her and I see her relax. She smiles more, she laughs and I get to hear her voice more and I look forward to those moments.

But if she's uncomfortable with something, she shuts down.

Like the time she asked me about my siblings.

That's partly my fault, I shouldn't have shut her out. I should have told her why I wasn't close to them. I should have opened up about how my siblings live with my mom and her new husband and how my dad manipulates all of my free time so I can't visit them. I should have voiced how when my parents divorced, I made the wrong choice when I decided to go live with my father. All those things came to mind when I saw her smile dwindle down, but I kept it to myself, because nobody cares about that Hunter. The only one that matters is the football player.

Every one of her pictures is different. There is no rhyme or reason to them but I still feel as if they all go together.

It's mostly pictures of random things and places but the pictures of her are what catch my eyes.

Some of her smiling straight at the camera, some are candid moments of her.

In each of them, she looks beautiful, happy.

Out of all her pictures, there is one that is my favorite. It's candid, her smile is bright and big and even though it's a picture, I can see that her eyes are sparkling. Her hair is filled with curls and she's a version of herself that I haven't witnessed before and the pull I've been feeling for this girl grows even stronger.

And because I'm a creep, I screenshot the picture and make it her contact on my phone.

I'm about to go back to Instagram when I decide to shoot her a text.

HUNTER: I thought that you were an exercise science major?

It's after I send the message that I remember the time and realize that Selena might be asleep. I watch as the message goes from delivered to read and then to the little bubbles jumping up and down before a message comes in. I guess she was awake.

SELENA: I am...?

HUNTER: Why are you tagged on the psych page?

SELENA: Because I'm minoring in psych?

. . .

HUNTER: huh I didn't know that.

SELENA: Because you never asked, Jacobi.

Is it bad that I hate that she calls me Jacobi? I like it better when Hunter rolls off her tongue.

A notification from HEX has me stopping from telling Selena just that.

Opening the app again, I go straight to Len's reply and I swear my heart starts to beat rapidly when I read the words.

SENFULL94: Fine if you really want to know... I'm on the Central Coast.

HUN4ALL: Are you lying?

SENFULL94: No, why would I lie?

HUN4ALL: Where on the Central Coast?

SENFULL94: Umm ... in Seaside.

No fucking way. There are so many coincidences in the world and this one has to be one of them. Out of all the places this woman could possibly live, she's in the same part of the state that I am.

HUN4ALL: I live in Seaside.

What are the chances that I know this woman? That I've crossed paths with her?

Worse yet, what if this woman is someone from my past and is out to play me even more than she already has?

What are the chances that the girl I know as Len is really fucking Jenna?

CHAPTER TEN

SELENA

HUN4ALL: **I live in Seaside.**

Out of all the words that he could have typed out, those never crossed my mind.

He lives in Seaside? What in the actual fuck?

If he lives in the same city as me, that means that our paths are more likely to cross. Wait, what if he goes to Cal U? Oh fuck.

Why didn't I ever think that it was a possibility? I possibly shared my lady bits with someone I share a class with.

Nope. Nope. Not going there. This guy has to be someone I've never met before, there is no chance I know him. Seaside is a decent-sized city and Cal U is a pretty big school. Our chances of knowing each other can be slim to none.

Or it could be that you see this person every day.

Yeah, I'm not going to think about that. I look down at the message and type out a response.

SEN4ALL: well fuck. Maybe you might actually get your wish of meeting in real life after all.

I try to play it off as if this little bit of news isn't freaking me out. There are so many possibilities and each and every one of them is causing me to bite my nails out of existence.

HUN4ALL: Maybe we already have and we don't realize it.

SENFULL94: I doubt it

HUN4ALL: Why?

SENFULL94: Because I'm sure I would have remembered a body like that.

I may be joking on the screen but internally I'm having an existential crisis.

· · ·

HUN4ALL: This one? *photo attached*

Okay, he's teasing me. He has to be. The picture he sent is sure to make me forget about my mind working overtime. He's shirtless, shorts hanging low, low enough to see exactly where that happy trail leads to.

A happy trail that I would gladly lick.

Get your mind off his delicious body, Selena. You will never have it. Especially if you've met him out in the real world.

Oh my god, how embarrassing would that be if I know this guy and I'm not attractive to him in person? Total buzzkill right there.

I type out a reply.

SENFULL94: Yes, that one.

HUN4ALL: Maybe you have seen it, you just don't remember.

SENFULL94: Trust me, that is something that I would not forget.

HUN4ALL: Then I say we meet in person and figure that out for sure.

. . .

It's tempting. It's tempting to push through all my insecurities and say yes let's meet. But the thing that is holding me back is fear. Fear that he will see me and conclude that he may like me through a screen but doesn't feel the same in person. And that also goes for sexual attraction.

He thinks he likes my body because of what he sees in pictures but pictures lie. Pictures can be manipulated and posed and not what real life represents.

I think the fear of not only getting hurt but also embarrassed is what is stopping me from saying yes.

A guy like him will never be seen with a girl that wears anything over size-six jeans. For all I know, he's just stroking my confidence, telling me what I want to hear to get off.

But the conversations are deep.

They are, but that could be because he needs someone to talk to.

I respond with all the truth that I can muster.

SENFULL94: I don't think I'm ready to meet just yet. It has nothing to do with you, it's all me.

HUN4ALL: Are you scared?

Again I respond with the truth.

. . .

SENFULL94: Yes.

HUN4ALL: Of what?

SENFULL94: of not meeting your expectations.

Never have I put my insecurities out there for everyone to see, let alone a guy. I hold them in deep and only show the confident part because I have to. But there it is, all of my truths in five little words.

HUN4ALL: Okay, I respect that.

I nod to myself even though he can't see it. I don't respond but as I'm closing up the app, another message comes in.

HUN4ALL: But know that you will be beyond every expectation I set and spending a single second with you will be well worth it.

SENFULL94: You don't know that.

. . .

HUN4ALL: Yeah I do, Len. I really do know that.

SENFULL94: Good night, Chase.

HUN4ALL: Good night, Len.

Before I close off the app, I snap a quick picture and send it in his direction. If there is a chance of meeting him in real life, I'm going to bask in how he makes me feel every time I show him a part of me that many others have not seen before.

It's a glorious feeling.

My phone dings once again but there is no new message from Chase, it's one from Instagram.

Hunter Jacobi is now following me.

CHAPTER ELEVEN

HUNTER

I WALKED into anatomy tonight and I realized one thing.

Somehow and I don't know how or when, but somehow it happened, Selena and I have become friends? More than classmates? More than two people that walk to her car three nights a week after class? I don't know but she's definitely become something, and I like it.

And I like her.

In the last eight weeks or so since the semester started, she has become a constant in my life that I didn't know I needed.

The one thing besides football that I would interact with. Sure there have been days where she doesn't say a word, but that's who she is and I'm okay with that.

There are days though where I feel the need to bug the shit out of her, and sometimes I get rewarded with her laugh or a small smile. Sometimes I get a death glare but she has yet to tell me to shut up or to stop bugging her.

Today I feel that need and I can't help but wonder what type of mood she will be in.

I walk into class and walk down to my unassigned assigned seat next to the brown-eyed girl.

Has Selena captured my attention in an unintentional way? Most definitely.

I pull out my chair and I start to get settled when I look over at the girl.

She's not paying any attention to me. Her head is down with her hair serving as a curtain covering her face while she's most likely scrolling on her phone. Since she didn't look up, I'm guessing she has her earbuds in, which I notice are never far from her ears.

Tapping on her shoulder to get her attention, she jumps back, startled, as if I just caught her doing something she shouldn't be doing.

"Well hello to you too, Miss Jumpy. What are you doing?" I throw a smirk in her direction and I swear I see a hint of pink come across her cheeks. It's fucking adorable.

"Just reading," she says, taking out her earbuds, not looking in my direction. She reads? How did I not know this?

"Just reading? What exactly were you 'just reading?'"

"Nothing," she says and I see her slide her phone into her backpack, still not looking in my direction.

"Pretty sure nothing wouldn't have you blushing right at this very moment."

That is what finally makes her look at me and it's a full-on glare. Oh it's one of those days. I love those days. Those are the days that her lips get even more pouty than what they are and her eyes twinkle a bit.

"Come on, tell me, what were you reading?" I turn to face her, nudging her in the process.

"Nothing that you would find interesting." She turns to face the front.

"It's a romance book, isn't it?" I throw out there. I've seen them around social media over the last few months and I may have gotten curious about them once or twice, but I've never picked one up. If Selena reads them, then maybe I would have to.

The way her blush continues to grow and how she is trying her hardest to not turn her glare in my direction, gives me my answer. It is a romance book.

"Well damn, I guess the shy girl has more than one surprise up her sleeve. Is it raunchy, like the *Fifty Shades* stuff?" I nudge at her again, but she doesn't budge. She just starts getting ready to start class, paying me no regard.

Wanting to see how far I can push her, I lean into her ear. Right away, I get a whiff of her. She smells like cucumber and mint and freshness, and the combination of the three makes my mouth water.

Does she smell like that all over?

"Does the book you are reading have the word pussy and cock in it? Because I hear those are the best."

Selena's breath hitches. If it's because of my words or my closeness, I have no idea. And given that she doesn't answer my question, I'm going to take her silence as a yes.

Interesting.

Not what I expected from her.

She sits up straight when Professor Peppy starts class and tries to take in everything that the professor is saying. As for me, instead of sitting back in my chair and paying attention to class, I pay attention to Selena.

Being this close to her, I see things that I never really paid attention to before. I guess because I've never been this close to her.

The first thing I notice is just how long and full her eyelashes really are. They are long enough to touch her cheek when she blinks and they go perfectly with those brown eyes of hers.

She's wearing her glasses today, something that I notice she does as the week comes to an end. They frame her face and she looks sexy with them, I'm not going to lie.

I also notice that she has freckles on her cheeks and nose that give her a good girl type of vibe.

Given the type of book she was reading earlier, I would say that the girl next to me is anything but.

I must not be thinking clearly because I have this need to be closer to her. So I put my arm around her shoulders, sliding her chair even closer to me.

"What are you doing?" she hisses, trying to get out from under my arm.

"I want to know about the book you were reading," I say next to her head, taking another whiff of her scent.

Being the unpredictable person that she is, Selena stabs my leg with her finger, digging it into the material of my jeans, for sure leaving a bruise.

I don't budge.

"No," she says through her teeth when I don't move.

"Come on, at least read me a little snippet. I bet those words that had you blushing would sound sexy with your voice."

The glare she gives me makes me want to close the distance between us and see how soft her pout is.

"What the fuck has gotten into you?"

What, indeed.

I just shrug. "You interest me."

"I interest you? What the fuck does that even mean?"

I shrug again. "So are you going to read something to me?"

"In your dreams, Jacobi." She nudges me again, this time an elbow to the ribs.

"Trust me, I will dream about it," I mumble and I can tell by the way she's looking at me, she heard. "Just a few words."

Selena continues to look at me and I throw her a smile that I know makes women crazy.

Finally she rolls her eyes before reaching into her bag and taking out her phone.

Instead of reading to me like I suggested, she does a few things before sliding her phone over to me, already to an open page.

As I take the phone, she tries to push away from me but I don't let her. Eventually she just gives up and stays at my side.

I read the words that are on the phone screen and now I know why she jumped when I got here.

Holy shit, this is explicit and very detailed.

This is definitely a book that has the word pussy and cock and so many other colorful words.

Just on this one page, the dude is eating the girl's pussy and telling her how he wants her to ride his cock after she squirts on his face.

"Jesus," I say, adjusting myself slightly. I stop reading and slide the phone back to her. Don't get me wrong, I want to finish the scene, maybe even the book but having a boner during class is definitely not a good idea.

"Now, move." She takes her phone, before hitting me again with her elbow.

I give her a little more room but keep my arm on the back of her chair.

I can't tell you why there is a sudden urge to be so close to her but at this moment and time, I don't want to question it.

Close to the end of class, I lean into her again, this time just to keep annoying her.

"Come to the game this weekend." I feel a pen stab in my leg and as much as I want to jerk away, I don't.

"No."

"Go to the game on Saturday."

Stab.

"No."

"Go to the game."

"Why?" she says a little too loudly and gets the attention of the people around us. She cowers down with embarrassment.

Why do I want her at the game?

She hasn't gone to any of the other six games this season, why would she go to this one?

And how do I know she hasn't gone to any? One I've looked for her and two I've made it a hobby to stalk her Instagram. Which she hasn't followed me back on. Because of my stalking, I know what she does on game days and it's not going to games or watching them on TV, that's for sure.

But that still doesn't answer the question as to why I want her at the game?

"Because we're friends." It's the best I got and we are friends. Right?

Does only interacting with someone in class count as being friends?

I would say yes, but that's just me.

"Okay, that is all for today!" Professor Peppy says to the class. "We'll end it here. Remember that next week we have a test on Wednesday here and then a practical test on Friday. So study, study, study."

Shuffling of notebooks, chairs and backpacks start to sound through the whole room and as I'm putting my laptop away, I come up with an idea that puts a stupid grin on my face.

Selena and I head out of class together and start making our way over to her car. Again because we've developed a routine that we don't really talk about.

When we reach her car, she finally turns to face me.

"Okay, what's with the creepy grin?" she asks, sounding exasperated.

I shrug. "Just seems that you will be spending the weekend with me."

Her perfectly sculpted eyebrows shoot up. "Did you hit your head during practice or something? What makes you think I'm spending the weekend with you?"

"Well I figure after class on Friday we study and then on Saturday you go to my game and then on Sunday we study some more. So you, me, all weekend."

"That is the stupidest thing I've ever heard," she says, again rolling her eyes and starting to get into the car.

"Come on, it's perfect."

She sits in the driver's seat for a few seconds before releasing a sigh. "Yes to studying, and only because I'm a bad test taker, but no to the football game."

"The football game is the best part," I whine.

She just shakes her head at me and I watch as she rolls up the sleeves of her hoodie before starting her car. Dark lines that paint her wrist capture my attention.

Selena has a tattoo? How have I not noticed it before?

I take my attention away from the tattoo and concentrate on the girl it adorns.

"Will you read me something from your book?"

"No."

"You're no fun."

"Take it or leave it, Jacobi."

I'm not used to this kind of treatment from women but I don't hate it, especially coming from Selena.

"I'll take it, but know one thing, Montez, before the season ends, you will be attending at least one game. Mark my words."

Again with another eye roll.

"Whatever you say. Can I go now?" She looks at me, her eyelashes batting in my direction.

"Fine, but text me when you get home." She's nodding before I even get the whole sentence out.

"You're definitely not who people say you are, Jacobi." She pulls the door closed and with a small wave in my direction, pulls out of the parking spot, leaving me there.

"I could say the same thing about you, Selena."

It's as I walk over to my own car that I realize two things. One, I feel like there is something familiar with Selena's tattoo, I just can't pinpoint what.

And two, Selena Montez is wedging herself into my brain and every inch of me likes having her there.

CHAPTER TWELVE

SELENA

"YOU KNOW WHAT YOU NEED, LENA?" my sister asks me from across her dinner table, her fork pointed right at me.

It's Thursday night, which is the one night a week that my sisters and I get together to eat, drink and talk shit.

Tonight the wine is flowing and it seems that my sisters have all decided to gang up on me.

"What do I need?" As much as I want to take a drink of my wine, I don't because I know her next words are going to take me by surprise.

"*¡Un novio!*" Sara, my eldest sister, throws out. She even slaps a hand against the table for emphasis.

"Oh, yeah. I agree one hundred percent!" Gabriella, the second oldest, says. She even holds out a hand for Sara to high-five.

Did I mention my sisters tend to go overboard with the drink on our dinner nights? Like a lot, and without fail every morning, I wake up to hundreds of text messages yelling at

131

me because I let them drink too much. A perk of being the youngest.

"I don't need a boyfriend," I state, taking a drink from my wineglass, trying to avoid my sister's eyes as much as possible.

"Oh come on, yes you do," Sara eggs on and I just shake my head at her, trying really hard not to laugh.

"No, I don't." What is it with Mexican families that always want you to have a boyfriend? Why is that so important? Like really, why does a woman need a man to be happy?

It would be nice though.

It would be nice to go to places with someone and not be by myself all the time. Or having someone to talk to when I'm having a tough day. Or to have someone at my side when I don't want to be close to someone that makes me uncomfortable.

You have Chase to talk to.

I do, but it's not the same. Chase knows a persona, someone that is like me but isn't completely me. As much as I want to tell him everything about me, let him know about everything that makes me tick, I don't. Who I am online and who I am in real life are two completely different people.

Online, I'm confident and free and don't have anything from my past or childhood holding me down. The online version of me is everything that I want to be.

Sara chugs down her wine before giving me her full attention. "Yes, you do. You need someone that can pound into your body! Just like—"

"Nope!" I stop her before she can say anything else. "Nope. I don't want to hear it! I don't want that visual of what your husband does to you or to your body. Nope, sorry."

"Are you into girls?" Stella, my third sister, asks, her eyes filled with wonder.

"What?"

"It's okay if you are, and it's okay to come out right now if you want. We will love you times a million, no matter what," Gabriella says in return.

"I'm not into girls." I can appreciate a woman's body, but there is no sexual or physical attraction there.

"Then why are you twenty-two and single? I don't think I've ever seen you with a guy before," Sara whines.

That's because they haven't.

I've dated, but nothing serious enough to call a relationship or to use the boyfriend/girlfriend labels or to bring around my family.

I'm about to answer her, but Gabriella stops me. "Or maybe she already has a boyfriend and she doesn't want to tell us."

My sisters are seriously crazy.

This time I let the smile and laugh come out. "I don't have a thing for girls. I don't need a boyfriend, nor do I have one."

"Really, then who's Hunter?" Stella asks, one of her eyebrows rising in a knowing way.

"Wha-what? I don't know what you are talking about. I don't know a Hunter," I say, as I feel my eyes go wide and my throat starting to close.

How does she know about Hunter? Never, and I mean never, have I mentioned him before.

"There's a Hunter in your contacts and he's calling you right now." She nods toward my phone. I follow her line of sight and sure enough, Hunter Jacobi is calling me right now.

Why is he even calling me?

Quickly, I silence the call and act as if no call ever happened.

All three of my sisters are currently staring at me with eyebrows raised.

It's times like these that I wish that we had these types of dinners in public, and not at one of their houses, because then I could walk away.

Maybe if I act nonchalantly, they will drop the subject.

"So who is he?" Sara asks, definitely not dropping it.

"No one," I say too quickly.

"Doesn't seem like no one. Maybe we should look him up," Gabriella says, taking out her own phone.

Oh god, please don't. Why do I feel the need to label my contacts with both first and last name? Now they can easily find him with a simple Google search.

Before I can say anything to stop them, my phone starts to ring again. Hunter Jacobi once again.

Sara laughs. "Might as well answer it. The boy seems eager."

I roll my eyes when she throws a wink in my direction, but I grab my phone and leave the table to answer the call.

"Hello?" I answer the call when I'm halfway to the spare bedroom.

"Get it, Lena! Get that dick, baby!" Sara yells and by the cough that I hear on the other side, Hunter heard it.

"'Get that dick'?" Hunter says instead of a greeting.

"Sorry." I slip into the spare bedroom at Sara's house and swiftly close the door behind me, locking it in the process so they don't come in. "I'm at my sister's house having dinner and well, they're a little drunk."

"Oh, I didn't mean to interrupt anything. I can call you back later."

If he's calling me, something must be up. So whatever it is, I rather have him tell me now rather than later.

"Um, no. It's okay. I already got teased anyway. What's up?" I sit at the edge of the bed, waiting for whatever he's about to tell me.

"I just, um, wanted to, um..." Why does he sound nervous? "I wanted to make sure that we were still on for tomorrow night. To study after class, I mean."

"You called me twice... to ask me a question you could have asked me tomorrow? During class?" I'm pretty sure he could have texted me and he would have gotten a response a whole lot faster.

"Yeah," he sighs out.

"Why?" I can hear the confusion in my voice.

"I don't know." I can picture him holding his phone to his ear and scratching his head, looking for an answer. "I guess I wanted to hear your voice or whatever."

Hear my voice?

"You heard my voice yesterday and I'm going to be seeing you tomorrow."

"Don't judge me, Montez. If I had it in my mind that I wanted to hear your voice tonight, then I wanted to hear your voice. Don't overthink it."

I can't help but laugh a bit. This guy surprises me more and more every time I talk to him. Take yesterday during class for example.

All last night and today while I was at work, I was trying to figure out what had gotten into him. I felt his gaze on me and then he touched me. It was innocent but he had never

135

been that close to me before. Never had actively touched me or spoken to me so close that I could feel his lips move against my earlobe.

It threw me off.

But I loved every single second of it. I liked being that close to him and I only acted to be bothered or to push him away because I didn't want him to suspect anything.

Then his words.

The words he said made me want to squirm and for a little while, I was able to pretend that I actually had a chance with someone like Hunter. I pretended that the size of my clothes or the fact that I had a stomach with stretch marks didn't matter.

Then class ended and I was brought back to reality.

The reason I said no to the football game was because I didn't want people to judge him for inviting me. They probably already judge him for walking me to my car after class, that should be enough.

"Fine. I won't judge you for it, but you got to admit, it's a little weird," I tell him, taking my mind away from my insecurities.

"Yeah, you might be right," he says and then he pauses for a second before he speaks again. "Did I hear correctly, or did your sister really tell you to get that dick?"

I groan. "Here I thought that you were going to forget that part and not mention it."

"Nope, for some reason when it comes to you and the word dick, I can't avoid it." He laughs, the bastard.

"I'm never going to let you read one of my books, ever again." That might actually be a lie. It was hot knowing that he was reading a romance book and was affected by it. I even saw him adjust himself when he passed me back my phone.

"You're mean. Now tell me why your sister, I think, told you to go get some dick."

"You're not going to drop it, are you?" I ask, lying back on the made bed, looking up at the ceiling.

"Not a chance in hell." I can't help but snort at his comment.

"Like I said, my sisters are drunk. They have it in their mind that I need a boyfriend. Or at least someone that could 'pound my body,' their words not mine."

The call goes silent. Silent enough for me to pull the phone away from my ear and check if the call is there.

Eventually Hunter clears his throat and responds.

"You don't have a boyfriend that can do those things?" he asks, clearing his throat a few more times.

"Um, no. I'm as single as they come," I answer. The fact that I'm talking about this with Hunter of all people is messing with my mind.

"And do you want a boyfriend?"

I snort. "Why? Are you offering, Jacobi?"

"I mean, if you wanted me to, yeah, I would offer."

He's dead ass serious.

"I was joking," I whisper, trying really hard not to be affected by his comment.

"Yeah, I knew that," he says, sounding a little defeated.

"It would be nice though, not the pounding." I cringe slightly, trying to figure out why I'm telling him this. "But the companionship. The whole not being alone all the time would be nice."

"Yeah?"

137

I nod even though he can't see. "Yeah."

"Well, I hope you find that one day soon."

Yeah, me too, I don't say to him.

"Lena! Stop with the phone sex and come back out! I found another bottle I'm making you try." Sara's voice flows through the room.

I can't help but let out a groan. "I'll be right out."

Hunter's laugh makes her comment even worse.

"Shut up," I tell him, contemplating hanging up on him for laughing at my teasing.

"Sorry." He chuckles. "I guess your sister really wants you to get laid." I let out another groan. Out of all people, I really don't want to talk about sex with Jacobi, he probably has stories left and right. "Also, did she call you Lena?"

I sigh. "Yeah, that's what my family calls me."

"I like it."

"Are we done here?" I get up from the bed, ready to face even more of my sister's teasing.

"You haven't answered my question."

"What question is that?"

"Are we still on for tomorrow?"

I don't say anything for a solid moment, but then I find myself nodding. "Yeah, we're still on for tomorrow after class."

"Cool. Then I guess I will see you tomorrow, Lena."

"See you tomorrow, Hunter."

I hang up the call and head back into the dining room. The second I turn the corner three pairs of eyes are pointed at me.

"So, who's Hunter?" Gabriella asks as soon as I sit down.

As much as I try to hide my smile, I fail. "He's a friend and only a friend."

And that's all he will ever be.

"Well, he's one hot friend. I say you hit it. No way in hell will a man like that say no to a woman with your ass and *chichis*."

I groan.

I should have stayed in the room.

CHAPTER THIRTEEN

HUNTER

I LOOK at my screen and I can't help but smile like the biggest doofus on the planet.

Also given the content on my screen, I shouldn't even be looking at it in public, or in the locker room for that matter. Yet here I am, not able to pry my eyes away.

Len and I are becoming more and more comfortable with each other and started talking outside of our usual window of ten at night to two in the morning. Messages during the day have started to become a thing between us and I'm not mad about it.

Especially if I continue to get pictures like the one she sent me about an hour ago while I was at practice.

The picture is dark, but I can still make out every single inch of her glorious body. She's leaning back on her bed with slightly open knees, her head is thrown back, and her chest is on full display along with her bare pussy.

It's fucking mouthwatering and painful given that I'm currently wearing a cup, but I can't look away.

This woman's body is what I would describe as my

personal heaven, and I want my hands and tongue all over her.

She has soft curves and they look absolutely perfect on her.

If she gave me the chance, I would worship every single inch of her as much as humanly possible.

And I tell her just that.

HUN4ALL: I want every single inch of you. Tits, pussy, ass, everything you want to give, I will take. Fuck that picture is gorgeous.

This isn't a message that I should be sending in a room full of men but fuck it. This woman is worth getting caught with a boner. A reply instantly follows.

SENFULL94: I'm glad you think so. I took it with you in mind.

HUN4ALL: Oh yeah? What exactly were you thinking about?

SENFULL94: How if I took you up on that offer to meet, you'd do stuff to me...

. . .

HUN4ALL: And what kind of stuff would I be doing? Say the words, Len.

SENFULL94: You would lick my pussy

HUN4ALL: And then what would I do?

SENFULL94: Make me come and because you wouldn't be done with me, you would slide your cock in me and make me come again.

Holy fucking hell. This most definitely isn't a conversation I should be reading in public.

HUN4ALL: Fuck. You know how to make a guy hard with just some words.

"Jacobi!" someone yells, taking me out of the conversation and grabbing my attention. Right away I turn off my screen and shove it into my bag.

Jax is in front of me, looking at me with confusion. He's probably trying to figure out why I jumped when he called out my name and hid my phone right away.

"What's up?" I ask, trying to push any form of arousal down and not have it be visible.

"You okay?" he asks, his brows bunching up.

I nod. "Yup. What's up?"

He gives me a look like he doesn't believe me, but thankfully he drops it. "Some of the guys are going to grab dinner after our night class. Like a team dinner of sorts. You coming?"

I heard a few guys talking about it earlier but I didn't pay much mind to it. I just thought that it was a regular night out, not an unofficial team dinner.

After the big deal I made with Selena last night about still meeting up, no way I can cancel on her.

"I can't this time, but tomorrow after the game, win or lose, drinks are on me," I offer.

It's not that I don't want to be with my team, I do and I kind of have to but I also want to be with Selena for reasons I can't explain.

"We'll hold you to that, man." Jax holds out a fist for me to bump and when he has his back turned to me, I take out my phone again.

A message waiting for me.

SENFULL94: You're hard?

I smirk. This girl doesn't know the sorcery that her body is capable of.

. . .

HUN4ALL: Very and it's fucking painful because I have a cup on. I'm going to take a cold shower

SENFULL94: If you would have said a hot one, I would have asked if I could join you.

What the hell has gotten into her? She's laying everything out there and it's a fucking turn-on.

HUN4ALL: Great, now my cock is going to be hard in the shower and I can't do anything about it.

SENFULL94: Maybe I will message you later tonight and I can walk you through how to take care of it just right.

HUN4ALL: You fucking better. Your body and my dick will be the perfect combination.

I don't wait for a response, I close the app and head straight to the showers and take the coldest shower that this locker room can muster.

If that isn't enough, I'm not against rubbing one out in my

truck before my next class, because I won't survive until tonight.

———

Anatomy was the most uneventful it has been in a while. I think if the cold shower hadn't helped with my hard-on brought on by Len, it would have been a little more exciting.

The only thing that Selena has said to me during class was to ask if we were still on for studying. When I told her yes, she just nodded and stayed quiet for the rest of class.

Part of me wonders if I did something wrong.

I'm still wondering that because class is over and I'm just standing here waiting for her to finish putting her things away.

"Should we go see if there are any tables open upstairs?" She breaks the silence finally, when she stands from her chair and looks at me from under those lashes of hers.

"I was thinking maybe we can head back to one of our places. You know, since it's more comfortable and we don't have to worry about being quiet all the time," I throw out there.

Was this my original plan? No, but I said it already so I can't take it back. And besides, given that it's halfway through the semester, tables are going to be scarce.

"Oh," she says, her shoulders falling a bit. "I don't live on campus. It's actually thirty minutes from here, and room-mates and all."

How did I not know that she didn't live on campus?

"Then we can head to my place. I live over on the west side, by the student apartments. And no roommates." I give her a smile, trying to reassure her but it doesn't do anything. She just continues to stand there and bite her lip nervously.

"Okay," she finally says.

"Or we can go upstairs and look for a table, if that's what makes you more comfortable." I'm not going to force her to do something that she isn't comfortable with. Even if that is studying at my place.

She shakes her head. "No, it's cool. We can head to your place. I don't mind. Really. I'll just follow you there."

"Okay then." I wave for her to walk out of the room in front of me.

Once we hit the parking lot, the silence is back, and I hate it. I'm used to silence when it comes to Selena, but this feels different, like something is off.

"Are you mad at me or something?" I try to rack my brain for something that I might have done but I can't think of anything.

Selena turns to me, her perfectly sculpted eyebrows popping out from behind her glasses. "No, why would I be?"

I shrug. "I don't know. You're a quiet person, that I know, but you're being overly quiet tonight and I can't help but feel like I did something wrong."

She continues to look at me as we walk, eventually sighing. "I'm not mad at you and you did nothing wrong. I just overheard Jaxton talking before class about a team dinner and how you weren't going. I felt bad. I don't want you to miss something with your teammates just because I'm a bad test taker."

That's it? That's why she's been shutting me out?

I grab her hand and pull her to a stop and when she looks

down instead of up at me, I place a finger under her chin and show her I mean business.

"Don't feel bad. Jax told me about the dinner and even after I thought about it, I still decided that I wanted to study with you. Should I go to that dinner? Sure, but I would rather study. Besides, I'm making it up to them tomorrow after the game."

She's looking at me with those big brown eyes of hers, with her bottom lip between her teeth and I have to fight not to lean forward and replace her teeth with mine.

I bet her lips are soft and her mouth would fit perfectly against mine.

"Are you absolutely sure you want to study?"

No, I want to see how her mouth tastes and how she feels in my hands and her body grinding against mine.

Fuck.

I guess this train of thought is enough to tell me that Selena has indeed wedged herself in my brain and I'm developing some very, very deep feelings for her.

I have no idea how it happened though, it's not like our interactions are over the top. We talk, I walk her to her car and yet I can see myself falling for her in every form of the word.

"I'm completely sure. Now forget about it and let's head to my place."

"Okay."

The whole drive to my apartment, I keep thinking of ways to keep my feelings for Selena at bay.

I have a feeling that if I made them known, she would get scared and never talk to me again.

CHAPTER FOURTEEN

HUNTER

TWENTY MINUTES after we leave the library parking lot, we are in my living room with books and laptops sprawled out on the floor in front of us.

Since we've stepped into the apartment, Selena seems a little bit more relaxed but she's still quiet. I don't like her quiet, at least not in moments like this. I like hearing her voice and listening to the rasp of it. It's soothing.

"So you have roommates?" I ask while I open up the lecture slides from last week.

"Yup. Two," she says as she writes something on her study guide.

"That's cool. Are they okay people?"

"I would say so. They haven't killed me yet, they might be planning it though. But it's taken them this long so I think they like me. I see that as a plus."

If I was eating or drinking something right about now I would have spit it out.

She can't be fucking serious.

I turn to look at Selena, where she sits next to me on the floor and I see that she's trying her hardest not to laugh.

"What?" I have to clear my throat a bit.

"My parents. I live with my parents. I grew up thirty minutes from here." She lets out a laugh that is like music to my ears. If only I could record it.

I can't help but laugh with her while I shove her shoulder.

"I was already picturing putting on the news and them saying they discovered your body," I let out before it gets drowned by her laugh.

She wipes her eyes from a few tears that have escaped. "I mean, they do have four daughters, it's no wonder that they haven't gone crazy."

"Your poor father," I say, shaking my head at her and this time I get shoved.

"My poor mother. She had to deal with the four of us and my dad on top of that."

"But I bet she loves having each of you home all at the same time." I know my mom loves it when I come home the few weekends a year I visit. She never wants me to leave, but that may be because I don't visit enough.

I should though. I should visit her and Jainie and Blake every chance I get, but I don't.

"She does. She loves having everyone home and now that my sisters are married and are having kids, she loves it even more."

I nod, wishing I had that. "Is that why you stayed close by? Because of your family?"

Selena puts her notebook on the coffee table and turns to face me, so I turn my body to her to give her my full attention.

"Yes and no," she says and I watch as her eyebrows come together before she continues. "I wanted to go away for school and I part of me wishes I had for the experience but staying close has had its benefits. It's helped me save money for the future while I still get a great education and get to be close to my family if anything were to happen. And with nieces and nephews in the picture now, I get to see them grow up and I think that makes not leaving for school worth it."

I noticed it before, when we were in the library a few weeks ago, she smiles whenever she talks about her family.

"Family must be very important to you," I muse.

She gives me a nod. "Yeah, it is."

We look at each other for a long minute, neither of us turning away. There's a small smile playing on her lips. It's inviting and enough to spill my secrets to her.

"I wish I had what you had. My only thing is that I wish I had stayed with my mom when she and my dad divorced."

Instantly her smile disappears, and I regret speaking.

"Why do you say that?" she asks as she leans her head against the couch and waits for me to speak.

She's giving me the option of opening up.

Am I going to take it?

"My parents divorced when I was fourteen. At that point, Dad was in and out of the house, but he was always there for anything that had to do with football. Even when my brother started to play hockey, football was all that mattered to him. Mom hated it. Mostly because when it came to Blake and Jainie, Dad didn't seem to care as much. At the time, I didn't see the other stuff. I didn't see that Dad would never go to Blake's games or Jainie's dance recitals, I only saw him at my stuff. My games, my practice, my coaches' meetings. Mom grew tired of it, and I heard some of the fights but chose to ignore them. When it was finally a done deal, and they were separated, they fought about who I was going to live with. They didn't fight about my brother and sister, they fought about me, because Dad wanted me to concentrate on football. I was fourteen, I didn't see things like grown-ups did. I saw it as I either give up something I love or I continue to play it as long as I could. I wanted to continue playing and because I chose that, I moved with my dad about four hours away from my mom."

"But you continued playing." Selena's voice breaks through my memories. I look over at her and I see that she is looking at me with the kindest expression anyone has ever given me. She looks so beautiful this way.

So breathtaking.

I place my arm on the sofa cushions, extending toward her, and without a word. I move pieces of her hair out of her face. She doesn't move away from my touch.

"I continued to play. And I loved it. I loved everything about it, the attention from girls, attention from both college recruiters and NFL scouts. It felt like I was something else besides the rich kid that was handed everything."

I continue to play with a strand of her hair as I talk. It's soft like I thought it would be.

"When did that change?"

I let out a sigh. "I started to notice around the time that I had to pick a college to attend. Dad wanted me to go to a school that was known to draft NFL players, but I didn't want to. When I chose Cal U, he accepted it but still made everything possible to make scouts notice me. Becoming friends with people at networks that would broadcast our games, sending me off to training camps during the summers to get better and stronger as he put it. The more games that went by the more I noticed that all that mattered to him was football. He didn't care that I was starting to hate the sport, or that I was burning out. All he cared about was the titles and the money that would come his way when I eventually signed with an NFL team. The tipping point wasn't my dad though. It was the weekend before the semester started that I found out Jenna was cheating on me. That's when I realized that all people saw me as a football player that would pave the way for them. That would make them rich. They didn't care what I was feeling, they just cared about what they wanted and how they were going to get it."

I give her a small smile when I finish, not really knowing what else to do.

"Jenna's a bitch for cheating on you," Selena mumbles.

I snort. "It is what it is. I'm over it at this point."

Selena nods, dropping the topic of Jenna. "I have a question, but you don't have to answer if you don't want to."

"Ask anything you want."

"Do you want to continue playing football? I know you didn't redshirt so your eligibility is over after this year. But after the season is over, if a professional team approached you, would you want to play?"

I had one other person ask me this question and that was my mom a few months ago. I had gone to visit her at the beginning of summer before I went to training camp and she asked me this.

At the time my answer was yes.

"Football is all I've known. Since I was seven years old, I

have never gone without it for more than a month. I want to say that yes, I want to continue playing but I want to do it for me. I want to play for myself and not because someone is forcing me to do it."

Selena smiles at my answer. "You are a rare species, Hunter Jacobi. If you continue to play, any NFL team would be lucky to have you."

"And how would a girl that has never seen me play know that?"

Her smile grows. "Just because I haven't gone to a game this season, doesn't mean that I haven't seen you play. It is a football school after all."

"If you've seen me play, then why are you so adamant about not going to a game this season?" I pull her hair and she lets out a small laugh but still doesn't push my hand away.

"Truth?"

"Always."

I watch as Selena sits up, the strand of hair that I was playing with falling out of my grip, and comes closer to me, leaning in until her mouth is so close to my ear that I can feel her breath on my skin. Feel her chest brush up against my side.

"I don't like football," she whispers and when she starts to back away from me, my hand falls to her waist, holding her in place.

"I'm sorry. I think I just heard you say that you don't like football."

How can someone not like football? It's like a staple, like apple pie, everyone likes football.

Selena pulls back slightly, sitting on her knees but still in my touch, and shrugs.

"Never got the appeal of it and frankly it's confusing, so I tend to stay away from all things football."

She's serious.

"There is nothing confusing about football."

I get a playful eye roll. "Says the star quarterback."

"I'm afraid to ask this, if you don't like football, then what sport do you like?"

She shrugs. The girl seriously gives me another shrug. "I'm more of a baseball girl."

"Do you even know what an ERA or RBI stands for?"

"Earned run average and runners brought in," she answers in the most serious tone that she can muster. "I played softball."

Un-fucking-believable.

"That's it. It's decided by the end of this class, you will be a football fan. I fucking guarantee it." I will strap her to a chair and have her watch a football game if that's what it takes to make her a football fan.

Baseball can kiss my dick for all I care.

"Nope, sorry, not going to happen."

"Oh," I say, placing my other hand on her ribs. "It will happen. I will make sure of it."

She leans in, a smirk taking over her face. "I want to see you try, Jacobi."

That's when I attack. My fingers start moving across her rib cage and she falls into my lap as I tickle her.

"Hunter!" Her laugh fills the room and I can't help but smile when I hear it.

"Say you'll go to a game," I demand as she squirms in my lap, trying to get away from me.

"No." A giggle slips out, her hair flying all over the place.

"Say it and I stop." I continue my war against her ribs and when she tries to get away, I pull her back.

"No!" The smile on her face doesn't disappear.

"Say it, Lena." I use the name she says only her family uses which just causes her to laugh even harder.

"Fine!"

I press my fingers just under her rib cage. "I'm sorry, I didn't hear you. What did you say?"

"I said fine! I'll go to one of your stupid games." One last giggle is released before I stop my attack.

Selena stays with her head on my lap, completely out of breath, a smile on her face, and hair all over the place. The way that she is looking up at me is my undoing.

Because one second, I'm staring at the beautiful girl with her head on my lap and the next I'm leaning down and pressing my lips to hers.

The second my lips meet hers, I want to sink into everything that she has to offer, but I pull back the second that I realize what I'm doing.

"I'm sorry," I say against her lips, her eyes open wide with surprise, her pout begging for more.

Selena stares up at me, not moving or saying a word.

We continue to stare at each other until Selena starts to move. I think she's going to pull away from me completely when she kneels in front, places a hand gently on my cheek and places a chaste kiss on my lips.

It's sweet, but not long enough for me to enjoy the feeling of her mouth against mine.

Selena pulls away, giving me a nervous look with her bottom lip going between her teeth.

"Why are you nervous?" I ask her, reaching to release her lip and rubbing my thumb against the skin.

"Because I'm scared," she whispers, leaning slightly into my touch.

Scared isn't what I thought that she would say.

"What scares you?"

She looks at me for a few seconds before she answers. "I'm scared of getting too close to you, because nothing will ever come of it."

I don't have to hear the words to know that she's scared that I'm going to hurt her. That I'm going to get close to her and walk away. That I'm going to use her.

Shifting, I come closer to her and place my hands against her face, leaning in until my lips and my words are a whisper against her lips.

"When it comes to me, you have nothing to be scared of. I promise you that. Whether it's just one kiss or more, I will never hurt you."

And because I want her to believe me, I show her.

Once again, I press my lips against hers, but this time I do it with everything that I've been feeling these last few weeks for her. Every raw emotion that she has made me feel, I give.

At first she is hesitant but after a few seconds, she is giving me everything that I'm giving her.

Her hands land in my hair, holding my lips to hers, not letting me pull away. Like I even want to.

My hands travel from her face down her body.

They glide along the side of her full breasts, her hourglass shape until I land on her waist. I bring her to me, settling her so that she is straddling my lap and I'm feeling every single inch of her. She fills my hands perfectly and I never want to let her go.

Her tongue sweeps along my lips and when I open up for her, it's as if she becomes hungry. As if she has wanted this as much as I have.

When I take her bottom lip between my own teeth, like I've wanted since I first saw her do the action in class, she lets out a sweet moan. I don't know if I love the sound of her moans or giggles more.

My hands move from her waist to her ass when I move my mouth down her neck.

"Fuck. I'm going to be having dreams about this ass. It's perfect."

She lets out a breathy chuckle, and her body starts to grind against mine.

"Hunter," she breathes out, her body not stopping.

"Yeah?" I move my mouth from her neck down to where her shirt exposes her chest.

She wears a lot of V-neck shirts and each time she does, I have a hard time concentrating on anything in class. This girl has it all. The ass, the tits. She's a man's dream.

My dream.

As much as I want to strip her of all her clothes, I don't. So instead I suck on any exposed skin that I can and enjoy everything that I can get.

"I need..." Selena pants, her own lips landing on my neck.

Fuck, that feels good.

"What do you need, Lena?" I bite down on the top of her breast and another moan fills the room.

Then it all stops.

One second my hands are on her ass and her lips are

against my neck and the next, she is off of me. Her eyes wide and lips swollen.

I'm about to ask what just happened, when she speaks.

"I need to go." She gets up from the floor and starts gathering all of her things.

"Len," I say trying to stop her but she doesn't. Selena continues to get her stuff all together as if there were a bomb in the room and it's about to go off.

"I'm sorry," she says, getting her keys out and heading to put on her shoes. That's when I finally get over the shock of what is happening and stand up to go to her.

"Did I do something?" It feels like I do something wrong every time she shuts down on me.

She shakes her head. "No, you didn't do anything wrong. I promise."

I grab her hand and start pulling her back into the living room.

"Then stay. I promise I will keep my hands to myself."

My thumb finds her wrist and starts rubbing small circles on her skin.

She's wearing just a regular T-shirt, so when I look down at where my thumb is sliding along her skin, I get a clear view of her tattoo.

It's a daisy. Hand-drawn, intricate and delicate and exactly what Selena is.

"I can't," she says, taking my attention away from her piece of art. "I have to go."

She comes closer to me and because there is only about a five-inch height difference between us, she leans up slightly and places a kiss against my lips.

It's soft and over way too quickly and soon with a final wave she is out the door, leaving.

What just happened?

I didn't even walk her to her car.

Not even thinking about it, I grab my phone and send her a text to let me know that she made it home safely. Once the message says delivered, I wait for some indication that she is going to respond but after five minutes of looking at the screen, I give up.

Deciding to check my notifications, I see one from HEX telling me that Len has replied.

When I'm about to open the message, I freeze.

Len.

I called Selena "Len" when she was getting her stuff together. She didn't even question it.

Len. Lennie. Lena.

Selena.

No.

The girl that I'm talking to online can't be Selena, can it?

Nope. No chance in hell those two are connected.

But they can.

Len said she lives in Seaside. Selena said she's lived here her whole life.

They would be around the same age and from the pictures that Len has sent me, I know she has dark hair. Just like Selena.

No fucking way.

Yet the more I think of it, the more it becomes a possibility.

I open up the messages between Len and me, ignoring the new one, and scroll through them until I find the pictures.

Usually any pictures that get sent my way have no identifying features. None of them except one.

The night that we told each other where we live. It was the last thing she sent that night and now that I look at it, I see it.

I see the intricate and delicate daisy on Len's wrist.

The same as Selena's.

That's why her tattoo had looked familiar when I first saw it in person, because I had seen it before and it wasn't in class.

It was in this photo.

Fucking hell.

The girl I've been dreaming about meeting from online is the girl that has been sitting next to me all semester.

How the actual fuck did I not figure this out sooner?

Before closing out the app, I send a message to SENFUL-L94, completely ignoring her previous message.

HUN4ALL: I want to meet and soon.

CHAPTER FIFTEEN

SELENA

I'VE BEEN AVOIDING HUNTER. It's been a little over a week since we studied at his apartment and I haven't spoken to him, except for a text message telling him I got home safely that night.

He's been trying though. For the last three classes that we've had, he's tried to get words out of me.

Why did I leave his apartment?

Why am I not answering his text messages?

Why am I avoiding him and not saying a word unless asked?

Question after question comes out of his mouth and all I do is shake my head and throw a small smile his way.

After our second class together, he kept his distance. One thing that surprised me though, is that even though I'm actively avoiding him, he still walks me to my car. It's a silent walk but he still does it.

I want to tell him why I ran from him that night. I want to tell him that I wasn't lying about what I was scared about. I want to place my hand on his face and give him another kiss as I tell him that he did nothing wrong and me leaving had nothing to do with him.

It was all me.

It was me and my insecurities and years of overthinking and silence that came into play.

The second he leaned down and placed his lips against mine, I felt like I was on a cloud and everything that I have ever wanted was coming true.

The boy that was bringing on the butterflies and that I had a crush on, was kissing me. It was simple and sweet and it was the trigger I needed to be bold enough to claim a second kiss.

Then his hands landed on my body and for the first time in my life, I was feeling things that I had never felt before. Not even with Scott, who ghosted me at the beginning of the semester.

Hunter Jacobi was kissing me and grabbing my ass and I was feeling wanted the whole damn time.

But like every good thing, the thoughts started rolling in.

His hands were close to the hem of my shirt. What if we went further and he took it off? The stretch marks that line my belly's lower half are going to be the first thing he sees.

What if he wanted to have sex and he noticed the dimples that are on my thighs and on my ass?

What if me being on his lap was crushing him?

So many insecurities started to pop off, one after the other. I tried to push them away but after a while I just couldn't.

That's when I pulled away from him and left.

And for the next week, I felt so much embarrassment every time I saw him.

Just because I show confidence on the outside, that doesn't mean I don't get embarrassed. I do, and a lot.

Now it's been over a week and I have to face him again and this time I think I'm ready to actually speak a few words. I know he's pissed at me by the way he's been looking at me, but I just hope that he isn't mad at me for shutting him out and just mad I left him high and dry. And if he is mad, I may be willing to grovel for him to forgive me.

Fingers crossed it doesn't come to that.

I walk into the nearly empty classroom for anatomy and take my seat.

Usually while I'm waiting for class to start, I read a book off my reading app on my phone. Today though, the first thing that catches my attention and takes my thoughts away from my most recent hockey romance, is a message from HEX.

Chase.

Another person that I've been avoiding.

I don't know what happened, but he has become more persistent in us meeting each other.

It threw me off at first because I thought we had an understanding of sorts about waiting, but I guess I was wrong.

Every other day, he asks a variation of the same question.

HUN4ALL: Have you changed your mind about meeting?

I sigh as I read the message and let out another sigh as I start to type out a response.

. . .

SENFULL94: Not yet... Why the sudden urge to meet?

A reply from him is instant.

HUN4ALL: Maybe I want to put a face to the gorgeous girl that has me jerking off in the shower every time.

I feel my cheeks get hot as I read the last message. I'm sure if we met in real life he wouldn't be saying words like that. And also, he jerks off to me? Never did I think I anyone would do that with me on their mind.

SENFULL94: you think of me in the shower?

HUN4ALL: Why is that so hard to believe?

SENFULL94: Because if I were you, I would be picturing someone that looked more like a model.

. . .

HUN4ALL: I picture you and only you and besides I need something to grab on to and mark with my bite.

Okay, not a conversation I should be having when class is about to start.

SENFULL94: You say that now, but we haven't met.

HUN4ALL: Then let's meet and I will show you exactly what I picture as I hold my dick in my hand.

For some reason, I'm kind of getting the feeling that he's angry in his texts. I've been noticing it more as the week has gone by. Does me pushing off meeting up in person piss him off that much?

Thud.

I jump at the slamming down of the book next to me. Swiftly turning my phone over, I turn to see Hunter pulling out his chair with narrowed eyes in my direction.

Okay, so he's mad at me.

I wonder if it's something in the air.

"Hi," I greet him expecting a greeting back, but all I get is a grunt.

Okay, then.

"How was your weekend?" I try to break the silence. He turns to face me and all I see is indifference on his face.

"Fucking fantastic," he says, placating me.

"That's good," I say, turning away from him. He's more than just pissed off.

I guess after a week of silent treatments I deserve this. Deserve it or not, it does hurt. Hunter Jacobi may be described as a jerk and asshole by most of our campus, but he has never been like that with me.

I turn to face him and see that his attention is on his laptop. Checking the time really quickly on my phone, I see that we still have a few minutes before class starts. Because I don't want anyone to hear our conversation, I send him a text.

SELENA: I'm sorry I've been avoiding you this past week.

I know he reads it off his laptop because the little bubble starts jumping up and down right away.

HUNTER: It's fine.

SELENA: It's not. And I owe you an apology and an explanation.

. . .

I listen to him type away before another message comes through.

HUNTER: We'll talk after class.

I can handle having that conversation. At least I think I can.

Professor Leininger starts class and I put my phone away, opening up my laptop to take notes.

It's halfway through class, as Leininger is talking about the difference between veins and arteries when a text message comes in.

HUNTER: How many tattoos do you have?

Tattoos? He wants to talk about my tattoos?

SELENA: I have four

HUNTER: Four? Seriously? Where?

SELENA: My ribs, thigh, wrist, heel.

. . .

HUNTER: Never would have pictured you as someone that has that many tattoos.

I shrug since he can technically see me doing it.

SELENA: Nobody really knows that they are there. They are mostly for me.

If someone were to look at the art pieces that I have on my body, they would say that they didn't go together. But to me they mean everything.

HUNTER: Will I ever get to see the other three?

SELENA: Maybe, I guess it all depends on if you hate me for leaving your apartment the other day.

I pull back and I don't hear his fingers hitting against the keys. I don't even chance it by looking over at him, I just keep my eyes straight ahead waiting to see if he will text back.
 He does.

· · ·

HUNTER: I don't hate you for leaving the apartment. I just don't know why you did it or did other things and the whole you not talking to me pissed me off. So I'm sorry if I seem like I'm on edge around you. I have a shitload of questions and I don't know how to handle not having answers.

Other things? What other things did I do? I try to think, but nothing is coming to mind. I type out a response.

SELENA: I get it. I do, and I promise to explain everything after class.

The typing stops when I send that message but it starts up again after a while.

HUNTER: You don't have to answer, but what does your daisy mean?

SELENA: It's the flower for the month of April. My birth month.

.   .   .

That's the generic answer that I give to anyone that asks me that question. The real answer will be followed by more questions that I want to bury and never have to hear again. Hunter has to sense that, because his next text has my shoulders getting stiff.

HUNTER: There's more to it, isn't there?

How did he know?

There is a slight hesitation that I feel before I send my next message.

SELENA: Yes.

HUNTER: Will you tell me?

I close my eyes and take as many deep breaths as I can. Usually people take the generic answer that I give them and leave it alone. I should have known that he wouldn't.

Do I tell him?

Do I tell him the truth that I've only told one other person before? Something that not even my sisters or my parents know?

I answer the text with as much honesty as I can without giving away my truths.

. . .

SELENA: There was a time when I was younger when a daisy was a symbol of not letting fear take over.

The most honest answer I have ever given someone and it so happens to be him. Over the years, I've taken a long while to open up to someone and somehow Hunter Jacobi was able to make me open up to him, even with something this small, within a matter of weeks.

HUNTER: Thank you for telling me.

I just nod in his general direction and the rest of class goes by without any more messages.

No more truths.

I guess I will save those for when we talk after class.

CHAPTER SIXTEEN

SELENA

IT'S COLD TONIGHT, but I guess that's what happens when it's nearing the beginning of November and the weather is changing.

Most people think that California is all sunshine and heat, but on the Central Coast, especially five minutes away from the ocean, it's foggy and below sixty degrees all the time. It's hot when it hits sixty-eight.

Hunter walks beside me as we make our way to my car just like every other night.

I thought that as soon as we left class that he was going to demand that I tell him why I left him all high and dry, but he didn't. He's been silent the whole time.

I guess we aren't having this conversation until we reach the car.

Fine by me.

When we reach the car though, he just leans against my trunk with his hands in his pockets, looking down at the ground. Not a single word comes out of his mouth.

As a quiet person, I'm used to not talking, and I'm okay

with it. I can put in my earbuds and go about my day without saying a word.

This though, this type of quietness, I hate. Things need to be said and everything is just hanging there waiting for it to happen.

Growing tired of it, I finally speak.

"I'm really sorry for running out on you like that." I mean it.

Hunter nods, still not looking up. "Can you tell me what happened?" He finally looks up, his eyes have a coat of sadness in them. "I thought that everything was going okay, but then it was like you shut down. You said that I didn't do anything wrong, but I must have, right? Did I pressure you into doing something that you didn't want to do?"

I'm shaking my head before he can even finish. "No. You didn't pressure me into doing anything."

I know what pressure feels like and what happened between us wasn't anything like that. Hunter was kind and we were doing something that we both wanted.

"Then what happened because I'm drawing a blank here," he says, and if I didn't know any better, I would say that he sounds just as angry as he did before.

I look at the person in front of me. If it was anyone else, they would have dropped it and gone about their day, but not Hunter because that's not the person he is. Even if people at this school have never seen that side of him.

Letting out a sigh, I go stand next to him, keeping my hand in front of me and I tell him everything that I wanted to tell him last week.

"I wasn't lying when I told you I was scared, but it was only the partial truth. I wasn't only scared of nothing coming from whatever we were going to do. I was also scared that you would see me differently once the clothes came off."

I look over to him and I see that he is looking at me with his eyebrows furrowed together.

"Differently how?"

"I'm not the skinniest girl in the world. I'm the girl that has the stomach and the girl that has to buy new jeans every few months because her current ones rip at the thighs. The one that has to shop for shirts that are XL or XXL because if I wear shirts that are actually my size, then people will judge me for showing too much cleavage. I'm nothing compared to the fangirls that throw themselves at you or even Jenna. I'm not a big girl but I'm not small either, you know?"

I turn back to face him and the look he is giving me and the way his jaw is ticking, tells me that he is pissed off by the way this conversation is going.

I continue either way.

"I've had a crush on you for a while, on and off for the last couple of years. It returned these last few weeks the more I got to know you and spend time with you. That night in your apartment, it was like everything that I had wanted for a while was finally happening and I was good with it. I even kissed you, but then things started to turn a bit and as much as I wanted to concentrate on being in the moment with you, my insecurities started to jump out of me. What would you think about my stretch marks or the cellulite? Would you be disgusted once the clothes come off? Everything that I was scared of was coming to fruition and so I did the one thing I thought of and that was to leave. I should have stayed and talked to you about it. Told you how I was feeling within myself, but I didn't. And then every time I thought about it after, I felt so much embarrassment, so I shut you out."

I keep my eyes on him, waiting for him to have some sort of reaction besides possibly breaking his jaw. But no such luck.

Hunter continues to stand there with his hands in his pockets looking out at the sea of cars surrounding us.

"And now you won't talk to me," I mutter.

He lets out a sound that sounds like a grunt before he speaks. "You were right. You should have told me that night. You should have told me a lot of things."

A lot of things? There he goes again with talking about other things.

What else does he think I'm hiding from him besides my insecurities?

"What things?" It's times like these that I think that my eyebrows will never go back to normal position. Because most of the time when it comes to Hunter, I'm beyond confused.

"Like maybe how you've been trying to play me since school started back up again?"

"Play you? How the hell am I playing you?"

"Answer me this, Selena. Did you know who I was when you commented on the picture? Did you think. 'oh hey, let me just not tell this guy who I am and see if he falls for me?' Did you really leave my apartment because of your insecurities or because you didn't want me to recognize you?"

Recognize me?

"What the hell are you talking about?"

How did we get from me telling him how I felt during our study session to here? I don't even know what he thinks I did.

"I'm talking about the conversations. The pictures and

endless hours of getting to know each other. Was that all a joke to you? Was I a joke to you?"

Finally he moves from his spot and comes to stand in front of me. His face red with anger.

"Okay, stop. I have no idea what you're talking about. What pictures? What conversations?"

Hunter rolls his eyes and pulls out his phone. "You know the ones. The conversations between Chase and Len. Or should I say you and Chase, Miss SENFULL94?"

I hear what he says. I understand the words, but it takes me a quick second to comprehend what he's saying.

He called me SENFULL94 and he mentioned Chase's name.

"H-how do you know about that?" I ask, my head spinning out of control.

How does Hunter know about SENFULL94 and how the fuck does he know about my conversations with Chase?

I never told anyone about that, but yet he knows. How?!

"Because like you're Len, I'm Chase." He holds up his phone for me to see. Message after message, picture after revealing picture is staring back at me, mocking me.

I sent my most revealing self to Hunter Jacobi. Everything about me was there for him to see.

"So tell me, how did you know it was me? Did you match the pictures I posted with the ones on my Instagram?" He comes closer, enough for me to feel his chest against mine.

If anyone passed by, they would think that we were a couple just doing what couples do and not revealing our secrets.

I'm still trying to comprehend that Hunter is Chase when his last accusation finally makes it to my ears.

"I didn't know who you were," I say, shaking my head.

"Bullshit," he growls out between his teeth.

Now I'm the one getting angry. "It's the fucking truth. Someone sent it to me because they thought that you would remind me of someone from the books I read. I just commented, I didn't think that out of all the hundreds of comments that post got that you would even acknowledge mine."

"You could have come and told me who you were."

Is he fucking serious right now?

"You could have too! You could have told me before class when you were messaging me as Chase and telling me those stuff about my body! But you didn't! It wasn't just me hiding who they were!" I say through my teeth. "Besides, telling you who I was would have defeated the purpose of trying to remain anonymous. For all I knew you were lying about your age and stealing someone else's pictures. I didn't tell you who I was for the same reason you didn't tell me, for fucking safety."

I try to shove him away from me, but he doesn't budge.

I knew this was going to bite me in the ass sooner or later. I knew that posting pictures online, especially nudes ones, was going to come back at me and hurt me. But I did it anyway. I did it because for a short period of time I felt confident. I felt worthy of someone's attention.

I felt fucking beautiful and now, now here I am in the middle of a parking lot at school trying my hardest not to break. Especially in front of an egotistical, arrogant football player.

"For all I know, you were the one using me. You were the one that started the messages. You were the one that started to flirt. How do I know that I'm not just a sick game that you came up with in the locker room with your teammates?" I can feel the tears in my eyes trying to find their way out, but I keep them at bay.

"You weren't," Hunter says.

"Really? Because you're also the one that sat next to me on the first day of class. Maybe that was just you adding to the joke. Not only make the chubby, shy girl fall for you online but in person too. Then embarrass her when the time was right."

I reach into my bag to grab my keys. I need to get out of here as fast as I can because I can't be here with him anymore.

"Selena," he calls out when I reach my car door.

I stop and turn to him. "You know what that was?" I ask him, pointing to the phone in his hand. "That was me being confident in myself. That was me not caring about societal norms and finally accepting myself for the way my body looks. I was happy to share that side of myself with you because for the first time in my life I had someone that didn't see me for my body structure or my weight, they saw me. For a short period of time, I felt beautiful because I was finally able to see myself through someone else's eyes."

Without my better judgment, tears slip out and I'm quick to wipe them away. He doesn't get to see me cry.

"I never played you, Hunter. It never crossed my mind that Chase might have been you. But maybe it should have, because then maybe it would have saved me from starting to fall for you. And I was falling hard. I hope you and your teammates have a good laugh with this."

I swing the car door open and throw myself into the driver's seat.

There's a knock on the window as I turn on the car, but I ignore it and reverse out of the parking spot.

The whole way home, I cry.

From the hurt.

The embarrassment.

All the insecurities that will forever haunt my life.

But most of all, I cry for the two boys that were never mine. The two boys that turned out to be the same person.

CHAPTER SEVENTEEN

HUNTER

I'M the biggest asshole in the fucking world.

If I was one when I found out that Jenna was cheating on me with Jax, this time is a million times worse.

And I don't know how to fix everything that I destroyed.

I fucking destroyed everything before it even started.

It's been almost seven weeks since Selena and I last talked. Since we were in the parking lot, she told me about her insecurities and how they made her run out of my apartment. Seven weeks since I accused her of playing me, of lying about the real reason why she left my place, and of knowing who I was when she was talking to Chase. Seven weeks since she blew up and accused me of the same thing and of her laying everything she was on the table.

She cried from all the anger that she was carrying for me. She cried because of me and I did nothing to fix it. I didn't go to her and tell her that I was starting to believe every word that she was saying.

I didn't tell her that I didn't see her in the way she saw

herself. That I saw her as the most beautiful woman I have ever seen and loved all the curves her body had to offer. I didn't tell her that she wasn't a joke, that she was very much real. I didn't do a thing but stand there and watch her storm away.

That night I went home and replayed everything that had happened between us in my head. The interactions on HEX, the conversations in real life, everything, and I came to two conclusions.

One, Selena couldn't have known I was Chase. I saw it in her face the second she told me she didn't know who I was. I saw it and I didn't say anything.

The second conclusion was that maybe my mind, subconsciously, knew that Len was Selena and that's why feelings for both of them developed so quickly. Why I had an attraction to Selena that I can't comprehend and had an urge to meet Len. It feels as if my mind knew they were the same person and that's why I finally noticed her the first day of class.

Even though I was avoiding Jax, there was something that pulled me toward Selena that day.

I should have put two and two together when SENFULL94 told me her name was Len, but I'm so fucking stupid for not seeing it.

And there is no way to tell her what I finally wrapped my head around. She hasn't talked to me since that night.

Not a single word, spoken or through message.

Nothing.

She even moved seats in anatomy so that she wouldn't have to sit next to me or interact with me.

I destroyed what was happening between us.

Now the semester is days away from being over and once finals are done, she won't have to see me anymore.

There's a possibility that we will be in the same anatomy course again next semester, but the chances are slim.

I hate not fucking talking to her.

Over these last few months, I've gotten used to talking to her on a daily basis. Both as Len and Selena.

I fucking miss her. I miss everything about her. The way she smells of cucumber and mint to the way she bites down on her lip when she's nervous. I even miss that blush she gets when I would catch her reading one of her steamy romance books in class.

I fucked shit up.

And as much as I want to make things right, I can't. One, because she blocked my number and on HEX and two, I have no idea where the girl lives, so I can't go to her house and beg for forgiveness.

I tried once at school, before Thanksgiving break, and let's just say that my balls haven't recovered yet and it's been weeks.

Even though she has a soft exterior, when she's pissed Selena doesn't take shit from anyone and that includes me. And fuck if that doesn't make her ten times hotter.

If I wasn't ass deep in finals and football, I would do everything in my power to apologize to Selena, but for right now that will have to wait. At least until after Christmas.

By some miracle, our team was selected to play in a bowl game next week, and that's with three losses under our belt.

Ever since Coach Young found out the news, he has been having us practice as if we were going to the Super Bowl. Never thought that I would see the day where I'm looking forward to ice baths, but here I am, silently begging Coach to end practice so I can soak every one of my muscles in ice.

The team is better than ever though and all the excitement for the game and seeing the dedication from everyone to win has me pumped. Not only pumped but also has me loving football again.

Sure, there are downsides to it, like my father being in town and promising not to leave until the game is over, but I've been trying to avoid him since he arrived yesterday morning.

For the first time all season, I'm excited about playing and he's not going to take that away from me.

I just wish that I could avoid him now.

We are currently sitting in a Mexican restaurant in downtown Seaside having lunch. Well lunch to me, and more of a business meeting for my father, since he has been talking about football scouts since we sat down.

"San Francisco is going to be there as well as Las Vegas. They're looking at you and the Stanford boy, what's his name? Gerald?" my dad muses while I half listen.

"Gary," I answer without looking up from my food.

"Whatever his name is. That boy has nothing on you. I'm positive that as soon as the game is over, we will be getting calls left and right."

I nod my head in agreement just to placate him.

For once in my life, I wish that conversations with this man weren't solely based on football. I'm sure we would have a whole lot more in common if that were the case.

"If everything goes smoothly, I think we will be getting offers from not only San Francisco and Las Vegas, but

Atlanta and Tampa Bay are good contenders too. If it's Cleveland or Seattle, we are going to say no."

We? Should that decision be on me and me alone?

And that's if I decide to join the draft.

"Why not Seattle or Cleveland?" I ask, trying to at least show some interest in the conversation.

"You can't be in the cold, Hunt. It's bad for your arm. Warmer climates are better. We would slightly push it with San Francisco but with their quarterback retiring in February, you would be the logical pick," he says, excitement forming in his voice.

If only I could be as excited as he is.

And the "can't be in the cold" comment is bullshit. I grew up in Montana for fuck's sakes. I strive to be in the cold.

"Have you talked to Mom? She said that she, Jainie and Blake will all be coming down for Christmas and staying for the game." I try to change the subject but looking at Roy's face, he doesn't care much about it. He's usually only like that when I mention my stepdad.

Does he forget he has two other kids besides me?

"No, I haven't talked to her," he says, taking a drink from his drink. "Is she staying in Seaside or up in San Francisco?"

"She said Seaside when I talked to her. They are going to be staying at the apartment with me and then drive up with the bus."

When I talked to my mom last week and threw the idea out there for the three of them to come visit, she was nearly in tears. She was so excited that I wanted her to come. Hearing her excitement made me realize that I needed to try harder to be a better son, so this is step one. And I didn't get the chance to tell her this, but I'm excited too.

"Your place is only one bedroom," Dad says and I can't help but sigh.

"Yeah, I figure that Mom and Jainie can take my room and me and Blake can camp out in the living room."

He just nods, not caring about his ex-wife and his other children. I wonder when I became more important, and Blake and Jainie stopped mattering. Just thinking about this makes me want to kick myself in the nuts for destroying my relationship with my siblings all because I wanted to continue playing a sport that I'm not sure I love anymore.

I'm going to try harder.

Especially if I don't join the draft and quit playing, then Dad will transfer all his energy to Blake and I can't have that happening.

"Anyway." The topic of his ex-wife and other children is over with. "I think that you should get your arm as ready as possible but don't overdo it. I think maybe skip a day or two of practice this week..." he continues, but I'm no longer listening.

The words that my father is saying are doing nothing to capture my attention.

No, that's on the beauty that just walked into the restaurant.

She has on a red dress, that lands just above the knee, it's covered in small flowers on them that from far away can't be distinguished, but I know they are daisies. Her legs are on display and on her feet are a pair of strappy heels that help accentuate every single curve that her body has to offer.

As my eyes travel, I see the tattoo that adorns her heel with how she is standing. From here it looks like a sun setting over the ocean on the outside of her right heel.

Selena.

In the months that I have known her, I haven't seen her in anything other than jeans and T-shirts and Vans. Never even close to what she has on right now.

Her hair is pulled back and she even has makeup on and she looks everything like the beautiful shy girl that caught my attention.

She looks mouthwatering and I can't seem to look away from her.

Why is she dressed like this on a Thursday at noon? Is she going to class dressed like that?

Selena looks around the restaurant, as if she is looking for something when she makes eye contact with me.

She's not wearing her glasses today, so I'm able to catch all the expressions that her eyes throw my way. There is shock, anger but also sadness.

A sad smile lands on her lips before her gaze drops from my face and she walks over to the counter.

My eyes never leave her.

That dress looks absolutely perfect on her.

"*Hola, mija,*" the lady behind the ordering counter says to her.

"*Hola. Vengo a recoger una orden para Marisol.*"

She speaks Spanish. I knew she was Mexican but I didn't know that she spoke Spanish. I have no idea what she is saying but I find it hot.

I watch as the lady nods at her and then goes to the back to retrieve what I'm guessing is Selena's order.

Selena just stands there, looking down at her hands, waiting.

I want to go to her. I want to tell her that she looks absolutely gorgeous and I'm sorry for being the biggest jackass in the world. But I don't move an inch.

Within a few minutes, the lady comes back with a few trays of food that look a little too big to be in her arms.

"*Aquí tienes, mija.*" The lady heaves the food platters onto the counter and Selena has to be wondering the same thing I am. That's a lot of food for one person to carry. Especially in heels.

"Um." Selena shifts from one foot to the other. "Okay. *Gracias.*"

I watch as Selena moves to get the trays but then one starts to slide from the top, so she puts it back down.

Ignoring what my dad is saying about what to do on game day next week, I get up from my seat and head over to the counter.

"Let me help," I offer in a whisper. Instantly, Selena turns to look at me with her eyes narrowed. She looks like she is going to fight me on it. "Please."

After a few seconds, she lets out a sigh and steps out of the way for me to get the trays. She helps place the trays on my arms and once I get everything, I follow her out of the restaurant and to her car.

She doesn't say anything. She just continues walking until we reach her car and she opens the trunk, unloading the trays from my arms.

She won't even look at me.

When everything is secure in the trunk, she looks over my shoulder and gives me a smile that barely brings up the corner of her mouth.

"Thanks." It's a barely there word and I hate it.

Selena turns to head to the driver's side door when I speak.

"I'm sorry," I say the second her hand meets the door handle.

She doesn't turn to face me, she just stands there looking down to the ground.

"What are you sorry for exactly?" For the first time since she walked into the restaurant, her eyes meet mine.

"For not believing you when you said that you weren't playing me."

"How do you know I wasn't?"

"Because if you were, you would have exposed my pictures to the school by now." That's something I thought about for weeks. I saw the shock on her face when I told her that I was Chase. That isn't something that you fake. That was genuine shock.

Selena opens her mouth, but she shuts it right away. I guess she doesn't know what to say, so I continue.

"I'm also sorry for invalidating what you were feeling. Invalidating your insecurities. I'm sorry that I made you believe that I was playing you, that you were a joke. You never were, Selena. When it came to talking to you as Selena or Len, it meant something to me. It was as if I could be myself and you didn't care about the fact that I was the star football player. I'm sorry for hurting you. Maybe one day you can forgive me for it."

She still doesn't say a word and that's okay. I deserve her silence.

But her silence doesn't stop the next words from coming out.

"You look beautiful, by the way."

A small smile appears on her face again, but it's not enough. I need to see a smile that reaches her eyes and makes her brown eyes sparkle.

"Thank you," she says and turns to face the car door.

She's leaving.

I nod, even though she can't see it and turn to head back to the restaurant.

"Hunter," Selena calls out and I turn around immediately. She is still standing by her door but now she's pulling at her fingers. "Good luck next week."

Her words take me by surprise. All semester when it has come to a football game, she never wished me luck.

I nod. "Thanks," I say, throwing a smile in her direction. "Hopefully I get to see you next semester and tell you all about it."

She gives me one last nod and she's in the car. I stay on the sidewalk, watching her drive away. When she turns the corner, I finally head back into the restaurant and take my seat again across from my dad.

"You know her?" he asks, nodding toward the street. I guess he noticed how eager I was to help.

I nod. "Yeah, she's a friend from school."

"Be careful, Hunter. You don't want any distractions this close to the draft. Jenna was distraction enough."

Nodding, I pick up my drink and take a swig before answering. "Don't worry. She isn't a distraction."

Selena is anything but a distraction.

She's... she is everything and more.

And I ruined everything I possibly could have had with her.

CHAPTER EIGHTEEN

SELENA

"WHY DO YOU LOOK SAD?" Stella asks as she comes to sit next to me.

We are currently in the middle of a holiday dinner for my dad's construction company. Why he always insists on having it on a Thursday is beyond me, but here we are in our backyard having a Christmas celebration.

Usually I don't mind having to dress up and interact with my dad's employees, but I'm not feeling it this year.

"I'm not sad," I say, not looking up at my sister as I do.

"Yeah you are. You've looked sad since before Thanksgiving. So what gives?"

Why did it have to be Stella that had to come talk to me? She's the perceptive one out of the four of us. Why couldn't it be Gabriella?

"Nothing," I say, keeping my eyes on my legs as they swing from the bench.

"*Mentiras*. Is it a boy?" Her voice goes up an octave like she's excited about the possibility.

I don't say anything but I guess my face must have because Stella lets out a sigh.

"Who is he so I can send Jonathan to take care of him and bury the body?" she says as if that's the most normal sentence in the world.

"And here I thought that you were the one capable of hiding a body."

"Oh, honey, I am, but my husband is better suited for prison, and he loves me so he would take the fall."

I sometimes wonder about my family and their love for anything true crime.

"Now tell me, what is going on with you?" Stella asks.

Stella is six years older than me and ever since she got married about four years ago, she constantly wants to know what is going on with me. She says it's her way of making it up to me for deciding to marry a boy and leaving me with the parents. Her words exactly.

We've always been close and when I need to talk about boy problems, she's the one to go to. Not that I've had a whole lot of boy problems in my lifetime.

"Remember a few weeks ago, I got a call while we were having dinner?"

"Oh yes, Hunter! I looked him up and let me just say the dude is hot. He's posted a lot of pictures of his abs. I'd let him have his way with me."

I look at my sister, a smirk playing on my lips. "You're married and he's seven years younger than you."

"Seven?" I nod. "That makes you the older woman. A cougar. I like it."

"You do realize this it's the same guy you were planning on sending your husband after, right?"

Stella lets out a sigh. "Tell me what the bastard did."

Do I really want to explain to my sister that I was exchanging nudes online with someone that I thought was a stranger but turned out to be the guy that sat next to me in class?

No, I really don't, so I give her half the truth.

"My insecurities got the best of me and I got scared." Okay, so I gave her half of a half, but that is still better than nothing.

"Selena." Stella takes my hand in hers and gives it a reassuring squeeze. You know it's serious when my family calls me Selena. "How strong were your feelings for him? Or should I say are?"

I let out a sigh. "Are. And pretty strong, I would say."

I've been trying my hardest to squash any feelings I have for Hunter Jacobi these last few weeks, but nothing I do actually works. It's easier to get over a crush on someone you don't know but once you get to know them and see the type of person they really are, it's hard as hell.

For a few short weeks, I got to see the real person that Hunter Jacobi really is and I liked everything that he let me see.

"And if the opportunity came up, would you want to see where it could go between the two of you?" I feel her thumb rubbing against my daisy.

I shrug. "Sure, but it wouldn't."

"Why not?"

I look up to face my sister. "You've seen his pictures. A guy that looks like that would never be with someone that looks like me."

Stella drops my hand and before I know it, she's taking my face between her hands.

"Listen here, you little shit. Any man should be fucking lucky that you decided to grace them with your presence. If they say otherwise, then they are a bunch of *pendejos* that don't know of a good thing when they see it. You are fucking gorgeous, so don't let a *estupido* tell you otherwise. Do you understand me?"

Not going to lie, I'm a little scared of my sister right now.

I nod.

"Okay good, now let's go get drunk before I really go find the fuckboy and cause him physical pain for hurting you."

I love my sisters.

———

I stare at the screen, contemplating if I should do it.

If I should push the button and finally make up my mind about attending this stupid thing. Well stupid for me. Some people might think this is the greatest event in the world. I know at least one person that would think that.

Do I really want to do this though? Do I really want to spend two hours driving, only to sit in the sun for hours on end?

As I sit on my bed and really think about it, the answer is yes. I very much want to do that.

Like the last time that my finger hovered over a button, my emotions are running rampant. It's just that this time, I don't feel sadness or the urge to cry. I feel excitement and nervousness.

I also feel like I need someone to talk me into actually pressing the button.

Moving my laptop off my legs, I reach for my phone and dial my best friend.

Thankfully, I don't have to wait long for her to answer.

"You're calling me. What did you do? Do you have to hide a body? I can be there in two hours. I just need to stop to get some gas." Jennifer's voice comes through from the other end and I can't help but snort.

Jennifer has been my best friend since freshman year in high school. We bonded over stupid nonsense and were attached at the hip for the next four years. Then college came and we went to different schools, me to Cal U and her to San Francisco State, but we still talk, maybe not every day like we used to but we're still close. I don't get to see her as often though and that sucks, but we handle it.

"No 'body.' I do need you to convince me to do something," I tell her instead of a greeting.

"Yes, you can run over whatever professor you want," she says, her tone filled with seriousness.

I can't help but laugh. "I was thinking something along the lines of visiting you next weekend. If you're in town, that is."

"Yes! One hundred percent, yes, you can visit me!" Jennifer cheers in my ear but then she goes silent. "Wait, why do you need me to convince you to come to San Francisco? That should be an automatic yes from you."

Moment of truth. "Because there's a certain football game I want to attend, and I don't know if I should."

The line goes silent for a bit and I know she is trying to piece together what I'm not actually saying.

Finally, Jennifer sighs. "Have you talked to him?"

Out of all the people in my life, Jen knows it all. She knows all the secrets I hold and why the insecurities that I have are so strong and why, at times, I let them tear me down.

She knows everything there is to know about me.

She's one of the only people that does. She even knows about HEX and SENFULL94 and when I told her about it, she encouraged it, if and only if, I was being safe.

So, when things went down with Hunter, I called her and I told her everything. I couldn't hold it in and talking to her was my saving grace.

"More like he talked to me."

"When?"

"Earlier today when I went to pick up some food."

"And what did he say?"

I tell her. I tell her everything from when I walked in to when I sped away. I tell her about the words he said and how he apologized for everything and how he ended it by telling me how beautiful I looked. And I tell her that when I heard him speak, the butterflies came bursting in even when I tried not to be affected by him. I voice how seeing him today was different than seeing him any other day in class or around campus and I have no idea why.

"Buy the ticket," Jen orders when I finish speaking.

"But what if I go up there and nothing comes of it?" I start biting my nails just at the thought.

"Then we will find you a boy that is just like the ones you read about to pick up all the pieces and put you back together." I've known her long enough to know that she is either rolling her eyes at me or she has a big smile on her face. There is no in-between.

195

"Funny," I mutter.

"I know you're scared, Sel. I know the possibility of putting yourself all the way out there is fucking terrifying, especially for the introverted person that you are. But you won't know what is going to happen until you're at the game and he sees you."

She's right. I won't know what will happen unless I try. I can't keep coming up with these stupid scenarios in my head and scaring myself with the thought that they will or will not come true.

Nodding to myself, I grab my laptop and hover over the Pay Now button.

"Come with me?" No way in fucking hell am I going to a sporting event like this all by myself.

"Sign me up. I got you, boo."

I click on the button.

I guess Hunter finally is getting his wish of me going to one of his games this season.

CHAPTER NINETEEN

HUNTER

THE ENERGY of the game is vibrating everywhere. The stadium, the locker room and every inch of my body.

It feels like I can feel the fans' cheers and screams down to my bones and I fucking love it.

I've played a number of high-profile games throughout my years of playing college ball, even two bowl games before this one. Yet this one feels as if it's on a whole different level.

This is the feeling that I've been missing. However I've been feeling about football lately, it was all erased the second I stepped foot onto this field today. No way in hell am I going to let this feeling go.

I look around the locker room and see that everyone is as pumped as I am. We're ahead by seven in the half and we have a chance of winning this thing.

As I continue to look around the room, I catch Coach Young glancing at me, so when he nods in my direction, I know what to do.

"Alright! Listen up!" The second my voice flows through

197

the room, the only noise that we hear is coming from the stands.

All of my coaches and teammates expect me to keep the energy up, to say something that will push us through to the very end so that we can come out as victors.

"This is a big stage, it may not be Super Bowl level but for some of us this is as big as we will get. So let's go back there and do what we do best and fucking win. Let's beat Gator asses and show them exactly who we are. Let's give every single sports network out there something to talk about."

"Let's fucking go!" Jax yells out and within seconds, every single person in the room is chanting and ready to kick some ass.

The team runs behind Coach as we head back onto the field. Somehow the energy in the stadium feels a lot stronger than it did before.

I fucking love it.

Looking over to the Cal U section, my eyes instantly scan the sea of people until I see my mom, Blake and Jainie. All three of them have huge smiles on their faces and I can't help but be proud that I put them there.

I don't bother looking for my dad since he got box seats to impress some of the people from his company that he dragged to the game. Those fuckers probably never watched a game of college football in their lives.

Grabbing my helmet, I raise it up and I give my mom the biggest smile that I can. She blows me a kiss before the people behind her start to cheer.

It's go time and it's time to win my Super Bowl.

I've only heard a stadium erupt in chaos once before in my life. It was during an actual Super Bowl game when I was twelve. It was New England and New York and I remember that day as if it had happened yesterday. When the Giants won, the stadium felt like it was shaking under my feet and I thought that the field would split open. I thought that I would never feel that excitement, that energy, the stadium shaking like that again.

I was wrong.

The second the clock hit zero and the ball was intercepted by Jax, it was done.

I felt the crowd before I heard it. The vibrations were hard and heavy and it's something that I know I will never forget.

If this turns out to be the last game of football I will ever play, I will be happy. I came out on top.

After celebrating as a team on the field, all the players and coaches go their separate ways. Either to celebrate with their families or to do an on-the-field interview.

I get stopped by a few reporters and after three interviews, all of which I talked about the motivational speech I gave to the guys at halftime, I go looking for my mom and siblings.

The field isn't as packed as it was when the game ended, most people heading to the locker room or heading out, so it's easy to spot my family where they stand by the tunnel entrance.

But I'm not only seeing my family though.

My eyes travel from my mom, who is wearing a big smile, to the brown-haired girl wearing a jersey with my number a few feet behind her.

No fucking way. My eyes must be playing tricks on me.

I start making my way over to the tunnel, not taking my eyes off the girl when I feel a hand on my arm. Stopping, I turn to see Jenna standing right next to me with a smile taking over her face.

"Oh, Hunty! I'm so proud of you!" She throws her arms around my neck and clings to me, her body against mine.

Hunty. A stupid nickname that she coined for me and just hearing it make my ears want to bleed.

I sure as hell didn't miss hearing it.

"Thanks, Jenna," I say, peeling her body off mine, but she is still close enough to me that I can smell her cotton candy perfume. I hate that too. All I want to smell is cucumbers and mint.

"I got a hotel for the weekend. We should celebrate." She flutters her lashes at me, but I look right through her.

She only wants me back because of what this game will do for me once it comes to scouts and the draft.

"No thank you. Excuse me." I turn away from her and turn back to the tunnel.

My sister approaches me first. Unlike with Jenna, I actually hold out my arms for my sister to jump into. Hearing her laugh and her excitement over the game makes this win even sweeter.

When I place Jainie back on the ground, our brother is next in giving me his congratulations. He's gotten bigger since the last time I saw him and soon he will be giving me a run for my money.

My mom is the last one to approach me. Her smile never disappears.

"I'm so proud of you, my baby boy! That game was insane."

As I hug my mom, my eyes drift to the person behind her.

My eyes weren't playing tricks on me.

She's really here.

Selena Montez is really at one of my football games wearing my number over her hoodie.

Her hair is down in perfect waves that go well past her shoulders, with a school beanie covering the top. She's in jeans and Vans and looks very much like the Selena I know.

She keeps her eyes on me the whole time, even throwing a smile in my direction.

Her gaze only disappears when the girl next to her whispers something in her ear, but it's only a second before it's back on me.

"We'll meet you out in the parking lot, okay?" Mom tells me as soon as she releases me. "We'll grab some dinner if you're not going to celebrate with the team."

It's my mom's hand on my face that finally pulls my attention away from Selena.

I nod at her, giving her a bright smile. "Sounds good. I will be out there in a little bit."

With one last kiss to the cheek and a few waves, the three of them are making their way out of the stadium and I focus on the beauty in front of me.

Her lip goes between her teeth as I approach.

"Hi," I say, my heart beating as fast as it was during the third quarter.

"Hi," she answers with a small smile that almost reaches her eyes.

"Well, this isn't weird," a voice says from next to Selena. I turn to the girl standing next to her. Her hair is a dirty blonde, and she looks like she just left the snow. It's only fifty degrees outside. "I'm Jennifer, the best friend of the girl you're trying to eye fuck."

Jennifer holds out an outstretched hand for me to shake, which I do, but she lets go of my hand before I can even comprehend what is happening and turns to Selena.

"You good?" she asks her and Selena answers her with a nod. "Okay good. I'm going to leave you and go find my own football player that is looking to celebrate. Whistle if you get lost."

Without another word, Jennifer turns and leaves through the tunnel, most likely going to find a football player to celebrate with like she said.

"She's an interesting friend." I muse.

Selena nods. "Yeah, she's something else."

I watch as she follows her friend with her eyes as she walks through the tunnel and when she is out of sight, Selena turns back to me. A nervous smile playing on her lips.

A part of me is fucking elated that she's here, but another part is wary. Is she here just to cheer me on or is she here for a whole different reason?

"What are you doing here, Selena?" I ask, stepping a few inches closer to her. The game may be over but it's still loud enough that I may not hear what she says.

"I wanted to cheer you on," she says with her smile growing a bit.

"Is that it?" The question comes out a little harder than I intended and by the way Selena takes a step away from me, she heard it too.

She shakes her head. "I was wondering if you wanted to

talk. I know it's a bit unconventional since you just won a big game and all that but I figured it was worth a try."

Talk. This is what I wanted to happen since that fateful night in the parking lot.

"And what do you want to talk about?"

I see her contemplating something, and by the way she is wringing her hands, I'm guessing it's big.

I'm about to ask her, but the words never make it out because Selena presses her mouth against mine, shocking the ever-living shit out of me.

There is a second of hesitation on my side, but I quickly get over it and slide an arm around her waist, the other holding my helmet and bring her closer to me.

Her hands slide through my sweaty mess of hair and I feel her bringing herself closer to me.

My tongue is about to slide along the seam of her bottom lip to ask for access when she pulls away. Her eyes are wide and the nervous lip biting is back.

I don't let her go or take a step back.

"I wanted to talk about that."

"Yeah?"

"Yeah." She gives me a curt nod and a bright smile that I've been dying to see for weeks.

I lean down and place a chaste kiss on her lips. I fucking love the feeling of her mouth against mine, but her body. Fuck. This girl might ruin me.

"I'm about to have dinner with my mom. Maybe we can talk after that?" As much as I want to invite her to dinner, I keep it in. I think we need to talk first, see where we're really at, and then we can see about the whole family introduction thing.

"Just text me when you're done."

I give her a nod and lean down once again and place another kiss on her pout.

She turns to walk away and before she is halfway through the tunnel, I call for her.

"Selena!" I yell out. Instantly she turns back to me. She raises an eyebrow at me and throw her a smirk. "I finally got you to one of my games."

A smirk likes the lips I just claimed as mine. "I guess you did."

I guess this really is my Super Bowl.

I got the win and there is a chance I'm going to get the girl.

This might be one of the best fucking days of my life.

CHAPTER TWENTY

SELENA

A TEXT MESSAGE came through a little after ten at night.

Jen and I had dinner at a custom mac and cheese place and then came back to her apartment. Right before my text came in, she told me that she had in fact found a football player to "celebrate" with. Before she left to meet said football player, she told me I was welcome to bring *my* football player over, but I turned her down.

No way am I going to be bringing a guy over to an apartment that wasn't mine and disturb Jen's roommates.

So when I got the message from Hunter, telling me that he was free, we came up with a plan. Since I had my car, he was going to take an Uber to my location and then we will take my car somewhere to talk.

Now, I'm waiting for him to get here, and I feel like my body won't stop shaking.

Going to the game was an impromptu decision I made after drinking a little too much with Stella.

After I purchased the tickets, I didn't know what my plan was.

As the game got closer, I still couldn't think up anything. The best I could do was decide to get a jersey with his number from the student store and just show up.

And that's what I did.

I showed up to the game, with Hunter Jacobi's number on my back and cheered him on the whole time. I also got death stares from Jenna and a few other girls while I was there, but I brushed those off.

When the game ended, I was back to having no plan. I was getting ready to leave when Jen suggested that we head down to the field. For some reason, I agreed.

We stayed by the tunnels and the whole time, my eyes didn't leave Hunter.

I watched as he celebrated with his teammates, and how he flawlessly went from one interview to the next as if he's done it a million times before. My eyes also stayed with him as he spotted his family and then when he was stopped by Jenna, who also happened to be wearing his jersey.

As much as I wanted to look away when she threw herself at him, I didn't and for a second, I thought me being on the field was pointless.

But he let her go and then started walking in our direction. Well, more like in the direction of who I concluded to be his mom and siblings, but I was only a few feet away from them.

The second that his eyes met mine, he didn't look away and my stomach started to flip as if it were jumping on a trampoline.

Then he approached me, and his eyes moved up and down my body as if he were hungry. I may have wanted to hold my thighs together a little tighter.

When he asked me if there was more to me being at the game, I did the one thing I could think of.

I kissed him.

I kissed him and then he kissed me back.

When he pulled back from me was when I realized just how terrified I was that he was going to reject me, but thankfully he didn't.

Now here I am. A nervous fucking wreck waiting for him to get here.

Maybe we should have waited to have this conversation when we were both home.

Where the hell are we going to go and talk when we are in a strange city?

I don't know San Francisco all that well.

And why is this the thing I'm panicking about?

The vibration of my phone has me forgetting about everything.

HUNTER: The car just pulled up.

Is it weird that I missed his name coming across my phone?

SELENA: I'll be right down.

I guess it's time to pull up my big girl *chonies* and put all my shit out there.

Grabbing my purse and my keys, I make my way downstairs and as soon as I open the door, I see Hunter leaning up against a lamppost.

Dressed almost exactly as I am.

In a hoodie with his jersey over it and dark jeans that look like they are barely hanging on to his hips.

His dirty-blond hair looks like it's no longer sweaty from the game and styled perfectly.

As soon as I step out the door, his dark-blue eyes meet mine. He gives me a grin that I've only seen a few times before, and it was always directed at me.

"We're wearing the same thing." Is the first thing that comes out of my mouth.

Hunter's smile just grows. "I think I like it better on you. Actually, I vote that you wear that outfit more often."

"Why?"

He shrugs. "I like seeing my number on you. And if it were my name, I would like it even more. It would tell everyone that you were mine."

My eyebrows shoot up at his comment. I don't respond to it, I just turn in the direction of where my car is parked.

"So the car is this way." I wave for him to follow. I hear him chuckle and then he's walking next to me.

"Do you want me to drive?" he says, leaning in to speak into my ear. I let out a shiver at the breath he releases against my earlobe.

Without saying a word, I grab my keys from my hoodie pocket and hand them over to him.

He lets out another chuckle but doesn't say anything else the whole way to my car.

Want to know what I hate about San Francisco? The

parking situation, especially near San Francisco State. It's worse than driving a stick shift up and down the hills.

When we reach my car, Hunter unlocks it and heads to the passenger side door and opens it for me. Before I can even get into the car, his hand lands on my hips, stopping me.

"I didn't get my kiss hello," he says when I give him a questioning look.

A smirk places on his lips. It's always the smirk that gets you.

I roll my eyes. "I gave you one earlier."

"Yeah, but a few hours have passed, and I think I deserve another one."

I resist the urge to roll my eyes again. I have a feeling that if we decided to proceed into something more, I'm going to be rolling my eyes a whole lot.

But I still give him what he wants.

I lean up on my toes to close that small gap between us and place a small kiss on his lips.

"I would have gone with more tongue," he says with a shake of his head. "But I'll take what I can get. Also"—the hand that's resting against my hip travels down slightly until my body is plastered against his—"I think I've told you I like when girls roll their eyes at me. So do it again and I will show you exactly what that means."

I feel a blush creep up my cheeks but that doesn't stop me from responding. "Promises."

With that, I slide into the car and leave him standing there.

"Son of a bitch," he mutters before he closes the door and I see him adjusting himself before he slides into the driver's seat.

Then we just sit there.

"How well do you know San Francisco?" he asks, looking over to me.

I can't help but laugh. "I know how to get to four places. The airport, the baseball stadium, Pier 39 and Jen's apartment."

"So neither one of us can get around without GPS, got it."

I watch as he pulls out his phone and starts looking for a place to go.

"Are you hungry?" he asks as he scrolls through the endless food options that the city has to offer.

"Not really."

He nods and then starts looking up bars.

"Do you want to get a drink?" he says a little too quickly.

I guess I'm not the only one that is nervous about this.

Placing a hand on his, I try to grab his attention. "Jacobi, relax."

He looks up at me, and I hear him let out a sigh.

"Sorry."

"It's all good. Let's just find a beach and we can talk there. Let's not stress and get lost in a city neither of us knows." I offer.

He looks at me and gives me a smile before he nods.

Soon we are on the way to a random beach that he found, that overlooks the Golden Gate Bridge. The only sound filling the car is the oldies playlist I had playing when I drove up here.

"You like oldies?" Hunter asks, breaking the comfortable silence between us.

I nod. "My dad is always listening to them, and they became my comfort music."

He nods and he continues to drive for a few more minutes before he speaks again.

"I hate it when you call me Jacobi."

That takes me by surprise. "You do?"

"Yeah, which is weird because I'm fine with everyone else calling me that, but with you, I hate it."

It's because you care. Those are the words that I want to say but I keep them to myself.

"Then no more Jacobi, at least not when we're by ourselves." It's the least I can do for him.

"And for you? Are there any nicknames I should steer clear of?" He throws a wink in my direction.

I think about it. "Not really. Pet names, on the other hand, there are a few."

He continues to maneuver the car through the streets of the city. "Really? And what would those be?"

Even from where I'm sitting, I know the bastard is smirking.

"Anything but kitten, sweetie, cupcake or anything cutesy, I'm good with."

"Have you had guys actually called you kitten?"

"One guy and he would ask me to send him videos of me purring." I gag a little at the memory.

A sound comes from Hunter and I can't distinguish if it's a growl or a groan. I'm going with the former just so I can think that was him being possessive. Which by the way, I like.

"Please tell me you're joking."

"Oh, how I wish I were." I sigh. There are parts of my life, like talking to certain people online that I want to forget.

"I guess I have a whole lot to learn about you."

I turn to face him as he looks straight ahead at the streets in front of him.

He doesn't look anything like the cocky football player that everyone has made him out to be.

To me, I don't see a star athlete. I just see him for just him. I see him as just Hunter.

"Then it's a good thing we have all night."

And hopefully longer.

CHAPTER TWENTY-ONE

HUNTER

THERE IS something soothing about being at the beach at two in the morning with no one else around. It's just you and the waves and the darkness.

It makes the world feel a whole lot bigger.

"One of the reasons I chose to go to Cal U, besides my family, was because of the distance to the water. There were a few years where I needed to be alone and going to the beach was the only place where I was able to find myself again. There's even one close to campus with a patch of daisies growing by the sand."

Selena's voice breaks through the sound of the waves crashing against the shore.

Her words feel heavy, as if there is something more she wants to say but doesn't.

We've been out here for over four hours and all four hours have been filled with just getting to know random parts of each other.

It started with questions about family and she told me all

JOCELYNE SOTO

about her sisters and their husbands and how they looked me up after I had called during one of their dinners.

She was embarrassed by the whole thing, but I thought it was funny.

Then she asked me about mine, and I told her what I've told her before. The difference this time is that I told her how in the last few weeks I've made it my mission to get closer to Blake and Jainie, which has made my mom happy.

From there it was like a rapid-fire question game.

Favorite colors. Favorite bands. First concerts. Everything that we could think of, we asked.

I even asked her about her other two tattoos but that is the one thing that she wouldn't tell me. All she said was maybe I will get to see what they are one day.

I will hold her to that. Any piece of art that is adorning Selena's body, I will love to see and study every inch of her. I mean, her tattoos.

As the questions continued, we talked about almost everything except what led us here.

"Do you still do that? Escape to the beach?" I ask, bringing myself back to the present.

She curls herself around one of the blankets she has in her car. Thank God for them too because it's cold as shit out here. We live by the ocean in Seaside but for some reason, the ocean breeze hits differently two hours north.

Selena just shrugs. "Sometimes. Not as often as I did though. I guess I haven't been losing myself as often."

"Did you go after the night in the parking lot?"

She is silent for a few seconds before I get a head shake. "No. I didn't feel the need to. The way I see it, I lost a piece of myself but not completely."

214

What I wouldn't do to close this small space between us and wrap my arms around her and apologize profusely for how that night played out.

But I don't.

Instead, I hit the subject that will hit both of us hard.

"So, tell me about SENFULL94. How did she come to be?"

I don't have to have my arm around her to feel her sigh from where I'm sitting.

"So I read, right?" she asks and turns to me in the process. I don't know if it's a question I'm supposed to be answering but I do anyway.

"Right."

"Do not judge me for what I'm about to tell you." She gives me a pointed look.

"I won't."

She nods and is silent for a few seconds before she continues. "I was doing this edit for a book I was reading. Getting pictures online and putting them together to fit the story. One of the things that I looked up was the word DILF."

I can't help but snort at her admission. A death glare gets thrown my way. "Sorry."

Mental reminder to ask her what book made her search up the word DILF.

"Anyway. As I was looking through the search results, I found a picture of a guy that I had seen on a dating app. I got curious and clicked on it and somehow landed on the *Confidence NSFW* page. For a while, I was just looking and then I started hyping up the women that posted and then the men. I was in awe that there were people out there that had that amount of confidence to do that. Something that I didn't have."

"You have confidence," I throw out there.

She just shakes her head. "I can do this thing where I can be the strongest, most confident person on the outside. But on the inside, I judge every little thing about myself even when my head is held high. My stomach is too big, my hips are too wide, I wish I could wear jeans that are under a size ten. When I posted my first picture and I saw people commenting and saying how much they liked what they saw, I started seeing myself in a different light. So I posted more, but as the weeks went on, it felt more like I was required to post to keep feeling the elation. After a few more than enough creepy messages and conversations that didn't lead anywhere, I stopped. I grew tired of it. SENFULL94 is just a play on words. Sen for my name and it was instead of sin, it felt fitting given what I was posting. I had put her away but she came out when you appeared. For the first time in a year, I felt the confidence that I thought I would never feel again. "

I gave her confidence and then I took it away. If I didn't feel like an ass before, I sure feel like one now.

"Now your turn. How did HUN4ALL come to be?"

I snort. "First, that name should have been your first clue as to who I was."

She lets out a laugh. "I'm sorry that I was too distracted by your abs to see the clue you placed in your username."

"I forgive you." I chuckle but I somber up and tell her how HUN4ALL came to be. "It was mostly a fuck you to Jenna and Jax. I found out about them that night. I guess I wanted to feel like I was worthy of someone, even if it was a complete stranger."

"And the name Chase?"

"My middle name." I guess if she knew that little piece of information, my identity would have been a little more clear from the beginning.

"Do you regret posting?" she asks, leaning closer to me.

I look her right in the eyes. "No, because it brought me to you."

"I could say the same thing about anatomy."

She's right. If I hadn't posted on HEX, I would have still met her in class. But I fell for Len first and the fact that she was Selena, it just added to the attraction.

"You're right. And I'm sure I would have fallen for you either way." I reach forward and brush a lock of hair that was pushed out of her beanie by the wind, away from her face.

"Fallen for me?" Her voice is small, but I still hear it.

"I've fallen for you so fucking hard, Selena, that seven weeks without talking to you pissed me off more than finding Jax and Jenna together. I hate that I fucking hurt you and I will keep apologizing for that day even after you forgive me."

I place my hand on her cheek and lean my forehead against hers.

"Please forgive me, Lennie."

That's the first time that I have used that nickname on her. When Len first told me her name, that was one of the variations that I used in my head, but I never used it. Not until now, because Len and Selena are the same person, and that name fits the girl that I've spent all semester getting to know.

Of course I'm going to start using the names interchangeably.

Her breath hitches slightly at the name, but she quickly recovers and her hand lands on top of mine. "Okay."

"That's it?"

"That's it. Don't hurt me again, Hunter."

"I fucking won't." I look into her brown eyes and try to convey all the truthfulness that I can so that she can believe me. Because I will never hurt her like that again.

I close the distance between us and kiss her. I kiss her like I've wanted for months now. How I wanted to kiss her after that night in my apartment. How I wanted Chase to kiss Len if we ever met in person.

Her tongue slides along my bottom lip and I give her all the access she wants.

The blankets are forgotten and we are trying to touch as much of each other as we can.

Then Lennie pulls away.

Is she going to leave again? "What?"

"It's cold. Do you think we can go to the car? I rather not freeze." Her body is shaking even though she is wearing a hoodie.

I jump up right away and grab the blankets all while Len is still on the sand.

"Come on." I grab her hand and drag her up. She laughs the whole time we run to the car. Reaching our escape from the cold I open the passenger door, but I don't let her go in. No, I just open the door to throw the blankets inside. I open the back door and push her inside before I slide in behind her and take her face between my hands.

"Are we doing this? Me and you? Are we really doing this?"

I look into her eyes and all I see is brightness and possibilities.

Please say yes.

"I mean I don't think we can tell people that we technically started this by exchanging nudes, but yes. I want to. What do you say?"

I don't use words, I use my mouth in all the places that I can. Her mouth. Her jaw. Her neck. Every piece of visible skin, I mark as mine.

Her hands are in my hair and my hands are on her hips, pushing her hoodie and jersey up to reveal more of her.

"You are wearing too many layers," I say against her neck.

"Then do something about it," she pants out and if I wasn't falling for the girl already, I would be.

I slide the hoodie farther up her body until it's over her chest.

She's in a black lace bra that fits her perfectly. Seeing her tits in pictures has nothing on seeing them in real life. They are fucking spectacular and so full. The sight of them is so fucking mouthwatering that I can't help myself but lean forward and grope them through the lace.

"Hunter," Selena moans when I bite down on her nipple through the fabric. She tries to move her hands but they are trapped by mine where I'm holding up her sweater.

I lean back enough to pull the sweater and jersey right off her and I start to drool.

I've seen pictures of her body, but pictures don't do the real thing justice.

"Fuck. You are fucking perfect," I tell her, looking at what is exposed.

Hearing my words though, she starts to shield herself

from me, her arms going automatically to her stomach, but I stop her before she can cover up fully.

"Listen to me." I place a finger under her chin and make her look up at me. "You are one of the most beautiful women I have ever seen. I want to mark every inch of you as mine. You are fucking beautiful and I will tell you that every single day for as long as you let me."

Her eyes still look unsure.

So I show her further what she does to me.

Grabbing her hand, I slide it down my chest to where the bulge is behind the zipper of the denim adorning my lower half.

I place her hand there and I know she feels it and when she closes her hand a bit and applies pressure, I let out a moan.

"You make me so fucking hard, Len. You've seen the pictures I've sent you. You know how you affect me. I'm trying to restrain myself so much right now, I don't know how much longer I can take it."

She starts to stroke me through the denim. "Then don't hold back."

"Our first time isn't going to be in the back of a car," I growl out and I swear she lets out a whine at what I just said. "But that doesn't mean that I'm not going to devour and mark these fucking glorious tits that I've been dreaming about for months or look forward to this pussy you've teased me with."

With one swift movement, her bra is off, followed by my own hoodie and jersey. I just wish taking off her pants was that easy. It took a second but eventually, she's in front of me, slouched on the back seat with only a pair of panties that match her bra.

Fuck, I never thought of her as someone who matches her panties and bra. It's sexy as fuck.

Her legs are spread and I settle between them and start to ravage every single inch of her tits.

They're soft and supple and exactly how I dreamed.

I bite down on one mound, sucking on the smooth skin. Then I do the same thing with the other.

Keeping my mouth in place, with her nipple in my mouth, I move my hand down to her center and stroke her just faintly through the lace.

"Hunter."

"What do you need, Len?" I say, biting down on her other nipple, while my fingers gently draw circles around her clit.

She's wet and hot and it's just for me.

"Just touch me already. Please."

"Anything you want, Len. Anything you want."

I mark every inch of her tits as I apply more pressure to her core and slide my fingers down to her entrance and tease her a bit before sliding a finger in, then two.

Moans fill the car. The windows fog up from all of our heavy breathing.

The more I touch Selena, the more I want. The more I want to take everything but I don't.

I will go slow with this girl, this woman, because that's what she deserves. She deserves to be cherished and handled with care, just like how I told her the first time I was talking to her as HUN4ALL.

"I'm almost there," Selena pants out and I abandon her breast and kiss her lips with hunger. Our tongues dance together and we suck and nibble on each other as much as we can.

Her hips move against my hand, seeking a release.

So I give her what she's seeking.

I slide my fingers in and out of her, pressing my thumb to her clit and within a minute she is shaking all over, panting out my name.

"Holy fuck."

I bring my fingers into my mouth to wipe them clean and the single taste of her isn't enough, I want more, but for tonight, it will suffice. I slide my nose along her jawline as she comes down from the high.

I place a small kiss just behind her ear when I feel her hand against my chest.

Before I know it, I'm getting pushed off her and my back hits the door. I'm about to ask what she is doing when she settles herself between my open legs. Even in the dead of night, the moon still shines bright enough for me to see the glimmer in her eyes. A glimmer of lust.

"What are you doing?" There's a rasp to my voice.

"Repaying the favor," she says, her voice has a seductive tone to it and just hearing it makes my rock-hard cock throb.

I don't stop her. I sit back and I watch her as she unzips my jeans and takes me out. I swear my cock twitches in her hand when she looks at me through her dark eyelashes. And the second that she licks the vein that travels along the under-side, one of my moans fills the car.

If the windows weren't fogged up before, they sure as hell are now.

My eyes stay on her as she takes my tip into her mouth

and sucks on it just a bit. It's a small motion, but fucking shit, this girl is going to make me come undone with it.

Soon, she is taking me whole. Her mouth is warm around me and all I can do is reach forward and grab at her hair.

She slides her mouth all over me, the mixture of her spit and my precum leaking all over and when I feel the tips of her fingers against my balls, I about lose it.

"Baby. Lennie." I pant out, grabbing at her hair, trying to pull her off.

But she doesn't budge. She just hums against me and continues to move my dick in and out of her mouth.

Fuck. We should be doing this in a bed. Not out in public, in the back of a car, in the middle of the night.

But damn does it feel good.

"Lennie, I'm going to come. Pull away." I pull at her hair some more but she still doesn't move.

She just continues to hum, sucking me hard, caressing in all the right places.

With a grunt and more hair pulling, I fill her mouth with my seed.

"Fucking hell," I groan when the last drop leaves me. Her mouth is still slowly working me.

Selena finally pulls away once she has me all cleaned up and gives me a smile as she wipes at the corner of her lips.

"That was fun."

"That was more than fun, baby. That was like going to fucking *Disneyland.* I don't even want to know where you learned to use your mouth like that." The thought of her with anyone else doesn't sit right with me.

"Porn and books."

"Porn?"

She gives me a curt nod. "Porn."

Well, I'll be dammed. I would have never thought she would watch porn.

I brush her hair out of her face, before leaning in and kissing her, tasting myself on my tongue.

We kiss until she's back on her back, her legs circled around my waist.

"Want to know something?" I say against her jaw.

"What?" She's still breathless.

"I was right. Spending even a second with you is well fucking worth it and I'm not giving it up."

And it's one hundred percent the truth.

She's mine now and nothing is taking her away from me.

CHAPTER TWENTY-TWO

SELENA

WHEN IT COMES TO SCHOOL, I hate spring semester. Maybe it's because the weather is changing and the sun is out for longer, or maybe it's the fact that the school year is almost over. Or maybe the fact that it's spring and given the proximity to the coast, I have no idea how to dress.

I think it's the combination of all three.

But this semester I hate it a little more, because I'm only a few weeks from getting my degree. One step closer to being in the "real" world and looking for a corporate job.

That's the part that scares me. I have no idea what I want to do after graduation.

But I'm not going to concentrate on that right now. For now, I'm going to just concentrate on my capstone project and finish out the year strong. I'll think about the grown-up shit later.

At this moment though, I'm just going to stress about how I'm going to pass my second semester of anatomy.

I passed last semester with a C-plus, so this semester should be fun, not.

Keeping my headphones in, I make sure I'm walking into the right room and head in. There are a few people in the room but it's not too crowded, which I'm sure will change in a few minutes.

I make my way down to the fourth row of seats and take a seat in the second to last chair in the row. Easier access when it's time to leave the room.

I'm barely in my seat, getting to the best part of the book I'm reading off my phone when I feel someone move my hair away from my neck and place their lips on my skin.

Hunter.

He's been doing this every single chance he gets, especially when we're in public. According to him, he's marking his territory. He won't hear any complaints from me, even if it is my tickle spot.

It's been a month since the football game and since we decided to give it a shot.

In that time, we had a month off for winter break, so we've been spending almost every day together. I even followed him back on Instagram when he posted a picture of me from a trip to the aquarium. It's been a lot.

And by a lot, I mean if we aren't together, we are either texting, talking on the phone or on FaceTime.

My sisters have even called me out on the fact that a smile has been semipermanent on my face. They keep asking if I have a boyfriend and I tell them no.

Technically, Hunter and I haven't talked about labels in the month or so that we've been hanging out? Dating? We're doing something that involves a whole lot of making out and exploring each other below the belt with our mouths and hands. Even if we kind of came to the conclusion of trying something between us.

Do I want a label? I mean, it would be nice.

My overthinking brain wants a label for sure.

I turn to face Hunter slightly and smile when I see that he's wearing the grin I love so much.

"Hi," I tell him as if I didn't see him this morning for coffee before my first class.

"Hi." He leans down and places a kiss on my lips before he pulls away and brings out the chair next to me and sits.

As I watch him get settled for our one and only class together, I'm slightly aware of the eyes that are currently on us. Or on me, I should say.

Turning my head slightly, I see a girl that I know is on the track team, sitting on the row above us, looking at us with her mouth wide open.

I guess I don't need to ask how the female population at this school feels about me and Hunter.

"How was your first day of your last semester of college?" Hunter asks, causing me to ignore the stares.

"I've been texting you all day about it." I raise an eyebrow at him. It was a question he asked me twice.

"Yeah, but I missed hearing your voice. So be a good girl-friend and let me hear it."

I feel my eyes go slightly wide at his comment.

"That sounded a lot dirtier than I intended." He chuckles as he throws an arm around my chair, bringing me closer to him.

But the insinuation of the comment isn't what has my eyes going wide. It's the fact that he called me his girlfriend.

There, you have your label.

Never thought getting Hunter Jacobi to call you his girl-friend would be that easy.

I lean in toward him and place a chaste kiss on his lips. "My day was fine," I say before pulling away.

"Just fine?" Why is how my day went so important? Is this what it's like to have a guy in your life that actually cares? He's just super invested in your day?

I just shrug. "I did have this random football player that kept texting me throughout the day. But that's about it."

The way he narrows his eyes at me has me holding back a smile.

"Oh yeah, and who is this football player?"

"I don't know. He keeps spewing about how he's the star or something. I think I might have to block him."

I shrug again just for good measure, which I guess he doesn't like because he pulls me into his body again until his mouth is only inches away from my ear.

"Block me and you will be feeling me between your legs for two weeks straight."

I feel my face get hot. Squirming a little, I look around to see if anyone heard what he just said. There are still eyes on us, but they just look even more confused by our closeness than anything.

As the professor walks into class, I try to push myself away from Hunter and his touch but he doesn't let me. All of class he keeps me at his side with his hand over my shoulders and not even an inch of space between us.

Usually, when it comes to being close to others, I tend to put as much space as possible between me and them. I don't want to feel like I'm invading their space or anything. I get nervous when I'm walking next to anyone, for crying out loud. But with Hunter, I don't feel the nerves and I like the fact that he likes to keep me close like this.

By the time class ends, I know nothing about what to expect for the semester. The only thing I was able to concentrate on was Hunter and Hunter alone.

This is going to be a long semester.

We start making our way out of the room, and Hunter grabs my hand and interlocks our fingers. It takes me a second to remember that we are together and the walks to my car are going to be a little different now.

Walking to my car holding hands isn't the only thing different now because as we make our way out of the building, someone calls out Hunter's name which causes him to stop.

Turning, I see Jax running over to us, a big smile on his face. That smile gets directed at me when he comes to stop in front of us and greets me.

"Hi, Selena."

"Hey."

Jax and I have had a few classes together through the years but never really had a conversation. We know each other but that's about it.

I don't think I can remember the last time I said a word to him.

"What's up?" Hunter asks his friend. Or should I say best friend? I've come to find out in the last month that Jax and Hunter have been best friends since freshman year and that little fact made my head spin since the whole Jenna cheating on Hunter thing. When I asked he told me that they're cool but definitely not at the level they once were.

"Having a party at the house this Saturday. You two should come. Celebrate the new year and all that." Jax says, his smile somehow growing.

Party.

A college party at that. I would rather suffer my sisters talking about what their husbands do to them in bed.

"Yeah, man. We'll be there." Hunter gives him an affirmative nod.

We will?

"Cool, man. See you both Saturday." Jax says before he throws a head nod in our direction before he turns to head to the library.

"Why is your face all scrunched up like that?" Hunter asks as soon as we're alone.

I didn't realize that it was. I fix it and give a small smile. "No reason."

He narrows his eyes at me. "Lennie."

Damn this man and the use of that nickname, hearing it is like a weakness.

"I'm not a 'going to college parties' type of person."

"Did something happen at the ones that you've gone to?" There is concern on his face.

I shake my head. "I've never actually been to one."

"How is that possible?"

"Um, because I've never been invited? I wouldn't classify myself as the most approachable person on this campus." The headphones and the quietness tend to make people a little wary when it comes to talking to me.

"You've never been invited to a college party?" I shake my head. "Okay, we are definitely going on Saturday."

He grabs my hand and starts walking again and I'm groaning the whole time, which earns me an eye roll.

I guess I'm going to my first college party. Yay me. Looks like when it comes to him, I will do anything.

Including going to parties I don't want to go to.

CHAPTER TWENTY-THREE

HUNTER

I DON'T KNOW WHY, but when I pictured Selena getting dressed for a party, I pictured her in her everyday jeans, tees and Vans, just dressed fancier. Her hair would be down and in waves and maybe she would have her contacts in. Maybe even a small amount of makeup or something

That's what I pictured, because what else would she wear? She's not the type of girl to wear dresses on any given day.

Even though I would fucking love it if she wore that little red summer dress I saw her wear in December, again. Especially if I get to see it around her waist as I devour her glorious tits. Fucking melons those things.

But that's not her.

So tell me why, as she's walking out of her house, as I'm picking her up to go to the party, she's wearing a damn skirt.

One that fucking accentuates every inch of her delectable curves and makes her legs look a mile long. Sure, she was still wearing her white Vans, her hair is just like I thought it would be, and she is in fact wearing her contacts.

But her clothes are different and I want to skip the party, head to my apartment and peel every scrap of material off her body.

"What?" she says as she approaches my spot by the passenger door of my truck.

I would have gone to the door to pick her up but she said her parents were already in bed and didn't want to disturb them.

"You're wearing a skirt," I state.

"I am. Is that bad?" Selena looks down at her legs and I know for a fact that my stupid ass just made her doubt how good she looks.

"No!" I say too loudly. I clear my throat and try again. "No, it's not bad. You look fucking perfect. I just think I'm going to be struggling a bit tonight."

I scratch my head. There are already scenes playing out in my mind as to what I can do to her without taking off the skirt. Or with it. The picture of her in the red dress comes back to mind but this time the black skirt is in its place.

Selena raises an eyebrow at me. "Oh yeah, and why is that?"

I look over her shoulder at the house to make sure that there is nobody standing at any of the windows before I approach her. Placing my hands on her hips, I bring her closer to me. Her soft body against my hard one aligns perfectly so I just have to lean down a bit to whisper in her ear.

"Because all I can picture is the skirt bunched up at your waist and having my tongue or cock slide into you."

Her breath hitches and I can't help but smirk when I hear it and run my tongue along the column of her neck.

Cucumber and mint and everything that is Selena.

Since the beach, we haven't done a whole lot. We've fooled around, both in my apartment, in our cars and over the phone. The over the phone part getting a lot more sexual than what HUN4ALL and SENFULL94 ever did. Fingering, making out, a blow job here and there but nothing were I'm licking every inch of her pussy and pounding into her.

I did find out what her other two tattoos are though, so that's a win in my book.

She stated once that we were somewhere between second and third base.

Her and her damn baseball analogies.

I think we've both wanted to go further but we are going slow and that is something I'm perfectly okay with. With Selena, I'm happy with just spending time with her, I don't need it to be sexual.

My dick has other ideas though.

Lennie's hand goes around my waist and starts rubbing circles against the material of my shirt.

"Maybe we should make the picture come alive."

Have I mentioned that this woman has a dirty mouth? It's one thing hearing it through text messages but hearing it in person is sexy as hell and makes my dick hard. Those words are not what you would expect to come from a girl like Selena.

I let out a groan, detaching myself from her body. "Let's get to this stupid ass party before I do something stupid. Like fuck you in front of your parents' house."

That would be a first impression that I would never be able to live down.

Selena laughs but gets in the truck. Once she is settled

and I'm in the driver's seat, we start making our way over to the football house.

The second we hit the main street to head in the direction of Cal U, Lennie grabs my hand and places it on her thigh.

On her upper thigh.

On direct skin.

Her smooth, caramel-colored skin.

It's fine. I'm fine. No way am I distracted by where my hand is. Nope, not at all.

I try to concentrate on the road ahead of us, and I'm able to do that for a whole three seconds before my hand starts to move.

Except, I'm not the one moving it. It's Len. She's moving it unconsciously, or at least I think it's unconsciously, up and down her thigh, creeping closer to the hem of her skirt.

Breathe, Jacobi. Just breathe and you will be able to survive this.

That is easier said than done, especially when I feel fabric over the top of my hand.

"Selena," I grunt out, grabbing her thigh and digging my fingers into her smooth skin.

Her thighs are so thick, I just want to sink my teeth into them. Leave bite marks that are hidden by her skirt.

"What?" she asks innocently and I'm sure that if I turned to her, I would see her throwing a smirk in my direction.

My fingers dig deeper into her skin, which I'm sure will leave a few marks. "I know what you're doing."

"What am I doing?" I hear her shift and next thing I know she lets go of my hand for a second to push up the

235

center seat. Selena scoots closer to me and my hand lands back on her thigh.

My fingers start to peel from her skin as she asks the question and I'm rendered silent when she grabs my hand, stopping me and moves it to the edge of her panties.

"Fuck." I groan once my fingers meet her heat.

I've touched her, I've made her come countless times with my fingers, but this is the first time that she's initiating it like this.

"What am I doing, Hunter?" she asks again, this time placing my fingers on the wetness of her panties.

"You're asking for me to pull over," I say through my teeth, rubbing her through the material, her hand never leaving mine.

"Why would you pull over? Things can be done without stopping the car."

Did I mention that this girl is perfect?

Fuck it.

I give her what she wants, what she is asking me to do.

My hand moves off her core only for a second to open up her thighs a bit more. To do things with my fingers that I want to do with other parts of my body.

I move her panties to the side and like our first night together, I move my finger through her slit.

"You're so wet." Her arousal coats my hand and her moan fills the cab of the truck.

"It's what happens when I'm around you," she pants out, opening her legs more by placing a foot on the seat.

I should pull over.

There is no way I can give her all the attention she seeks while driving, but I keep one hand on the wheel and rub circles over her clit with the other. Her hips start to move along with the motion of my fingers moving in and out of her.

"Take my fingers, baby. Take everything you want to. Use my hand."

My dick is hard as fucking stone and is pressing against the zipper of my jeans. It's painful, but the pain is the only thing I can concentrate on instead of driving this truck off the road and replacing my fingers with my mouth. Or better yet with my cock.

Lights and cars move past us and I try to do everything to make my girl come.

"Hunter, I can't—" She stops to moan, grabbing my hand and holding my fingers in her.

"You can, baby. Release it. Come on my fingers." I do a come-hither motion with the fingers that are in her and after a few more swipes of my thumb against her clit, I can feel her legs shaking under my touch.

Fuck, I really wish I could turn to face her and watch her unravel under my touch.

"Shit!" Lennie yells out, still holding my hand to her as she tightens around me and starts to drown in her release.

Her pants and the sound of the tires moving along the asphalt are the only things that I hear. I continue to work my fingers along her pussy, coating them with her orgasm. Once her breathing is more stable, I finally pull away from her, my fingers going directly into my mouth.

Her taste on my tongue is something I will never get tired of.

"Hmm, I think you should wear skirts more often," I tell her, licking every inch of my fingers clean.

A chuckle escapes her lips as she readjusts her skirt and situates herself back in her seat.

I have to do some readjusting myself.

"Well, there is always after the party."

After the party.

I don't know if I will be able to make it that long.

———

Selena

I really don't want to be at this party.

Everything that I thought a college party would be, it is and it only took a whole five minutes for me to realize that.

But I'm here for Hunter and as much as I want to leave this space, I will keep a smile on my face and continue to act like I really do want to be here.

I could deal without the constant stares from the girls that are here, especially the ones that are coming from Jenna.

Not even the drink that I have in my hand is distraction enough to forget about her. I get it, I'm with her ex-boyfriend, but she cheated on him. She hurt him, and he's moved on. She needs to get over it.

"She has nothing on you." Hunter's voice breaks through the music. His hands are on my hips and his mouth is close to my ear.

"You were with her for three years." I take a drink of my beer, looking at a spot on his chest.

Three years is a long time to be with someone.

"Three years too long." Hunter pulls back slightly, moving his hands from my hips to my face. "The moment I met you, I realized that. So, when I tell you that she has nothing on you, believe me." A small kiss lands on my lips. "She." Kiss. "Has." Kiss. "Nothing." Kiss. "On you."

"Okay," I say, taking another sip.

It's not that I don't believe him. I do, but comparing myself with Jenna, she wins every time. She has the body of a dancer and all that.

"Good. Now dance with me."

"Excuse me?" Is the music playing with my head?

"Dance with me," he states, his hands landing back on my hips, swaying them with the music.

"You know how to dance?"

"Baby, I'm an athlete. I can do everything." That cocky smirk I love so much makes an appearance.

"And what if I can't dance?"

"Lennie, I've been watching you all night, you've been moving these hips like you want to forget about every person in the room and dance your heart out. You can dance."

Stupid music playing through the house. Whoever made the playlist knows how to get the Mexican girl's attention.

"*Quieres bailar, pues vamos a bailar.*"

"I don't know what you just said, but it sounds sexy as fuck."

"*Si vamos a estar juntos, vas a tener que aprender español.*"

"Again, sexy as fuck. What did you say?" I can't help but laugh a little at his excitement.

"I said that if we're going to be together, then you're going to have to learn Spanish."

"Deal, now let's dance." He grabs my hand and drags me

over to the makeshift dance floor in the middle of the living room.

A few seconds in and I find out that Hunter knows how to grind. I wouldn't call it straight up dancing but the electricity between us is so damn intoxicating, I love every single minute of it.

I sway my hips against his body, trying to feel every inch of it against mine. His hands never leave my body, not even when I turn and grind my ass against his hardness.

Every inch of it.

We dance four songs and after each song I get sweatier and sweatier.

"Okay, I need a break and a drink," I say when I turn and place a kiss against my boyfriend's lips.

I see it as a good sign that I thought of him as my boyfriend. Finally.

Hunter agrees, grabbing my hand and walks us to the kitchen to where the keg is. Once beers are in hand, we make our way outside for some fresh air.

Hunter takes one of the open lawn chairs that overlooks the yard and pulls me onto his lap.

Not for a second do I question his actions. For the moment, I feel comfortable just being with him and not worrying about anything else.

We sit like that for a few minutes, just the two of us holding each other and living in our little bubble.

Eventually someone comes by and pops the little bubble.

"Hey," Jax says as he comes by and crouches down next to our chair and addresses Hunter. "We're about to start the tournament upstairs. You want in?"

Tournament?

"Sure, we'll be up in a bit." Jax nods at Hunter's answer and leaves as quickly as he appeared.

"You guys have tournaments at parties?" I ask when we're alone again.

Hunter shrugs. "Just guys playing video games. Sometimes a little money is involved."

"And you called me a nerd because my ideal date was going to the bookstore," I tease him.

He pulls on a small strand of my hair. "You are a nerd."

"A nerd that reads things that are beneficial to you." A thing that not many people understand is that reading something like a romance novel teaches you things. A romance book shouldn't be just enjoyed by one person.

And in the last month or so, I may have shared a few books with Hunter. Some very explicit scenes included.

He will probably say otherwise if other people were around, but he loves every single minute of it.

"And they better be for me and only me," he growls into my neck and I can't help but laugh a little.

"Possessive, but yes only for you."

"Good." A kiss lands behind my ear.

He stays in the position for a little while before he finally lets out a sigh and pulls away from me.

"Let's go upstairs and play some video games before I change my mind and drag you to my place."

It's when I'm back standing on my feet that it hits me.

His words are simple, a suggestion that is said on a regular basis.

But they hit me so hard that I have to remind myself to breathe. So hard that I find myself rubbing at the daisy on my wrist.

"Selena." Hunter comes into view, his eyes filled with concern. He must have called my name more than once because he doesn't call me Selena all that often anymore. "You okay?"

"Huh?" I try to shake the cloud that has filled my mind but it doesn't move.

"I asked if you were okay?" He places a finger under my chin and forces me to look up at him.

"Yeah, I just, um," Am I okay? "Yeah, I'm fine." I don't even believe the words as I say them and given the look Hunter is giving me, he doesn't either.

"Are you sure? You look a little pale."

I try to take a deep breath, but it feels like nothing is going into my lungs.

I nod either way. "Yeah, let's go play video games."

My voice is shaky and it's not as strong as I want to convey but it's enough for Hunter to take my hand and lead us into the house.

When we reach the stairs, and start going up to the second floor, I'm taken back to a time that I thought I buried away. It's like a hammer hitting a nail over and over, making sure I don't forget.

I'm in a different space. I'm not back there.

That's what I keep thinking the closer we get to where the video game tournament is taking place. I repeat the words in my head, and I hold on to Hunter's hand as tightly as I can.

Every few seconds he looks back at me, silently asking me what is going on, but I don't say anything. I just keep my eyes forward and continue to walk.

It's a different place. It's nothing like it was before.

We walk into a room that is closer to a movie theater than

it is to a bedroom. It's filled with chairs and guys and girls all around looking at the big screen that's on the wall.

Nothing about it is familiar, I've never been here but yet I'm still transported to a place that was messy and filled with darkness and pain.

It's not the same, I know it's not, but my body says otherwise.

I need to get out of here.

I need to breathe. I need to get the hammer to stop moving. No matter how much I touch my daisy, nothing helps.

Before walking fully into the room, I tug my hand out of Hunter's grip, causing him to turn to me right away.

"What's wrong?"

"I'm going to go outside." I point over my shoulder, not really looking at the man in front of me.

"Selena." He starts to close the distance between us, but I step back.

"It's okay, play with the guys. I'll just be by the car." I give a small smile before turning and walking away from the room and the memories as fast as I can.

"Selena!" Even over the music, I'm able to hear Hunter call after me. I just don't turn to face him.

I just keep walking.

I just keep pushing the memories out of my mind.

But as much as I keep pushing, they aren't going anywhere.

I really shouldn't have come to this stupid party.

CHAPTER TWENTY-FOUR

HUNTER

FOR TEN MINUTES, I kept telling myself that all she needed was air. That the number of people in this house was beginning to be a little much for her and she needed a break.

Yet every time I thought that, her face popped into my line of vision and all I could see was the fear in her eyes.

She was scared. Something happened that scared her and I have no idea what it was.

I lasted ten minutes watching my friends play video games before I told myself that Selena was more important. So now I'm walking out of the house trying to find my girlfriend and make sure she's okay.

"Hunty." I hear the second I step foot onto the porch.

I don't know what enticed me to stop but I do. I turn to see Jenna leaning against the railing, with a drink in her hand. She's looking at me like she used to when we first started dating, with lust-filled eyes.

"Jenna," I say through a sigh.

"You look like you're having fun." She takes a sip of her drink but keeps her eyes on me.

"It's a party." I shrug.

"I wasn't talking about the party. With your piece of ass." Jenna spits out.

She's talking about Selena.

Instantly, I push my shoulders back, ready to fight her on anything that has to do with Selena.

"She's not a piece of ass," I spit back, before turning away from her and stepping off the porch. "And she never will be."

"That girl won't be able to give you what you need!" Jenna yells as I walk farther away from her.

I ignore her words and continue toward the truck, looking in every direction to see if I catch sight of Selena.

Getting to the truck, I don't see her. She's not by any of the doors or by the tailgate. She's not even sitting on the sidewalk.

Where the fuck did she go?

I look over at the other cars, but she's not anywhere near them.

Could she have gone home?

It's possible. She could have called a car to pick her up or one of her sisters because there is no way she would have walked, it's too far and she's wearing a skirt for fuck's sake.

I'm starting to panic. I start patting my pockets for my phone to call her, but I come up empty, I must have left it in the truck.

Ignoring the fact that I don't have my phone, I start walking around the neighborhood, trying to find her. I walk down the street a bit when a park comes into view. I let out a sigh of relief when I see a silhouette. There, surrounded by the darkness of the night, is Selena, sitting on one of the swings, motionless.

Closing my eyes, thankful that I found her, I walk over to her, trying my hardest to make sure that she knows I'm approaching so that I don't spook her.

Something is going on and I hate that I don't know what.

There is an eerie silence as I close the distance between us. I call out her name, but she doesn't turn, she just keeps looking out to the empty space in front of her.

I walk over to face her and that's when I see the silent tears that are rolling down her face. The fear a lot more prominent than it was inside the house.

I close the distance between us just by a bit, and when I place a hand on her shoulder, she flinches.

"Selena, it's just me," I say as gently as I can muster. She still doesn't look up at me.

Crouching down, I make sure that I'm at eye level with her before I speak again. "Lennie, look at me."

When I say Lennie, she finally looks at me. The fear isn't only in her facial expression, it's also in her eyes.

"What happened, Selena? Did someone do something to you?" I stand there staring at her for a second, and when she finally nods, my heart sinks.

I try to rack my brain as to who could have done something to her. She was with me all fucking night, always within a foot or two from me. I always had eyes on her because I knew she didn't want to be at this party. I kept watch just in case she wanted to go. How the fuck did someone do something to her without me noticing?

"Baby, you have to tell me what happened. Tell me what happened and who did it and I promise you that I will take care of it." I hope with all my might that she can see the worry in my face.

But she just shakes her head. "You can't."

"Like hell, I can't." I feel myself becoming unhinged. I try to reel it in as much as possible because if I go off on her, she's going to shut off again. I need to keep her talking. "Just tell me, Lennie. Please just tell me."

She looks up at me with those big brown eyes of hers and seeing the tears flowing out of them is breaking every inch of me.

I reach out and wipe them away, this time she doesn't flinch from my touch.

After a few long seconds, she speaks. "The daisy isn't taking the fear away. Why isn't it working? It always worked before."

She says the words but it's more like she is saying them to herself instead of to me.

"I don't know why the daisy isn't working," I say to her, wiping away a few more tears. "Did something happen to you, Selena? Is that what you're scared of?"

She nods.

"Did it happen tonight?"

A shake of her head.

It didn't happen tonight. Whatever she's scared of, whatever is causing this manic state, happened sometime in the past.

"Did something trigger the fear tonight?"

That has to be it, right? That's the only logical explanation. Something at the party had to trigger the emotions that she is currently feeling.

Again, she nods.

Fuck.

She didn't want to go to this party. She told me and I

247

heard her, but I still made her come tonight. Something triggered something from her past and it's all my fault.

"What triggered you?" I say after clearing my throat a few times.

When she doesn't speak for a few minutes, I think that she's shut down again but thankfully I'm wrong.

"I was okay. It just felt like another normal night with you, but then you said it and floodgates opened and I couldn't close them. Not like I've been able to in the past."

I don't know what scares me more, the fact that her voice sounds so level, so calm or the fact that I was the trigger?

"What did I say?" I grab her hand in mine and give her a reassuring squeeze.

"You suggested that we go upstairs and play video games. Such a normal sentence that should mean nothing, but yet the combination of them together sends me down a spiral."

Video games?

So many questions run through my head and I want to ask them all but all I can concentrate on is the fact that the mention of video games triggered her and sent her down a dark hole.

"Will you tell me why suggesting we play a video game was a trigger?" I need to know, so I won't do it again, I don't say.

She looks at me but then she looks away, staring at something in the park. This time I count to one hundred before she speaks, but she doesn't say what I thought she would.

"You never asked me." Her voice is low and for a quick second, I think that her mind might be in another place and not speaking to me.

I still answer her though. "I never asked you what?"

"You never asked me if I was a virgin." Her eyes meet me dead on. No sadness, no tears, no fear. Nothing.

Her question takes me aback a bit. "I didn't think that was something that I had to ask."

Her virginity was never something that crossed my mind. I just assumed with how she was over the phone and in person that she had been with someone before.

She nods and looks back to the park.

"Are you?" I ask, my curiosity about where this conversation is going getting the best of me.

"I don't know." Her answer almost knocks me off my feet, literally.

Is she saying what I think she's saying?

Please, God, tell me I'm wrong with this assumption.

"What do you mean, you don't know?" I ask but she is back to shutting me out.

Everything in me is telling me to shake her. To grab her by the shoulders and force her to tell me everything that is going on within her mind right now. But I can't. I have to be gentle with her. I have to use kid gloves on her right now or she won't tell me.

The way that this is going, I have an idea, but I need her to confirm it.

"I mean, I don't remember."

I close my eyes and swallow down the lump in my throat as I try to digest her words.

She doesn't remember.

She doesn't remember giving away her virginity.

Before I ask anything, she continues. "I don't know if I'm

still a virgin because I don't remember. I remember everything that led up to it. I remember what was done to me before I walked into the bedroom. I remember having lain on the bed and feeling the touching, but I don't remember the actual action. I remember looking up and seeing a daisy and thinking that if something so pretty was there, then maybe I didn't have to be afraid. I didn't have to be afraid of what was happening or afraid that I was going to get in trouble for being somewhere I wasn't supposed to. I don't remember it actually happening, so I don't know if I am."

My legs can't hold me up any longer, so I fall back until my ass is on the rubber padding of the park floor. There's a pain in my chest, like my heart is breaking just by hearing her speak.

I try to swallow down all the emotions flowing through my body and ask one question.

"How old were you when it happened?"

My heart breaks even more when I hear her answer. "I think it started when I was eight and then it went on until I was about eleven. I don't remember it clearly. It's as if my brain blocked certain portions of it, and I only remember a handful of things. But it happened. A lot. I know it did. I just don't remember all the details. But it happened. I swear, Hunter. It happened."

I'm on my feet the second she says my name. I take her in my arms, not caring about the chain of the swing she is sitting on being in the way. I wrap my arms tightly around her and she lets out a sob into my shirt.

"I know it did. I know it happened. I believe you." I lean down and place my lips against her hair. As I hear her cries and feel her body shake against mine, I have to hold back my own tears. She needs this and I can't be breaking down when she needs me to be strong for her.

After a few minutes, her sobs quiet down a bit but she is still shaking.

I shouldn't ask but I need to know. "How did the words I said trigger you?"

I feel her take a deep breath before she answers. "There were times before this one. It always happened at my grandma's house, but it was usually in a room on the first floor. I hated that room. Whenever my mom put me in a skirt or a dress and we visited, I would end up in that room. It was one cousin at first. He would just touch me, just slide his hand up the fabric. I didn't know what was happening or why. I didn't like it. Then I started wearing jeans, and I thought that would stop it." Selena pauses for a few seconds, taking a few deep breaths before she continues.

"I was ten when the video game happened. We were at my grandma's house again. My mom was in the living room with my grandma and aunt and my dad had gone to the store. I was in the next room playing with a few toy cars that some of my younger cousins had left behind. I was by myself when he came into the room. It was my other cousin's brother. He was older than me and my cousin, so when he asked if I wanted to go play video games with him upstairs, I went. The only hesitation that I remember having is knowing that I shouldn't have gone upstairs because my parents always told me not to. To never go to the second floor whenever we visited, not without one of them. But I went anyway, because I wanted to play video games since we didn't have any at our house.

"I thought that he was going to stop it. I thought that he

was going to stop whatever his brother was doing to me. He didn't, he continued it. The first time, he laid me down on the bed, unbuttoned my jeans, and the last thing I remember was that he pulled himself out. Then I don't remember anything, it all goes dark. After that, he would always say we were going to play video games, but in reality, something else was happening. I remember always going to the room but not the things that came after, not in detail anyway."

Her cousins.

Her damn fucking cousins took her innocence away and she has to live with that for the rest of her life.

If I ever meet the bastards, I will strangle them with my own hands and burn them alive.

Selena releases one more sob and I hold her as tight as I can. Silently telling her that I'm here for her, no matter what.

After what feels like hours, she finally lets go of me and wipes away the tears.

"I'm sorry," she whispers, sniffling.

"Hey." I take her face between my hands, making her look up at me. "Do not be sorry. I'm the one that is sorry. I'm sorry that you had to go through this. I'm sorry that I put you in a situation where you had to live through this again. I'm sorry about everything."

I lean forward and place a kiss on her lips, the taste of the saltiness of her tears still fresh on her skin.

When I pull back, Selena just nods.

"Come on, let's go," I say, holding out a hand for her to take. She hesitates for a second but she takes it. As we walk to the truck, I bring her into my side tightly.

"Where are we going?" she asks when I open the passenger door to the truck.

"I know a place."

A place where she can find herself again.

The beach.

CHAPTER TWENTY-FIVE

SELENA

WHEN MY EYES OPEN, I feel disoriented, partly because of the blinding light that is coming through from the window and partly because of an arm that is around my body.

Given that I've slept alone my whole life, the arm is messing with me more than the light.

Then all the thoughts from last night start to roll in.

The party.

The trigger.

The conversation at the park.

After Hunter and I got into his truck, he drove us to the beach closest to campus. The one with the patch of daisies growing by the sand.

I remember that I had told him about the beach, but I didn't think that he knew where it was.

I spent a good ten minutes marveling at the man for knowing what to do when I was losing myself in front of him. He brought me to the one place that I once told him I would go to that would help me find myself again.

That's when I realized that it took Hunter Jacobi only a month to make me fall in love with him.

At the beach, we didn't talk. There wasn't a word said between us physically, but I heard every silent word that he was throwing my direction as he held me.

We sat there for a good two hours, until it got too cold.

He wanted to take me home, but for some reason, I didn't want to go home. I didn't want to let go of him just yet.

So, I texted my mom and told her I was going to spend the night with my sister and Hunter brought me back to his place.

When we walked into his apartment, again no words were said. We just went through the motions of getting ready for bed. He handed me a shirt and a pair of shorts to sleep in and offered me the room to change.

I told him not to leave. For the first time, I undressed in front of Hunter completely and let him see all of me as I pulled on his shirt that should have fit big but didn't.

Every inch of me was on display, but he didn't care.

He didn't see the stretch marks that lined my lower stomach or the way that my thighs shook when I stripped off my skirt. He just saw me.

I fell a little harder at that moment.

Then we got into bed, and he gave me a kiss before he held me until we both found solace in the night.

Now here I am in this man's arms, as he continues to sleep.

I turn slightly, trying not to wake him. He's on his stomach, his face turned in my direction, with his arm thrown across my midsection.

He looks like a boyish version of himself. His hair is

standing up in every direction and his eyelashes sit just above his cheekbone. His skin has a tan to it because of the time he's spent in the sun because of football and small, light freckles line his nose.

This boy, this man, looks like every woman's dream man and even in his sleep, he exudes cockiness.

And he's here with me. Out of all the women that he could be with, he's here with me. He chose me.

I rub a hand over his bare arm until he shifts and turns onto his back, tucking me into his side so I can lay my head against his bare chest.

For the record, pictures do not do this man any justice. It's one thing seeing him naked and showing off every muscle he has in pictures, but it's a whole different thing to see them and touch them in person.

HUN4ALL is, in fact, real. Every inch of him is real and I get to touch him whenever I want.

I place a kiss just under his collarbone, and he must have felt it because he lets out a groan, telling me that he's waking up.

"Good morning," he says, sleep still very much in his voice, as he tightens his arm around me and places a kiss on my head.

"Morning," I say into his chest.

I can feel his body tense up a little bit, like he wants to say something, but he doesn't know how.

Last night was hard for me but I'm sure it was hard for him too. I let him see something that only one other person knows, so he probably has more questions than he can comprehend.

He was there for me, he still is. I owe him all the answers to all the questions he has.

Pushing off the bed, I turn so that I'm looking down at him, giving him a small smile.

He looks up at me with sleep-filled eyes and reaches up to push a few strands of my hair away from my face.

"Are you okay?" he asks, the concern still a prominent emotion on his face.

I nod. "I will be." I place a kiss on his palm when he places it against my cheek.

Hunter just nods, not allowing the question that I know is on the tip of his tongue to escape.

"I know you want to talk about it, and I'll tell you, but how about some breakfast first and I will tell you everything you want to know?"

Hunter continues to just look at me, his fingertips softly caressing my cheek. Eventually he lets out a sigh and nods in agreement.

We get out of bed and head to the kitchen, me still in his shirt and my panties and him in a pair of basketball shorts. He looks fucking hot without a shirt, and if there wasn't a cloud of rain over the two of us right now, I would take advantage of it.

"I don't have much that would be considered breakfast. Just eggs, ham, and broccoli," he says, turning to me, cringing a little bit.

"I can make something with just ham and eggs if you're up for it."

"Be my guest." He waves me toward the kitchen and within ten minutes, I have breakfast ready for us.

I plate the food and place it in front of him at that kitchen island.

"*Jamón con huevo*," I say before I take the seat next to him with my own plate.

We eat in silence for a few minutes before Hunter breaks it.

"Why is this combination so simple and yet so fucking bomb at the same time?" Hunter says through a big mouthful.

"I don't know but if we had green salsa it would be a whole lot better."

"Next time," he throws out there, wiping his plate clean.

I would have figured that seeing Hunter first thing in the morning would have been a little awkward, but it isn't. It feels really nice.

But I have to break that feeling.

"You can ask whatever you want," I say, keeping my eyes on the food still left on my plate.

Hunter is silent for a minute but soon he is putting his fork down and lets out a sigh. "Do your parents know?"

I shake my head, keeping my eyes on my plate. "I've only told one other person besides you, and that was Jen."

"Selena." The concern in his voice is back.

I finally turn to face him. "I know. I should tell them. I *need* to tell them. I just don't know how. Some of the stuff that they did are like faint memories and feel as if they were something I watched in a movie or a TV show. I'm scared they won't believe me and that they will think that I'm just making it up or something. Even if a part of me is telling me that they might have known something if they warned me not to go to the second floor without them. I've wanted to tell them so many times, but even after all these years, I haven't been able to find the words on how to tell them."

I don't tell him that telling my parents would be the first step in the whole recovery process. It may seem like my everyday life isn't affected by this, but it is. I'm just good at pushing that part of my life down. There's also a chance that I may need professional help, and I just keep acting as if it didn't happen.

I don't realize that I am crying until Hunter reaches over and brushes the tears away.

"Do you still see..." He pauses, closing his eyes, taking a deep breath in the process, before he talks again. His hand never leaving my face. "Do you still see them?"

"Not since I was fourteen. They and my aunt lived with my *abuela*, at her house. After it stopped, I would go over to my grandma's house less and less. The last time I saw them, I was fourteen. My grandma moved to the area a few years ago, so there was no need to visit her down south anymore or to see them."

I know that won't last forever. Especially with the relationship my dad has with his sister, but hopefully when that time comes, I will be mentally ready for it.

"How much older were they then you?" Hunter's jaw is rigid as he asks the question, like he wants to punch something.

I swallow down the lump in my throat. "The older one is seven years older than me and his brother is five years older."

Hunter is up from the stool he is sitting on within seconds, throwing the plate that's in front of him toward the wall.

The echo of the porcelain hitting the floor sounds through the apartment.

"That's why it stopped when you were eleven, isn't it? Because the older one turned eighteen and if he got caught his consequences would have been worse?"

I nod. "I think it also had to do with the fact that I started going into puberty."

The cousin that started it all stopped when his older brother took over. It made sense as I got older, that the older one would stop completely because of his age and the new changes happening in my body.

I can't imagine being that age and going to my parents and telling them that their baby is having one of her own. It makes me want to cry just thinking about it.

A loud thump takes me out of my head. I turn my attention back to Hunter.

"I hate that you went through this. I hate that they took something from you when you couldn't defend yourself."

Yeah, and he's going to hate it even more when I tell him the rest.

"There's more," I whisper.

Hunter lets out a grunt of frustration but nods for me to tell him.

"After..." *Can I get the words out? Can I reveal the one thing that I didn't even tell Jen? I have to.* "After the sexual abuse stopped, the verbal abuse started. That's where the lack of confidence I have in myself comes from, I guess. My older cousin told me things, like how I was ugly, how I would never have a boyfriend because he had touched me first. All these nasty things and I believed every single one of them. I was eleven or twelve and he was older. How could I not?"

Hunter comes over to me and wraps his arms around me as tightly as he can. My body molds against his as if they were meant to be put together.

After a beat of silence, I continue. "It took me years to figure out that he was lying to me, that he was trying to bring me down in every way he could. I've tried so hard to see myself in a different light, but after I stopped playing softball, it was hard. I started to gain weight, started to wear jeans above a size ten, started to see the stretch marks along my body, and all the progress I had made went out the window. That's why, even to this day, I still have trouble seeing myself as something other than what he told me I was. There are three hundred and thirty-five days in a year where I absolutely love the person that is staring back at me in the mirror. Yet there will always be thirty days where I wish I could change something about her."

Hunter pulls away from me only to take my face between his hands and lean his forehead against mine.

"Want to know what I see? I see the most beautiful woman in the whole fucking world that deserves everything that she wants in life. I don't see the stretch marks, or your jean size, if anything those things make you everything and more. You are everything to me. I know it will be hard to forget his words but concentrate on mine. Believe me when I say that I love your body, every inch of it. Believe me when I say that I love you and will show you that for as long as you let me be by your side. Let me erase his words with mine."

I stopped breathing. He said three words that I never thought would come out of his mouth, especially not to me.

"You said..." I stop, my mind overworking.

"I know what I said." He kisses my lips softly. "And I

mean it. You don't have to say it back, that's not why I said it. I said it because I wanted you to know that every inch of you is loved. Loved by me."

Another soft kiss to the lips.

I continue to sit on the barstool with my arms around his waist, holding him to me.

I don't need to say it back, but I want to.

"I love you too."

He pulls back just enough to see my face and his lips tilt up in a small smile. "Who knew that I would fall for the girl that left a comment on my nude picture online?"

"Who knew that I would fall for the cocky arrogant football player that sat next to me the first day of class?"

We stand like that for a few minutes. Forehead to forehead, eyes on each other, breaths intertwining.

"Hunter."

"Lennie."

"Give me something to remember. Something besides the words." I lean a little closer, my lips almost touching his.

"What do you want me to give you?"

"A real first time. I want you to give me a real first time. One that will replace all the dark memories that someone else caused. Touch me. Fuck me. Give me everything."

He is silent, looking at me. His blue eyes never leaving mine.

"I will give you everything you want, Lennie. Anything."

I don't wait for him to finish. I just press my lips to his and hold on to everything that he's talking about.

CHAPTER TWENTY-SIX

HUNTER

HER WORDS BROKE me but having her in my hands, feeling her skin against mine is repairing me.

I kiss her with fervor, my tongue sweeping every inch of her mouth, leaving no crevice untouched.

Selena wants me to give her something to remember, so I'm going to make that my mission. I will give her something to remember and so much more.

I swallow one of her moans and all I want to do is pounce.

"You feel so fucking good in my hands," I say against her lips before I move my mouth down her jaw until I glide my lips to her neck.

"You make me feel good," she moans as I keep my mouth on her neck but move my hands to the hem of her shirt.

Or should I say my shirt, the one that I will only picture on her from here on out.

I push the shirt up until it's over her chest, revealing her perfect tits. I pull away from her only for a second to discard the shirt, before going back to the mauling I was doing to her neck.

My hands find their way to her tits and I tease the flesh before taking her nipples between my fingers and pinching them. The moan she releases is a sweet escape that makes me want to bring out my phone and record everything that comes out of her mouth.

"Jacobi." Selena pants out. Her hand moves to my hair, pushing my head to go farther down.

I growl against her skin. "I told you to not call me Jacobi." I sink my teeth into her smooth skin, marking it as mine.

"Move your mouth and I won't." She pulls at my hair hard enough that to some people it would be painful. To me, it just drives me crazier.

"Where do you want it?" I place a small kiss on her clavicle.

"On my tits. They feel so fucking heavy right now. Touch them."

I can't help but smile against her skin. "For a shy girl, you sure have a dirty mouth."

"Blame all the romance novels that I read."

"Remind me to send those authors a thank-you letter."

"Hunter!" I release a chuckle at her exclamation of my name and give her what she wants. Placing my mouth on her tits.

I'm thankful that when she told me what she wanted me to do that I had the right mind to bring us to the bedroom. No way was I going to give her chest the attention that it deserves standing up.

I settle between her legs and I go in for my attack. My hands wrap around the mounds and moans, both mine and

Selena's fill the room. I grip them tight enough for my nails to leave a mark.

Her nipples are the next thing on my line of sight. I take them in my mouth and give them a good suck.

Lennie's tits are so full that I could spend all night worshipping them.

Removing her panties, I place my hands back on her breasts. I start to move my mouth down her body. Reaching her stomach, I kiss every single one of the stretch marks that make her lose confidence in herself.

I find them sexy. Everything about her is fucking sexy.

After giving her marks the attention they deserve, I continue to kiss farther down her body. Her belly and then down to her mound. There is no hesitation as I run my tongue along her slit, tasting her straight from the source.

"You taste so fucking good," I mumble against her, moving up to take her clit into my mouth.

"Hunter." Her hand pulls at my hair but she's not pulling me closer to her body, she's pulling me away. "I want your cock."

I don't stop the attack that I have on her pussy. I keep my mouth on her but my eyes are on hers. Fuck, I really like the way she says cock. It has me shifting to press my hard-on against the mattress.

"Be patient, baby. You will get it. I just need you to come in my mouth first. That way I know that you can take every inch of my cock."

She lets out a whimper as she bucks against my face. "I don't know how much more I can take."

"You will take everything that I give you," I command.

But because I'm the loving boyfriend that I am. I give her what she wants.

I place my tongue against her entrance and tease her until her thighs start to tremble against my head. Then I move back to her clit and go to town. I suck the bundle of nerves into my mouth and don't let go until she screams.

"Hunter!" she moans out, but I still don't move away until I feel her completely unravel under me. "Fuck. Fuck."

My hair has never been pulled so hard in my life, but you won't hear me complaining.

I wipe her clean as she comes down from her high and start to kiss up her body again. Doing the same thing I did when I went down.

When I reach her mouth, I kiss her, swiping my tongue against hers.

"Do you like the taste of your pussy? Because I sure do."

"Hmm, I think I only like it because it's coming from your mouth."

We kiss until we are both panting again. Until my cock is throbbing and itching to find a release within Lennie.

I break the kiss and lean my forehead against hers.

"Are you sure you want to do this? We can stop if you want. I don't mind."

She places a hand on my cheek and I lean into her touch. "I want this, I promise. Besides, you haven't had the chance to come yet. That makes me a bad girlfriend if I don't take care of it, doesn't it?"

We may have only been together for a short period of time, but I know she is trying to deflect. This is serious to her but she is trying really hard not to freak out right now.

"I can wait. You are what I care about. I want you to be

sure about this." I can handle blue balls, she is more important. If she wants to do this, then we will, but I need to know that she is sure.

My eyes stay on hers and she takes in my words. Tears spring in them and when a lone tear escapes, I kiss it away.

She nods. "I'm sure. Please give me something to remember."

I look down at the girl under me and expect to see fear in her eyes, yet I don't. I see trust and love and I want to pound my chest because she is gifting those two things to me.

I lean down again and kiss her, except this time, it's slow and everything she deserves.

I made her a promise when she was just SENFULL94 to me, that her body deserves to be cherished and handled with care, so that's what I do.

The manhandling that she wanted then, that will come later.

For now, I'm going to cherish every inch of my girl and the body that she entrusted me with. For now, I'm going to kiss away every tear that is escaping her eyes as I slide into her.

We have plenty of time for everything else later.

———

"Lennie, have you seen my phone?" I yell from the kitchen, looking around for the stupid thing. I try to remember the last time that I used it but the only thing coming to mind was before I picked up Selena last night.

"No, I haven't seen it." Len comes into the space, now fully dressed and back in her clothes from last night.

I don't know what I like better, seeing her in a skirt or seeing her in my shirt. Honestly, it's a toss-up.

"Have I used it?" I ask myself more than her.

"I don't think I saw you pull it out since the party. Maybe it's in the truck." She throws a shrug in my direction.

"Maybe," I say, looking one more time just to make sure before grabbing my keys and wallet. "Ready to go?"

Selena nods and starts walking toward the door.

After getting to know every single inch of her body, not once but twice, Selena thought that it was time for her to go home. As much as I wanted to keep her with me for another night, I respected her decision. So after we ordered some pizza and watched half a football game, it was time to take her home.

When we get down to my truck, I look for the phone but nothing. Selena even calls it and it doesn't ring.

"Maybe you left it at the party?" she suggests.

"That has to be it, because where else could it be?" We get into the truck and start making our way to Selena's place. My hand never leaves her thigh.

"Can I ask you something?" she says when we're only a block away from the house.

"Go for it."

"Have you made up your mind about declaring for the draft?"

And here I thought that she was going to ask if I wanted to hang out later.

I sigh.

The NFL draft is definitely not something I want to talk about, but it's Selena asking not my dad.

"Why?" I ask, only to buy me more time to come up with an answer.

"So don't get mad, but I was curious, so I looked it up. I saw that the deadline to declare was two weeks ago and they're going to send out NFL combine invitations soon. I just got curious about you and wondered if you changed your mind without telling anyone."

I quickly look over at her. "You don't know a thing about football but you know about the combine?"

I get an eye roll. "I know sports, okay? I just don't understand football. And you're deflecting."

I am deflecting.

"I declared about two weeks ago. After the season was officially over," I say, feeling my jaw tense up just thinking about it.

During the game, I felt some sort of happiness that I possibly played my last game of football, but with the happiness also came sadness and I couldn't see myself giving it up.

After much thinking, I talked to Coach to see what I needed to declare.

"Oh," Selena says, sounding a bit hurt. "Why didn't you say anything? That's a big deal."

"Because the second my father got wind that I was actually thinking about declaring, he went behind my back and sent in the application that I had filled out and signed." My hand tightens around the steering wheel and my knuckles go white.

"Isn't that illegal?"

I shrug. "Possibly, but it's done. Now I just have to wait and see if I get invited to the combine."

Which will most likely happen, especially with the

number of scouts at the last few games of the season. I should be receiving that invitation, I know I will.

"But if you get an invitation, would you want to go through with it? And I'm not talking about what your dad wants you to do, I mean what you want to do. It's your life, you have a choice."

I do have a choice. And I've thought about it so fucking much that it hurts my head every single time.

It's just not something that I've talked about with Selena. It's like a part of me was trying to shield her from that side of things. Shield her from the cocky football player that gets everything he wants. I'm not him when I'm with her, but she's a part of my life, so I have to bring the two together.

Especially if I see a future with her. It may have only been a month, but I can picture the whole nine yards with her. So my decisions could affect her too.

I stay silent though. I don't answer her question until we arrive at her house.

Shutting off the truck, I just sit in my seat, looking ahead and give her the most honest answer that I can think of.

"If I get the invitation, I want to go through with it. The bowl game made me realize that I love playing, and it was for myself and I couldn't see myself giving it up. I took my dad out of the equation and for the first time in a while, I was happy at the possibility of playing for longer."

I turn to Selena, who is looking at me with pursed lips and bunched-together eyebrows.

"Do you not want me to continue playing?" I ask because her face is worrying me.

"I really don't have a say. I just want you to be happy in whatever decision you make and make it for you and only you. Do I think you'll make a good NFL player? Yeah, but I don't want you to regret it in the long run with whatever direction you do go in."

She does have a say, though. That's what I want to tell her, that she does have a say in this but I keep it to myself.

She's right though, whatever decision I make, it has to be one that I'm happy with.

I just nod at her statement.

Selena leans over the center console and places a kiss on my lips. It's short and sweet and I can't help but want more.

"Do what makes you happy, Jacobi." She pulls away when a growl rumbles in my throat. She just chuckles and gets out of the truck. I'm turning on the ignition when she turns back to face me. "Oh by the way, you're invited to a family dinner in two weeks."

That has me sitting upright. "What?"

Are my eyes popping out of my head? I think they are.

She just shrugs. She just told me that I was invited to her family dinner and she just shrugs. Girl wants me to fail in front of her family.

"It wasn't up to me. I was cornered by four women. So you're invited. Okay, bye!"

The passenger door slams closed and I watch as she scurries inside.

Forget the fact that I declared for the draft.

How the hell does a white boy prepare to meet his Mexican girlfriend's family?

Shit, I have two weeks to learn Spanish.

And to find my fucking phone.

CHAPTER TWENTY-SEVEN

SELENA

I'M TRYING REALLY HARD NOT to laugh right now, but Hunter looks like he's about to shit his pants. And he hasn't even stepped foot into the house just yet.

"Stop laughing at me," he says through clenched teeth, looking at the house and not at me, standing like he has a pole screwed into his back.

"You look like you're shitting your pants." I hold my laugh in.

"Well yeah, I'm about to walk into a house that is filled with your family and all I can think about is how I keep defiling you in public and they somehow know."

I let out a snort. "Can we not say defile anywhere near my parents' house, please?"

Hunter turns to me with narrowed eyes and speaks through his teeth. "I had my fingers in your pussy this morning."

A blush creeps up my cheeks. I mean, he did. We went to breakfast this morning since it's Saturday and all and we might have fooled around a bit before he brought me back home. It was like dessert for breakfast.

Also, why am I just noticing that we have a thing for doing shit in public? Like we are always doing things in the car. He has an apartment for crying out loud.

I shake the thought of public sex out of my head and give him a smile. "Look, I know that this may seem like a big deal," says the girl that almost puked when the subject was first brought up, "But you have nothing to worry about. You will be fine."

He takes a deep breath. "Says the girl that's about to throw me in with the wolves."

Rolling my eyes at him, I step closer to him until my lips are closer to his ear.

"If you act like a big boy, I will show you my glass dildo," I say. The blush that is coating my cheeks is getting a little more prominent.

Right away, Hunter takes his eyes off the house and looks down at me with wide eyes. I mentioned that I had a glass dildo around when Len and Chase started to talk. Looking at how his facial expression changed, He hasn't forgotten about that little tidbit of information.

"Like you actually using it?" The excitement in his voice is something that you can't miss. Even his eyes brighten up at the thought.

I shrug. "I mean, you already defiled me in public, why not see how I get myself off?"

Actually this might be a good idea. I smile. The fact that this excites me, tells me that I read too many romance novels, and I'm okay with that.

"I have to ask, how did you come about having a glass

toy?" His eyebrows wiggle as if he's excited about knowing everything that has to do with said toy.

I shrug. "I read it a book sometime last year that had the heroine using one, and I got curious, so I looked it up. It seemed interesting, so I ordered it."

I don't tell him that I rarely use it because not only is it heavy, but it also feels heavy when it's inserted.

"Interesting." He has a stupid grin on his face probably picturing me using it.

I roll my eyes. "Do we have a deal or not?"

"Deal!" Hunter says, a little too excited.

"So are you ready to go inside?" I nod toward the front door where my family awaits. They are probably trying their absolute hardest to not peek out the window right about now.

"Yeah, I think so but I think I would be more ready with a kiss before we go in." The cocky smirk gets thrown in my direction and I can't help but roll my eyes. I love seeing it but it does trigger some eye-rolling.

Leaning up, I place a chaste kiss against his lips before pulling back just as fast.

"That was too fast." He groans.

"Too bad. That's all you get for right now."

He sighs, intertwining our fingers together. "Okay, I think I'm ready."

With a smile, I walk us over to the front door. The second that I open the door to my parents' house, it feels like the whole place went silent.

"I would like to apologize in advance," I whisper as I close the door.

Instantly his face is covered in fear. "What? Why?"

I don't answer. I just give his hand a reassuring squeeze

and walk through the house until we reach the kitchen. Where eight of my family members stand. All eyes are on us.

Might be just my mind, but I swear I hear Hunter swallow very loudly from next to me.

"Hunter, this is my family. *Familia este es mi novio*, Hunter."

The whole room stays silent and if I had one of my mom's sewing needles and dropped it on the floor I'm sure that we would all hear it.

Eventually the silence is broken by my dad.

"Hunter, *mucho gusto*," he says, holding out a hand for Hunter to shake. I have to nudge Hunter in the ribs to get him out of the stupor he is in.

Luckily he recovers fast enough to not miss a beat and shakes my dad's hand.

"It's nice to meet you too, Mr. Montez. It's nice to meet all of you." He waves to the whole room.

Within seconds, everyone starts talking and comes over to him and they introduce themselves.

Once the awkward portion of the night is done with, it's just like any other normal dinner night with my family.

The kids are running around and my brothers-in-law have taken a liking to Hunter. Or more specifically, that he plays football and that there is a possibility that he might get drafted.

Yeah, the topic of the draft came up, and it was only because someone asked Hunter if he was thinking about playing after college. So he told them what he had declared and how now it was just a waiting game.

Even my dad was impressed and the man only watches American football once a year.

Now the guys are talking his ear off while I'm in the kitchen helping my mom and sisters clean up. From where I'm standing it looks like he is having fun and is relaxed, so I know my brothers-in-law aren't razzing him too much.

"He seems like a good guy," Sara says as she hands me a few plates to put away.

I nod. "He is."

"So is he really joining the draft?" Stella asks as she puts some food away in the fridge.

"I think so. He's still waiting for his invitation for the combine thing so it might not happen, but I think if it does, he's leaning toward it." I put the dishes away and when I turn back, my sisters' and my mom's eyes are on me. "What?"

"What's going to happen if he gets drafted?" Gabriella asks.

I shrug. "He plays football?"

"And if a team from the East Coast picks him up?" Now Sara is throwing the question at me.

"Then he goes to play on the East Coast." What are they not comprehending about this?

"And what happens to you?" Stella asks.

"I'll stay here."

"So if he gets drafted and has to move across the country, you're just going to stay here while he lives in another state?" Sara asks as if it's the most ridiculous thing she has ever heard.

"I mean, I haven't really thought about it. We've been together for two months, that's not a whole lot of time to think about what is going to happen six months from now."

"Are you going to break up?" Gabriella throws out.

I expected them to interrogate Hunter this way, not me.

"I don't know. I don't think we will."

"Then you have to think about the bigger picture here," Stella says, crossing her arms across her chest and coming to stand next to my mom.

"What bigger picture? I have no say if he gets drafted or not. It doesn't affect my life." I'm trying really hard to stay calm right now. I feel like my sisters are ganging up on me for no reason.

"*Estás asustada.*" My mom speaks for the first time since this conversation started.

"I'm not scared," I answer, my voice wavering a bit in the process.

"Yeah, you are," Stella says, agreeing with our mother. "You've just always been good at hiding it. I've only seen you two together today, but every time he talked about being drafted you pulled back."

I did?

"You keep saying that whatever happens with him, that it doesn't affect your life, but it does. You want to support him but you want to keep your distance just in case he goes in a direction that doesn't involve you. And because you love him, you will tell him to choose football over you because you think that's what's best for him."

"It is what's best for him." My voice is small but all four of them are able to hear it. All of their expressions are filled with pity.

"He doesn't seem to think so," Sara says, so sure of herself.

"And how do you know that?" She raises an eyebrow at me when my voice goes up, a tinge of anger in it.

"Because, like Stella said, even though we've only seen

you two together for a few hours, I see the way he looks at you. He looks at you like you're his fucking world. Yes, it's only been two months since you've been officially together, but if that's how he looks at you two months in, my heart flutters with anticipation with how he would look at you on your wedding day."

I look at my sister, trying to believe every single word that she is saying. Does he really look at me like that?

Have I been so lost in my own feelings and thoughts that I didn't see it myself?

"*Mija.*" My mom comes over and takes my hand in hers. "This is a scary time. You are unsure of a lot of things but let me tell you this. When you told me that you had a *novio*, I was scared. I was scared that he wasn't going to treat you right, but that fear went away the second I saw you two together and he shook your father's hand. He cares about you, we can all see it. I know the possibility of him leaving terrifies you, but don't let your fear dictate how you support him. Be there for him through whatever gets thrown his way. You may think that football is what's best for him, and maybe it is, but you are a close second. Tell him how you feel, that way when the time comes, you're ready."

I look at my mom, and I see the sincerity in her face. Just like my sisters, she wants the best for me, she wants me to be happy. And they see me happy with Hunter, and they don't want me to give up on it because I'm not sure where I want to stand.

It goes to show that even if you are quiet around your family, they still know what is going on with your life. No matter how much you want to hide.

We continue to clean the kitchen and once all that is

done we all head back outside to sit around the fire that the guys started.

The stars are bright in the sky over us and as the night gets darker and colder, the crowd around the fire gets smaller and eventually it's only me and Hunter left.

"Your family is awesome," he says once my parents go inside the house.

I laugh a little, cuddling into his side a little more while extending the blanket over his legs.

"They like you. I'm surprised that my brothers-in-law didn't threaten you," I say, placing my head on his shoulder.

"I think they knew I could take them," he says with a smirk on his face. I can't help but laugh at the statement.

We sit in silence for the next couple of minutes, just watching the small fire. I'm content with just being in Hunter's arms.

"I have something to tell you," Hunter says, tapping on the leg that is swung over his.

I pull back slightly to look at him and see that he has a nervous look on his face. "What is it?"

"I got my combine invitation. I'm going to be spending spring break in Indianapolis," he tells me, his eyes looking into mine.

He's one step closer to possibly getting drafted.

Pasting a smile on my face, I lean in to give him a kiss. "That's awesome. You get to show how awesome you are, and I'm sure plenty of teams will be dying to have you be a part of their organization."

Hunter just nods at my words, moving his gaze from me to the fire.

"Can I ask you another question?" he says after a few minutes.

"Yeah, of course."

"If the combine goes perfectly and I get drafted, would you come with me to wherever that is?"

Come with him.

I open my mouth to say something but close it just as quickly when no words come out.

This is big and my first instinct is to shut down.

"Do you *want* me to come with you?" is the only thing that I can think about saying.

Hunter keeps his eyes on the fire as he answers. "I do. I know you're super close to your family, and that might be a challenge, but yeah, I want you to come with me. Wherever I land."

"But what if..." I start, but I stop when he turns to face me again.

"But what?" he prompts.

"What if we don't make it that far?" There, I said it.

"But what if we do?" he asks, shifting his body to face mine. "Want to know what I see when I think about my future?" I nod. "I see playing football, maybe not until I'm forty but still playing. Then I see you at every single home game with my name on the back of your jersey, cheering me on. Maybe I even see a kid or two. This isn't just something to have until I finish school. I want this with you for years to come, possibly forever. That's how much I love you. How much I want to be with you. And wherever I land, I'm sure we will be able to find a graduate program so that you can continue going to school."

He remembers that?

A few weeks ago, I made an off-topic comment about wanting to go to graduate school but not as soon as we graduate. Like in a year or two. I want to find my footing in the world first before I look for a program.

I'm a little surprised he remembered that.

We look at each other and I hope that I'm conveying the same love in my eyes that he is.

Because everything he said, I want that too.

"Would you come with me wherever I land?" he asks again.

This time I don't hesitate.

"Yes, I will go with you. Wherever you land."

I just hope that I don't get my hopes up and everything goes to shit later on.

CHAPTER TWENTY-EIGHT

HUNTER

MY PHONE BUZZES on the nightstand of my hotel room.

The same phone that I had left at the football house the same night of the party. How it ended up out of my pocket, I have no idea, but I was relieved when I got it back when I went to the house. It's a good thing I have a passcode on it, because there are a few things in my hidden folder I don't want anyone to see.

They're for me and me only.

Grabbing my phone, I see that two texts came in. One from my dad and one from Lennie.

I sigh. My dad has been texting me nonstop since I arrived in Indianapolis two days ago. Since the combine is being broadcasted online and ESPN, he is seeing everything I'm doing. Every single time I grab my phone a new text is there waiting for me, all of them with some sort of critique about me.

Ignoring his message, I open Lennie's.

. . .

SELENA: Tell me why I just got home from work and my dad is watching you on TV?

I can't help but snort. She's probably rolling her eyes as we speak.

HUNTER: It's because he loves me more than you. *Tongue sticking out emoji*

It's been a little over a month since dinner at Selena's parents' house with her family. In that time, I've spent a lot more time with her sisters and parents, even as much as going over for dinner every Sunday night. Sometimes when I have practice late during the weekday, Selena's mom sends me food with her.

And yes, I eat every last bite.

Never have I had real Mexican food and I think I'm in love. I just have to watch what I eat because these last few weeks I've been pulling double gym training to burn off those calories.

Everything between me and Lennie has been going good, and I think her opening up to me about what happened to her when she was younger, helped. She seems lighter at times, smiles more and comes out of that shy shell that encases her more often.

Yes, there have been days where the insecurities have

gotten the best of her, but she has become a whole lot more confident in herself and her body. She no longer just portrays being confident, she is it, and I love every single fucking second of it.

SELENA: If I'm going to watch you all sweaty and running around, I'd rather do it in person. *eye roll emoji*

HUNTER: You know how much I love it when you roll your eyes at me.

SELENA: *Eye roll emoji*

This girl. She's lucky I'm over two thousand miles away.

Instead of sending her another text, I FaceTime her.

The call is answered on the third ring and her beautiful face fills my screen.

"Now, roll your eyes at me," I say, leaning back against the headboard, an arm going behind my head.

Selena laughs and just like expected, she rolls her eyes but does it with a smile on her face.

That's my girl.

"I was told that you had a busy day," she muses as she moves her dark hair that is in soft curls out of her face. What I wouldn't do to have my fingers running through the softness right now.

I smile. "Your dad?"

"My brothers-in-law. I guess they all had the livestream on at work and thought it was necessary to give me a play-by-play whenever you popped up on the screen." She wants to come off as irritated, but she loved every second of it. I know she did.

"I fucking love your family," I say through a laugh.

"I'm sure they feel the same way," she says, throwing herself back on her bed.

From the way she is holding the phone, I can see her hair sprawled out against her white pillowcase and the shirt she has on does nothing to cover her cleavage.

Her tits look fucking perfect even when they are covered.

I look over at the time and see it's only a little after ten at night here. Meaning that it's only seven in California.

"Seven o'clock and the bra is off already?" I tease her, my eyes staying at the edge of the screen.

"The fact that that was the first thing that you noticed should say something," she says, adjusting herself, which only brings out her cleavage more.

"Baby, your tits are worth noticing. Show them to me."

Selena looks at me through the screen, her eyebrows raised, as if I just asked to do something ridiculous. There is nothing ridiculous about my request.

"Hold on," she says, putting the phone down. Now I'm staring at the ceiling instead of her chest.

"What are you doing?"

"Making sure that my parents don't hear this conversation." Within seconds, some music starts playing in the background, the lights are down and Selena is back, putting her earbuds in.

"And what type of conversation are we going to be having?" I raise an eyebrow at her, and from looking at the small screen I have a smirk playing at my lips.

"The one where I show you my tits."

Fuck yes.

I keep my eyes on the screen as she leans against her headboard and without taking her eyes off me, she lowers her tank top from the front.

Inch by inch, more of her skin is revealed until her dark-pink nipples pop out, looking like they need to be sucked.

"You should play with them," I suggest, licking my lips, thinking about what I would do to her if I were there.

"Like this?" She grabs her right breast in a strong grip, her fingers digging into the skin. I watch as she massages the skin, her breathing becoming slightly labored.

"I think you need to give your nipple a little attention," I suggest and she does what I say.

Her fingers roll against her nipple. She pulls at it, pinches it and twists it every which way.

Lennie brings out her chest more toward the screen, like she wants me to reach out and touch her. I wish I could.

"Now the other one," I order, my own hand sliding to the front of my shorts, stroking my cock through the material. It's throbbing and I have a feeling it's going to get worse the longer this call is.

Selena follows my order and gives her other breast the attention that it deserves.

"Hunter." She rolls her neck, her tit filling her hand.

"If I were there with you, what would I be doing?" The grip that I have on my cock grows tighter. Fuck, her hand would feel a whole lot better.

"You would suck on them." Pant. "You would bite down on my nipple." Pant. "You would be marking every inch of my chest."

"Do you like it when I mark you?"

Pant. "Yes. It's like always carrying a part of you."

Stroke. "What else would I be doing?"

"You would kiss your way down my body." Pull on a nipple. "Until you were between my legs."

"What would I be doing? Sliding my tongue along your slit? Shoving two fingers into your pussy? Biting down on your clit?"

"Yes," she pants. Her chest is red by her actions.

"Which one is it, Selena?" I slide my shorts off and take myself in my hand.

"Everything."

"Slide your hand down your body, Lennie. Pretend that it's mine. Touch yourself just like I would do it."

Selena pulls her phone away from her body so I can see her hand travel down her body. She caresses her stomach and the top of her mound through her panties. They're black and look flimsy and like a material that I could easily rip through.

Her hand slides over the material of her panties, the wetness coating the black material and giving it a slight shine.

"How does that feel, baby?" I pump myself at the sight of her hand on her pussy. I bet her fingertips are getting wet with pleasure that is seeping through the material.

"I want you to touch me." Her body shifts against the bed. She's looking for more friction.

"I want to touch you too. When I get home, I promise I will touch every inch of you."

My hand slides down to my balls, trying to relieve some tension before I explode all over my hand.

"More." Her panties get moved to the side and her fingers start to move through the folds of her pussy. It's covered with small strands of hair and mouthwatering.

"I think it might be time for you to have a little help." I feel the sweat rolling down my chest and I try to think of everything that I can so I don't come before she does.

"What kind of help?" Her chest is rising more and more, and I wonder how close she is.

"Bring out that glass toy, baby. Bring it out and let me see you use it."

I get a nod and for a second I'm back to looking up at the ceiling.

It doesn't take Lennie long to come back. Except this time, she doesn't hold up her phone, she props it up on something and positions the camera so that I'm looking at her straight on. Her legs are open, panties have been discarded and I have a clear view of her pussy. It's wet and glistening and I can't wait to lick it in a few days.

"Fuck, if that isn't a sight." My dick is throbbing in my hand, precum leaking all over the place.

"You want me to use this?" A glass object comes into view. It's long and thick and has what I would describe as a beaded surface to it. It's one thing picturing it but seeing it in person and knowing what is about to happen, is fucking exciting. "Or this?" she asks, showing me a small bullet that I can only guess is a vibrator.

I nod. "I want to see you using both. Are you sure you can take all of that glass?"

"I take you just fine. And I think you're bigger." Her next move surprises me. With a smile on her lips, she opens her mouth and slides the toy into her mouth, taking every inch of it.

"Fuck." I stroke, grip, everything that I can to ease the pain I'm currently experiencing.

She slides the glass toy out of her mouth, once, then a second time before she pulls it out fully and slides the wet glass down her body, circling her nipples then moving farther down until the glass tip reaches her clit and then her entrance.

There is lust in her eyes and she is panting, her legs are still wide open and I see her slide it in.

Her mouth opens wide, while a moan slips from the back of her throat, and her eyes close as she slowly moves the glass. I can't take my eyes off her. Everything that she is showing me is so fucking erotic that nothing will ever be able to compare.

After what feels like an hour, the glass is finally seated.

Before doing anything else, Selena grabs the small bullet toy and turns it on before placing it on her clit.

The way her moan fills in through the screen, makes me wish I could jump through it and replace the toy with my mouth.

Selena sits there panting, not moving, looking down at her phone. Straight at me.

I have to clear my throat a few times just so I can speak. "How does it feel?"

"Cold, and good." Her voice is filled with so much lust

and desire that it makes me believe that the simple action of sliding the glass into her entrance got her close to the end.

"Fuck yourself, baby. Fuck yourself, pretend those toys are me. Let me see it."

Selena keeps her eyes on me for a minute. We just stare at each other, sex filling up the distance between us.

With a lick of her lips, she gives me a nod, sliding her hand along her thigh before reaching the head of the toy.

Then she starts to move it.

Her legs open wider, her hips start to move and I hear every single sound that she makes.

Every moan, groan, as well as her juices as she slides the glass in and out of her pussy.

I follow her lead. I take my cock and fuck my hand in coordination with her.

"I'm close," Selena moans out as I cup my balls.

"Come, baby, I'm right behind you." Now I'm the one panting. My legs are starting to shake and I don't know how much longer I can hold off, but she needs to come first. Even through FaceTime fucking, she needs to come first.

"Right there. Right there. Fuck, Hunter. It's right there." I force my eyes to stay open when I see her legs starting to shake uncontrollably.

"Please, Lennie. Let me see it," I beg her. That does it. Her moan fills my ears and she holds her legs tight together. My name falls from her lips.

It's when I hear my name that I can't hold off any longer. Cords of my cum cover my stomach and chest and I feel like I just ran a marathon.

"Holy fuck," I say, completely out of breath.

"Okay, when you get home, we are repeating that at your

place," Selena pants and I just nod, having no energy for anything else.

"You won't hear me complain." Fuck, I can already feel how out of breath I will be if we do this in person. I'm ready to go to sleep from doing it over a damn video call.

"Hey. Hunter?" Lennie asks, the phone back in her hand as she lies on her back.

"Yeah, baby?"

"I love you."

I look at the woman that owns my heart through the phone, all exhaustion forgotten.

"I love you too, Lennie."

The smile she gives me is one that I wish I could embed into my mind so I can see it every single time that I'm away from her.

"Kick some ass tomorrow. Show those teams that you are worth it."

I smile.

Over the week, she has been more open with showing her support for anything football related. The complete opposite of what she was last semester when she wouldn't even go to a game.

Now she's my biggest cheerleader, even if she has trouble voicing it at times.

"I will. I promise." I blow her a kiss.

A smile comes in my direction. "I'll let you get some sleep. I'm sure you need it."

I nod and soon we are saying good night and hanging up the call.

After cleaning myself up, I head back to bed and shut off

all the lights. Lying there in the dark, I think about what Selena said.

Show the teams that I'm worth it.

I will but all I want to do is show Selena Montez that she is worth everything and more.

CHAPTER TWENTY-NINE

SELENA

I DON'T KNOW what scares me more. The fact that I'm graduating in six weeks and have no concrete plans for what to do after that or the fact that I turn one year older in two of those weeks.

Honestly, I think it's the former, since that makes me want to puke every single time I think of it. The only thing keeping me from totally losing my mind is the meeting I just had with my guidance counselor.

My application for graduation was approved and she told me about an intern position that was announced for the summer. She says I'm a shoo-in, so I applied. Just one more thing to stress about.

The only thing that is keeping me from going completely crazy is the fact that Hunter is back from Indiana and I get to see him today.

His flight came in late last night and because of my classes and meeting with my counselor, I haven't been able to see him yet. So now I have to go through all of class trying to keep my hands all to myself.

Having some time to kill, I decided to go get something to drink at the library café. Maybe a panini and a strawberry banana smoothie will take some worry away about my life in six weeks.

I walk over to the counter and place my order. Once that is done, I head over to a small table to wait for my name to be called. It's when I sit that I feel eyes on me.

As someone who lacks confidence, something that has been heavily increasing since Hunter inserted himself in my life, I always think someone is looking at me. Not in an "I want all the attention" type of way, but more along the lines of judgment.

Looking up, I see that my intuition was right because a few tables away sits Jenna and her stare is directed right at me.

It's not the first that I've caught her looking at me, but it is the first time she is giving me anything other than a murderous glare.

Her stare confuses me even more when she gives a small smile and waves at me.

The confusion must have gotten into the deep part of my brain because I smiled back. It was small, sure, but I still smiled at her.

And I guess the smile was a fucking invitation because, within a minute, her smile is growing and she is making her way over to me.

This should be interesting.

"Selena, hi," Jenna says once she's only a foot or two from the table I'm occupying.

"Hi, Jenna."

Jenna and I have never been friendly toward each other.

Actually, before this year, I didn't even know that she knew who I was.

That changed when Hunter and I became official. It was at the bowl game that she started giving me her murderous stare. I've tried to keep my distance from her but I guess that's about to change.

"Do you mind if I join you?" she asks, pointing at the chair in front of me.

"Um, sure. Go right ahead." I wave for her to sit. I'm not a rude person but at a time like this, I really wish that I was.

Before she gets too comfortable, my name is called and I get up to grab my order. When I turn back, the smile on Jenna's face is a tad bigger.

Great, I guess I'm entertaining this conversation until class starts.

"Do you love the paninis too? They are my absolute favorite." She places a hand on her chest and lets out a moan at the thought.

"Yeah, I do. They're the one thing that I actually like from the café."

"They are the best." She nods her head, her smile still in place.

What is happening here?

My phone buzzes on the table, taking my gaze away from her. Looking down, I see a text from Hunter asking me where I am. After sending a quick reply back, I turn to face his ex-girlfriend again.

"How are things going with him?" Jenna asks as soon as I face her.

I shrug, not really wanting to give her details. "It's going fine."

"That's good. I hope his rich boy personality isn't getting in the way of you guys. He sure loves to flaunt his daddy's money around."

He does? Is Jenna talking about the same Hunter? Because the Hunter I know doesn't give a shit about money or showing it off. When we've gone out, we have never gone to a fancy place or had a good bill over sixty. The man doesn't even have good beer in the fridge. Sure, there have been times where we've gone to the mall and he's bought two of the same hoodie but according to him he says he does it so when I steal his, he has another as backup.

The man I'm dating does not flaunt money.

"He's not that way with me." I'm not trying to show off or anything, it's just the truth.

"Really? When we were together he would always buy me designer stuff and when I told him to stop, he would get mad."

I'm pretty sure that comment is supposed to make me jealous. It doesn't. It just tells me that Jenna might have been the one that liked to show off her boyfriend's money.

"Maybe that's what he thought you wanted." I take a drink of my smoothie.

"Maybe," she says with a shrug. "But he treats you good?"

I nod, starting to grab my stuff. I just want to leave and be done with this conversation.

"Are you sure?" she asks, her eyebrows rising a bit. I think I would know if my own boyfriend treated me well.

"Yup, I'm sure." I grab my backpack and swing it over my shoulder and start to stand up when she grabs my hand, holding me in place.

"Wait. There's a reason why I came to talk to you."

I humor her. "Oh yeah? Why?" I sound annoyed and frankly I am. I'd rather not deal with Jenna and whatever bullshit she feels she needs to tell me.

"Look, I know you and I aren't the best of friends."

I stop her. "We have never been friends."

She looks at me a little dumbfounded. "Right. Well forget about that, I still wanted to come talk to you because I couldn't keep this to myself. Girl code and all that."

"Girl code?"

"Yeah, us girls need to stick together." She gives an affirmative nod.

I let out a sigh. "Jenna, just tell me whatever it is you want to tell me. I have class."

She looks at me, the smile she was wearing earlier gone. She stares at me for what feels like forever until she lets out a sigh before reaching for her phone.

"I didn't want to do this, but I felt like it was necessary for you to know." She does something on her phone before she looks up at me. "Necessary for you to see."

Jenna hands me her phone and the second I see what's on the screen I feel all the blood in my body drain.

"Ho-How did you get this?" My hand shakes as I grip the phone. Along with the feeling that all my blood has drained, my lungs feel as if they are being constricted by something tight.

I can't fucking breathe.

I'm looking at a picture of myself completely naked, standing in front of a mirror. A picture where you can clearly see my face.

A picture I had sent to Hunter a few days after we had made things official.

A picture that I absolutely loved because I liked the way my body looked. I liked how I could see the subtle changes from the running routine I had started a month prior.

A picture that is now staring back at me and is causing bile to rise up my throat.

A picture that I now hate.

"I heard a few of the guys from the football team talking about it, laughing at it, and when I asked, I was disgusted by what I saw."

An unwanted tear releases at the word disgusted.

"Not at you," Jenna quickly reassures me. "I was disgusted by what I was seeing on their screens. I was disgusted by where the message came from, to see that Hunter would do something so fucking disgraceful."

Everything in me is telling me to not believe her, that she is lying, that Hunter would never do that to me.

But I'm staring at the evidence. I'm staring at the picture, looking at the words that are attached to it.

Fat ass.

A good lay.

Fucking ugly.

There's a sob forming in my throat, but I don't let it escape. I won't let it, not in public, not in front of Jenna.

"I'm so sorry, Selena. Nobody deserves to be treated that way. Especially by someone that they thought cared about them. I'm so sorry that you found out that Hunter was using you this way. But I needed to tell you. I couldn't continue seeing you with him when I knew this was going on."

I hear her words, but I can't figure out what they mean.

All I can concentrate on is the fact that Hunter shared the most intimate part of me with other people, something that he had promised from the very beginning that he wouldn't do.

I don't share.

Those were his words.

And he lied to me.

He lied and shared me anyway.

I trusted him. We were planning, dammit. I fucking loved him and this is what he does to me. He used me.

I feel like I'm about to combust.

"I have to go," I say out loud, not directed at anyone, not even at Jenna. It's more for me because I can't be here right now.

I need to breathe.

I need to do something before I break down.

Without a second look at Jenna, I make my way out of the café, I think I'm free but the second that my foot hits the threshold of the two doors, I run into something.

Or should I say someone?

I look up and right away, I'm met with blue eyes that I thought were my solace but betrayed me in the worst possible way.

Hunter's face transforms from one with a bright smile to one filled with concern.

"What's wrong?" Concern not only coats his face but also his voice. Right away he places a hand on my shoulder and the other on my cheek, as if his touch is going to take all the pain away.

I step out of his reach and shove past him and head straight for the door that leads to the parking lot.

Fuck Hunter Jacobi. Fuck this school and fuck their football team.

"Selena!" Hunter yells after me but I don't turn. I just continue to run away from him and all the promises of a happy life.

"Selena, please! Stop!" He catches up to me and grabs at my hand and pulls me to a stop.

"Don't touch me," I say through my teeth, yanking my arm out of his grip.

"What the hell is going on?" he asks, the concern that was on his face a few seconds ago is now in his eyes, but there is also fear.

Fear that he might lose me.

He is right to fear that.

I don't answer him though. I don't give him the answers he is looking for. He doesn't deserve them anyway.

No, I just stand there, tears rolling down my face, staring at the man that I opened up to. At the man that I felt safe with, the man I saw a future with.

I shouldn't have listened to my mom and sisters when they told me how he felt. I shouldn't have gotten my hopes up. Because at the end of the day, they all went to shit like I thought they would.

When my bottom lip starts to tremble that's when I turn away from him, but it's not enough. Hunter stops me once again, this time coming to a stop right in front of me, moving every time I move.

"Selena, please just tell me what the fuck is going on? What happened?"

I don't know what caused it. Maybe it was the fact that he has tears forming in his eyes. Maybe it was the proximity of his body to mine. I don't know what it was, but I snap.

"You told me I wasn't a joke. You stood in front of me and

apologized for making me believe that I was. I heard your words and I fucking forgave you. But I guess you're a good liar, huh? Because you had me believing every single word that came out of your mouth. You had me believing that I mattered. That you fucking cared about me, but it was all just part of the game." I wipe at my tears. He doesn't deserve to see me like this.

"What the fuck are you talking about? Everything I said to you was the truth, all of it. I never lied to you," Hunter says through his teeth, a tear of his own escaping.

"I don't believe you. Not this time. Not after seeing what you sent your fucking teammates. Not after what you told them about me. Not after sending them pictures of me! Pictures that you promised not to share with anyone! You're a liar and a manipulator and a fucking asshole and I don't want anything to do with you. Good luck with your fucking life Jacobi, I hope you find someone that does to you what you did to me. Fuck you."

I shove him.

A few gasps sound around us but I don't give a shit. My most intimate parts have already been seen by the whole football team. Why would I care what random people at school think of me now?

Hunter calls after me as I continue to walk away but unlike before he doesn't follow.

I try to keep it as together as I can as I make my way to my car, but the second I'm behind the wheel, I lose it.

All the anger boiling inside of me comes out and tears come out as if I turned on a faucet. I rub at my tattoo but like the last time I did it, the daisy doesn't take the fear away, it's not making anything feel better.

Why was I so stupid?

I should have never accepted his apology.

I should have never fallen for him. I knew he was an arrogant jock and I still let myself fall.

Why do I keep falling for the guys that don't want anything to do with me?

My cousin was right. I am worthless. No one wants to be with me and no one is ever going to love me.

He's right.

A sob escapes my throat, filling the car.

I wish he was wrong.

I wish I was worth something. I wish I was worth someone's love.

Why do I have to be worthless?

I don't want to be worthless.

Yet I am.

CHAPTER THIRTY

HUNTER

LIAR.

Manipulator.

Asshole.

Those are three words that I never expected Selena to ever call me. Yet she did and here I am, standing here watching her retreating figure get farther and farther away from me.

I didn't go after her. I should have, but I saw the look on her face. I saw the anger that swam in her eyes. If I had gone after her, it would have only made everything a whole lot worse.

I don't even know what everything is in this scenario.

And what did she mean that I had sent them to my teammates?

I would never send them pictures that are supposed to be for my eyes only. I'm not that type of man, even if people think that I am.

So many questions are floating around in my head, nothing is making any sense.

Pulling out my phone, I open it up to the last message that she had sent me. It was just her telling me where she was.

I was on my way to find her because no way in fucking hell was I going to go through a whole class not being able to touch her after not seeing her in person for a whole week.

When she ran into me, I thought I was going to get the chance to take her in my arms and claim her lips like I've been dreaming about for days. How I've wanted to after a hundred FaceTime calls. Then I saw her face.

There were tears rolling down her cheeks. Her eyes were filled with sadness but it seemed like when she realized it was me, that sadness disappeared and it was replaced with anger.

There was anger in her eyes. Anger in her voice. Anger radiating off her body. So much fucking anger and I don't know why.

Once Selena is out of sight, I look around and see the number of eyes that were on us. Everyone is watching as if they were watching a reality show on TV.

"Don't you have other fucking shit to do?!" I yell out through the whole fucking courtyard in front of the library.

Right away, people start to disperse. As everyone starts to leave, I catch sight of someone by the main door.

Jenna.

I don't want to deal with her shit right now. I have to figure out how to talk to Selena. I have to know what the fuck happened and apologize for whatever the fuck I did, even if I don't remember.

"Fuck!" I pull at my hair and start making my way over to the parking lot when Jenna calls out my name.

I turn to face her and she's looking at me like I'm crazy.

"What the fuck do you want?" I say through my teeth. I have more pressing shit to take care of, like go find my fucking girlfriend and have her talk to me.

"Geez, you would think that you would be a little nicer to me." The girl has the fucking audacity to flip her hair at me and flutter her eyelashes.

Can't believe I fell for her crap for three years.

"And why the hell would I do that? You're the bitch that not only cheated on me but had no remorse about it. So fucking forgive me if you're not my favorite person to be nice to."

"Have I ever told you how hot you look when you're angry like this? Makes me wet and hot." She throws a smirk in my direction.

"What the fuck do you want, Jenna?" My fists are in tight balls at my side.

She shrugs. "I just figured you'd want to know what set your pretty little girlfriend off. Well, I wouldn't call her little, per se."

"What the fuck did you do?" I say through gritted teeth. Something happened with Selena and whatever it was, no way she got that mad on her own. Something or someone had to prompt her, and my money is on Jenna.

"I just showed her what you really thought of her." She grabs a piece of hair and starts to twirl it. If she had a piece of bubble gum in her mouth, she would be the perfect mean girl you see in the movies.

What I really thought of her?

I take a step closer to my ex. "I will not ask you again. What. The fuck. Did. You. Do? Do not fucking play with me, Jenna."

Jenna stands her ground. Nothing about her wavering. Her shoulders are back and she is staring me straight on.

"I don't know why you're mad at me. You should be mad at yourself. You are the one that sent a nude photo of Selena to half the football team and said she was a fat ass that was fucking ugly that you were only using for a lay." Her hand lands on my chest, her fingers wrapping themselves around the material of my shirt.

What she just said registers in my head.

I grab her hand and shove it off me and I reveal my teeth to her. "I would never fucking do that."

Not to Selena.

Not to anyone.

Jenna just smiles at me, her eyes filled with fucking joy. "You're right, but I would. Only I wouldn't send it to the whole team, I would just send it to myself and pretend that you were the one that sent it and had to show all of your friends her precious, naked body. You should really change your passcode, Hunty. Anyone who knows it can get into your phone and find the photos that you don't want the world to see."

How the fuck did she—

Then I remember.

I forgot my phone at the party that I dragged Lennie to. The night that she told me about the sexual abuse that she went through as a kid.

For hours I didn't know where it was until I found it the next day.

And Jenna was at the party.

For hours, my phone was left unattended. Jenna could have come across it and looked through it, because she knew my passcode. She had access to the most vulnerable part of Lennie that I keep for myself and she used it to destroy the one person that doesn't deserve it.

"Which photo?" I growl through my teeth.

"I don't see why that fucking matters." She shrugs.

"It matters. Which fucking picture did you send to yourself?"

Jenna rolls her eyes but pulls out her phone and a few seconds later she is turning the screen to face me.

Selena's body stares back at me. I know the picture, it's one of my favorites of hers. She had told me that she was feeling really good about herself and that she wanted to share that feeling with me. I kept the picture because I wanted to have it just in case she needed reassurance that she was fucking beautiful.

Out of all the pictures that Jenna had to pick to make Selena doubt herself, she chose this one. Jenna's a bigger bitch than I thought.

"Why the fuck did you do that? Selena hasn't done a fucking thing to you."

Jenna comes closer to me, her mouth so close to my face I can feel her breath on my skin.

"Because you're mine," she says through clenched teeth, a smile never leaving her face.

"I stopped being anything to you the second you decided to play with someone else's dick." I put my hands on her hips and move her away from me.

"You're the one that moved on!"

"You fucking cheated on me, Jenna! Of course I fucking moved on! I moved on and I found someone that I could actually see a future with and you fucking ruined it. You're an evil bitch that doesn't care about who she hurts around her, you just care about you and you only. So fuck off, and I hope you rot in hell."

I leave Jenna standing there fifty shades of pissed off and continue my trek to my truck.

The second I pull out of the parking spot and onto the road, I pull up Selena's number off the screen and dial her phone.

Four rings and it goes to voice mail.

I dial again and it's the same thing.

I call her phone three more times to get the same result. On the sixth time, it just skips the ringing and goes straight to voice mail.

She shut it off.

"Fuck!" I slam my hands against the steering wheel.

I should have gone after her before she got in the car. I should have made her tell me everything, because now she won't answer the phone and I have no idea where she is and it feels like my chest is constricting. My heart feels like it's going to explode and the only way to fix it is to talk to her. To have her in my hands and hear her say she loves me.

How the fuck could Jenna do this? What kind of person does something this fucked up? She's the one that cheated on me for crying out loud!

I leave campus and head to the beach closest to me. The one that she said that she would go to growing up to find herself. The one that I took her to the night of the party and held her for most of the night.

Getting to the beach is the easy part. It's the looking for her in a stretch that goes on for miles that is the issue. The one good thing that is on my side is the fact that it's April and the sun doesn't go down for another hour or two.

I drive along the shore, not spotting her car anywhere, that's when I get on foot.

After about two miles later, there's still no sign of Selena.

When I get back into the truck, I head straight to her parents' house. It's a low move, cornering her at home, but I need her to talk to me and that is the only way.

The whole drive to her house, I'm shaking. My hands can't stay steady enough and if I had passed a cop, I would for sure have been pulled over.

Thankfully I wasn't and I made it to Selena's in one piece.

I leave the key in the ignition as I jump out of the cab and head straight to the front door. My knocks are a little too aggressive, but I don't care at this point, I need to see Selena.

Footsteps sound on the other side of the door and I hold my breath when the door swings open. A pair of brown eyes stare at me when the door opens, but they are not the pair that I was wanting.

"Hunter, *qué estás haciendo aquí?*" Selena's mom asks me, confusion coating her face that looks so much like her daughter's.

"I'm sorry to bother you, Mrs. Montez. I was looking for Selena. Is she home?"

Please say yes.

Please.

Mrs. Montez's face just gets more confused.

"Selena just called and said that she was going to visit a friend. She's not here, but I'm sure that she will be back later."

A friend.

I give the woman in front of me a smile. "I guess she forgot to tell me. It's okay, I'll see her tomorrow. Would you tell her I stopped by?"

She nods. "I will."

"Thank you." I give her a small smile and head back to the truck.

From the cab, I watch as Mrs. Montez watches me for a few minutes before she throws a sad smile my way and closes the door.

I wonder if she can sense that I'm on the verge of fucking tears right now.

I sit here for god knows how long, just looking out to the street lined with houses.

It seems so quiet, so peaceful.

The opposite of how my mind feels right now. How my emotions feel.

As the sun starts to set, my phone vibrates on the center console.

I don't wait to pick up and when I see Selena's name come across the screen, I let out a sigh of relief. Her mom must have told her I came by.

The relief though is short lived after I read her message.

SELENA: Please. Stop. Nothing is going to fix this.

She's wrong. There are so many things that could fix this. If she would just listen to me, I could fix this.

But because Selena has the thought that she is not worth fighting for, that I couldn't possibly be with someone like her, embedded so deep into her head, she's not going to. I know the girl, she's not going to listen to a word I say.

Selena knows me, knows that I would never do something like this to her, but her overthinking mind will tell her otherwise.

I have to show her that I really do love her with everything that I have. How I'm going to do that, I have no idea.

For now, I place the phone back on the console and start the truck.

The whole way back to my apartment, I let the pain take over and let the tears roll.

Jenna had two goals with her fucked-up plan. Hurt Selena because she was with me and hurt me because I chose to be with someone that wasn't her.

She's a narcissist and I hate her, because she took the best thing that has ever happened to me away.

CHAPTER THIRTY-ONE

SELENA

DAISIES.

Two dozen of them currently sit on my nightstand. I should grab them and throw them out, but I don't. I just continue to sit here, staring at them.

Some of the petals are droopy, while others are getting dried out, but that's what happens when flowers sit for two weeks. They get sad and just end up dying.

The only thing that has any life left is the note that sits unopened on the cardholder. My name is scrawled on the front and every time I see it, my heart beats a little faster.

The second the delivery guy handed them to me, I knew who they were from. There wasn't a need to open the card. But everything in me was telling me I needed to anyway. To read the words that he had written because they might mean something and they could be a memory that I could add to the pile.

But I'm scared to.

It's been a month since Jenna showed me the text messages that were being circulated among the football team.

After I left campus in tears that day, I missed the next two days of classes out of fear that someone was going to come up to me and say something that would have the tears starting up again.

Well, that's one reason I didn't go back to class. The second was Hunter.

Unlike the first time, when I yelled at him in the parking lot and accused him of using me, this time around hurt me a hundred times more. There was actual evidence this time around.

I couldn't be around him and pretend like his actions didn't hurt me.

Because they did, beyond fucking repair. Every time I think about it or about him, tears spring in my eyes and I'm battling the big lump in my throat.

So I avoided going to school for a few days, just like I avoided every form of contact that he threw my way.

Texts.

Calls.

Messages on HEX.

Messages on Instagram.

Even emails.

I ignored them all. But I couldn't do it forever. So while communication was avoided, I had to go back to school. This close to the semester ending I couldn't afford to miss anymore.

Going back to school and avoiding him felt a whole lot like the first time all those months ago. The one difference, Hunter looked just as miserable as I did.

I could see it every time I looked up and saw him staring at me. His eyes were filled with disappointment, and I so badly wanted to take it away. Then I remembered what he did and that want went away quickly.

When my birthday came two weeks ago, my family could tell I wasn't in a celebrating mood. They asked about Hunter and why he wasn't there, and after I shrugged off their questions, they concluded that something had happened, so they stopped pressing.

Then the flowers came. I grabbed the bouquet and went straight to my room. I cried the whole night.

Now two weeks later, I'm just sitting here feeling miserable. I haven't even been able to pick up a book to distract me from the hundred pounds of heartache.

The note taunts me.

Did he send me my favorite flowers and call me names on the card?

Or did he write words of love and beg for forgiveness and I've just been sitting on them?

Honestly, I don't know how I made it two weeks without reading his words.

Shoving the lump in my throat down, I get up from where I sit on my bed and head over to the flowers.

Even as they are dying, they're beautiful.

Plucking a white daisy from the vase along with the card, I go back to sit on my bed. Leaning against the headboard, I place both items on the comforter in front of me.

I bite at my nails as I look at the items in front of me.

So innocent and yet they still have the power of destroying me until there is nothing left.

Letting out a sigh, I pick up the note. My hands shake the whole time as I lift it up, you would think that it was made out of glass.

I feel tears forming as I flip the little envelope over and pop the seal open.

My eyes close as I slide the little card out of its place, the piece of paper feeling thicker than the normal piece of cardstock.

Peeling my eyes open one by one, I see that the piece of paper in my hand isn't just a lone rectangle, it's a full page folded up to fit in the envelope.

I unfold it delicately, so I don't rip any piece of it. The second I turn the paper over and see the first sentence, the tears that I'm holding in fall.

Lennie,

I got my invitation to the NFL draft. When I got the email, the first thing I wanted to do was to go to your house and tell you in person. It sucked so much when I saw you in class the next day and I couldn't tell you.

At the beginning, I'd decided to declare because it was about finding myself again, about finding my love for the sport once more. Then you came. You came and it turned to a lot more than just something for me, it became something for you too. I saw the possibilities of me being drafted and what it could do for our futures. I saw you in the stand with my name on your back and I saw you standing next to me through all the shit life would throw at me. Football might have been my first love but having you in my life is far greater than anything football could give me.

One of the greatest moments in my life was hearing you say I love you. I would do anything to hear those words come out of your mouth right now, but I don't deserve them. Not right now, at least.

I don't deserve them because I failed you, Len. I'm supposed to protect you. From pain and hurt and I was supposed to show you that you are everything to me. Make you believe in the love I have for you. I didn't do it because Jenna was able to get in and destroy everything we had in just a few minutes.

She lied, Lennie. You have no reason to believe me but I swear to you, I would never do that to you. I would never do something that would hurt you, that would destroy you like that did. But she made it believable. So believable that it took you away from me. You believing her is something I can't fault you for because I would have thought the same thing.

I made her delete every picture of you she had.

I know that's not enough, and I know the anger you hold won't go away just like that. But know that I really do love you, Selena. I promise you from now on, I will never put you in a situation like that again.

How I wish I could be with you right now and hold you. But I know I can't.

Happy birthday, baby.

I hope that the 23 daisies take away any fear and sadness and the 24th one, I hope that it makes you smile and gives you all the happiness you deserve.

I know there's a chance of you never talking to me again, and that's okay. Just know I mean the next three words.

I. LOVE. YOU,

Hunter

· · ·

Tears land on his written words. If I wasn't in pain before, I sure as hell am now.

I should have read this note sooner, then I would have known that the anger I was holding inside of myself was directed at the wrong person.

Maybe if I had answered one of his calls or messages or had spoken to him on campus, I wouldn't be in tears right now.

How can I be so fucking stupid? What is wrong with me? How is it that I believed what Jenna showed me and never for a second questioned the authenticity of it?

That's what she wanted. It had to be. Jenna had to make me believe that Hunter would do that so that I would break up with him.

She probably wanted him back and thought that the only way to do that was to break me.

And break me, she did.

I fucking hate her.

I hate her just as much as I hate my own insecurities.

Because both those factors, combined, nearly destroyed me and if I don't do something about it, it will happen again.

And again.

I know it will. My insecurities have already affected my relationship with Hunter once before.

I fold Hunter's note back up again, placing it on my nightstand. I grab the daisy next, twirling the stem around with my fingers.

I have to find a way to fix myself before fixing anything else.

And if I'm going to do that, I have to do something that has terrified me for years.

Grabbing the daisy and holding it tight in my hand, I walk out of my room with fresh tears rolling down my cheeks.

CHAPTER THIRTY-TWO

HUNTER

I SPOT her from across the field. Her hair is down, going past her shoulders and styled in perfect waves.

Her black gown is open, revealing a white dress under it that goes to just above her knee. In her hand, she has a cap that has some sort of design on it, that I'm sure would look perfect on her.

Selena looks so fucking beautiful, and I wish I could go over to her and tell her.

"You know, if you want to talk to a girl, you have to move those pretty legs of yours and go talk to her," Jax says from his place next to me.

We are currently in the waiting area to start our graduation from Cal U. Every single person around us is dressed in the same black and white cap and talking with the people they met while attending school here.

I don't take my eyes off of Selena as I answer him. "She doesn't want me over there."

"And how do you know that?"

"Because if she did, she would have done something to grab my attention. A wave, a smile."

"Maybe she's scared to," Jax muses.

Maybe she is.

Maybe that mind of hers is overthinking and she is too scared to approach me without having thought up what to say. Or she thinks I don't want to talk to her. Knowing my girl, that's probably the case.

That or she didn't read the letter I sent for her birthday and she still hates my guts.

I won't actually know unless she talks to me.

Soon we are getting the signal to line up according to majors. The whole time, I keep my eyes on Selena. Jax and I decided to line up toward the back, because why not end this boring ass ceremony with a few star athletes?

Once in line, we start making our way into the stadium. The whole way to our seats, as everyone cheers and makes their excitement known, I keep my concentration on Lennie. The more we walk, the more I notice what's on her cap, daisies. Twenty-four of them. The number of daisies on the material can't be a coincidence, can it?

As we take our seats, I lose her but I know that she is only a few rows away.

I try to concentrate on what's going on all around me instead of the brown-haired beauty with the daisies on her cap.

All around me, I can feel the energy in the stadium. It's not like it would be for a sporting event but it's still something.

The ceremony starts and the university president starts to drone on about how spectacular these last few years have been for all of us. He goes on to talk about a few specific students that are in the audience and of course my name is at the top of that list.

The applause when he mentions a few key wins and the possibility of being drafted is deafening but I just take it in stride and pretend like I care about all of it.

When the university president goes to another topic, talking about the community and how it has helped the community grow, I feel my phone vibrate in the pocket of my slacks.

I take it out because it might be my mom asking me to distinguish myself in a sea of people.

Except when I check the notifications, I see that it's a message from HEX.

The only time I've used the app in the last few months was to send Selena a message when my text and phone calls went unanswered.

Putting in my new password, one that nobody but me know, I tap on the notification.

It's a message from SENFULL94.

The way my heart beats uncontrollably when I read her username is compared to the way adrenaline pumps through my veins during a game.

I waste no time opening it.

SENFULL94: Don't respond, okay? Let me get everything out.

I nod even though she can't see it.

. . .

SENFULL94: I know we're in the middle of graduation, but if I don't do this now, I'm going to get scared and this message will forever be saved in my notes. I got your note. For two weeks it sat unopened because I was terrified to know what it said. For all I knew you were sending me flowers to further rub it in my face.

I close my eyes and take a deep breath. If I ever meet her cousins, the ones that touched her, I'm going to fucking kill them. The oldest one first. If it wasn't for him, Selena would see her worth and she would never doubt something as simple as a bouquet of flowers.

SENFULL94: A few weeks ago, I finally got the courage to open it and from the first words you wrote, you had me in tears. Some of them were good tears, and others were ones that I never want to cry again. Not only did I cry, I was also angry, but not at you. I was angry at her, but I was also angry at myself. Angry for believing her. For believing that you would actually do something like that when all you've shown me was love. And angry at my insecurities because once again, they made me run before I was able to listen.

. . .

She's blaming herself.

I want to type out that she had every right to run away and that she shouldn't be blaming herself. But she told me to let her speak and not respond, so that's what I continue to do.

SENFULL94: Because of the anger, I told myself that I was going to do something. I was going to fix myself before fixing anything else. Because if I don't do that, then my insecurities will always win. They will always have me running away and believing in something that isn't true. For years when it has come to my trauma, I've always pushed it aside and pretended it didn't exist. It does and I couldn't avoid it much longer.

There's a pause in the messages. It's short but it's enough for me to notice. Every ticking second has me on edge, wondering what she is going to say next.

SENFULL94: I told my parents about what happened to me. That was the first step. I did it while I held that 24th daisy. The next step was, is, getting professional help. I started seeing a therapist. One that has been helping me get out of my own head and out of the bubble I put

myself into sometimes. It's helped but I don't think that I will ever get over the insecurities that plague me.

The speaker on the stage says something that has the crowd laughing, but the only thing that I can concentrate on are the words on my screen.

There are so many things to digest from that one message. Selena conquered fear and told her parents something that I'm sure she would have taken to the grave. And she's getting help.

If you'd asked me, I would have told you that Selena Montez is perfect the way she is. We all have insecurities. But hers are stronger than others and her finding it helpful is all that matters.

SENFULL94: you may be wondering why I'm sending you all of this through HEX at our graduation.

I snort a bit, because I was wondering about that.

SENFULL94: Because this is where we started. It wasn't in anatomy class. It wasn't in the parking lot or at the beach, or in a field of daisies, it was here. We started here. And I want to say I'm

sorry. I'm sorry for believing Jenna. I'm sorry for shutting you out. I'm sorry for thinking that you would call me names and share my photos with your friends. I'm sorry for not believing in you and in what we were starting to build. But most of all I'm sorry for letting myself get in the way and for thinking I'm not worthy. I want to be worthy. I want to be worthy of everything that life throws my way, and that includes you. I want to be worthy of you. I love you, Hunter. I really do. And I hope as I fix myself, I am able to fix this too. If you still want me, that is, I understand if you don't. Sorry for the long message. That's all I wanted to say.

I read the last words and I start to type out a message. One telling her that I do still want her, but then I freeze.

Do I really want to say that through a message?

No. No, I don't.

So, I pocket my phone and I sit there, looking straight ahead, hoping to catch a glimpse of the cap with the twenty-four daisies adorning it.

———

It's when names start getting called and we are lining up to go on stage that I catch sight of the girl of my dreams.

For a quick second as she walks past me, her eyes turn to me. It's short, but in that short time, I'm able to see so much.

Joy, sadness and uncertainty. She doesn't give me a smile or a wave, just one quick look before she turns in the other direction and heads for the stage.

My row follows right after.

It takes forty minutes to get through all of the names and now it's time for the university president to call it and say we're officially Cal U graduates. The sooner he does that, the sooner I get to tell Selena what I wanted to type out, right to her face.

"And with that, students. Faculty. Family and friends." Just say the damn words already, it's not that fucking hard. "I would like to congratulate the class of 2022. You did it!"

Cheers erupt both in the student section and out in the stands. Graduation caps get thrown in the air and everyone is jumping up and down, shaking hands or hugging their friends.

I just want out of this section and to head straight to her.

It takes me ten minutes, ten minutes too fucking long, to get away from the throngs of students and teachers. Somehow I lost her when people were dispersing to get to their families. I should really go and find my own, but right now I only have one thing on my mind.

And the thing that's on my mind steps into my line of sight, heading straight to the end of the field.

I run.

I run through family and people hugging, all to get to her.

Once I'm within a few feet of her, I reach out and pull her in my direction.

Surprise coats her face when she sees it's me manhandling her. Selena opens her mouth to speak, but I stop her.

"I still want you."

I don't know how it was possible, but her eyes got bigger. "What?"

Closing the distance between us, I place a hand on her waist and lower my mouth to her ear. "I still want you. I will want you and everything that you come with. Because I love you."

Her breath hitches at my words and for a cool minute, she stands there not moving. When I think that she is going to step away from me, I feel her hand go around my waist and she comes closer to me, closing any distance that there is between us.

"Wherever you go?" she asks, taking me back to the first dinner at her parents' house when I asked her to follow me wherever football takes me.

"Wherever I go, I want you at my side. What do you say? Come with me?"

There is no hesitation in her next words. "Yes. I'll come with you. Wherever you land."

I smile at her words, then do what I've been dying to do for the last six weeks.

I kiss Lennie.

I kiss her with everything that I have and show her that she is worth it.

She is worth loving.

She is worth being with.

Selena Montez is worth every second of my life and I will spend forever showing her, just in case she forgets.

CHAPTER THIRTY-THREE

SELENA

I'VE NEVER BEEN EXCITED about football.

Put me in front of a baseball game, a hockey game and I will be solid. Hell, going to every single bookstore in the country three times over is more exciting than having to sit through a football game. You would think that having a football player boyfriend would change that, but it hasn't. Something that he pretends pisses him off.

What does excite me about the sport though, is this moment right now.

Currently we are at my parents' house sitting in the living room with the TV turned to ESPN, waiting for the draft to begin.

By we, I mean my parents, my sisters and their husbands and kids and myself are all glued to the TV.

My relationship with my family has been a little different since I told them what had happened to me when we would go to my abuela's house.

I first told my parents together. They had to be the first ones to hear the words. My mom knew something was wrong the second I walked into their room. She saw the tears in my eyes.

They asked me what was wrong and after five minutes of trying to find the words, I told them.

I told them what had happen to me during those three to four years.

They both cried.

They were mad, but not at me. They were mad that it had happened and angry at who did it to me.

The question came up about why I didn't tell them sooner and I told them. As it turns out, my dad's relationship with his sister has been strained for a while and this just sets it back even more.

I cried in my parents' arms that night and the next day, I cried in my sisters'.

Ever since, it feels as if they have a better understanding of why I act a certain way. One thing that hasn't changed is how much they love me.

Now here we sit all together; all ready for the big day.

Today is the day that we find out if the one Hunter Jacobi will be drafted by the NFL and if he does, where he will land.

Graduation happened a week ago, but sitting here now, it feels like it has been a lifetime since I walked across that stage and received my mock diploma and then was in Hunter's arms not thirty minutes later. It's mind blowing how slow these last couple of days went.

After Hunter and I kissed on the field, we separated and went to find our respective families. For the days after that, we spent as much time together as we could, talking, reconnecting, everything that we wanted. Then it came time for him to head to Las Vegas for the draft.

He wanted me to go with him, but I told him that I would wait for him at home. He ended up going with his mom and brother and sister and I know that made him happy. His dad was also going to be there too, but he didn't seem overly ecstatic about that one.

So because I wasn't going, I sent out a text to my sisters and brothers-in-laws asking if they wanted to watch the draft with me.

That one text turned into a million regarding the status of mine and Hunter's relationship. I gave them one answer and one answer only, we were together, and as of right now it was going to stay that way. They accepted it and started planning on spending draft day at my parents' house so we can watch what happens.

Now we are only minutes away from the first round starting and I'm pretty sure I'm not the only one in the room biting their nails.

"I say San Francisco," my brother-in-law Jonathan states.

I turn to face him, my eyebrows furled together. "You sound so confident."

"Duh, I've been following his draft journey since I met the guy." He gives me a headshake like it was obvious.

I just roll my eyes and get up from my seat to grab something from my room.

When I'm about to head back to the living room, my phone starts to vibrate in my back pocket.

Taking it out, I see it's a FaceTime call from Hunter. Shutting my bedroom door, I answer it.

"Shouldn't you be at your table already, waiting for the thing to start?" I say instead of a greeting.

From the looks of it, he's in a single stall bathroom.

"Maybe I just wanted to see your face before all the craziness starts up." He throws a smirk in my direction and even through a screen, I love seeing it.

"How are the nerves treating you?" I say, taking a seat on the corner of my bed.

Hunter lets out a sigh. "Is it bad that I just want this to be over? The constant thinking about my placing and which team might choose me is making me want to puke up my breakfast."

"I think that's normal. I'm sure that every guy there is feeling the same way."

He nods at my words and within seconds, the smirk is back. "You know what would make it a whole lot better?"

"What?" If I can help calm him down, I will.

"You sending me a titty or pussy shot. Better yet, you can send me a trifecta. Tits, pussy and that delectable booty of yours."

I roll my eyes at this request. "Nope, sorry."

"C'mon. It's my big day. Let me see what's waiting for me at home."

"You're going to be sitting next to your mom," I throw at him. I'm all for sending pictures, but time and place dude. Time and place.

The truth is, I haven't sent Hunter a picture of myself since before all the shit with Jenna happened. That doesn't mean that in the week since graduation that we haven't done anything. We added a full-on car fuck to the things-we-do-in-public-list we have going one. That was fun. I just haven't able to push aside the fact that someone else besides Hunter has seen me in my most revealing state.

"She's not going to know," Hunter says, throwing a wink at me. He's being pushy, I know that and knows it too by the way his smile falters. He's most likely pushing the subject because he's nervous about what is about to happen and this is his way of forgetting about that even if it's for a second.

Do I feel okay sending him another picture?

The only thing that is making my mind lean to yes, is the fact that Hunter keeps his phone extra protected now since the incident. New passwords and password protection everywhere.

I nod. "Just cleavage and nothing else," I bargain and thankfully he's giving me a nod back.

"I will take whatever you want to grace me with." He gives me a smile, one of understanding why I said what I said and can't help but send one back to him.

Quickly I leave the video call and snap a picture of before sending it off to him.

A few seconds later he gives me a bright smile as a thank you.

"Hey, Hunter?" I say, bringing the phone back to my face.

"Yeah, baby?"

My smile is big and for the first time in my life, I'm excited about football. "Go get drafted."

"I love you, Lennie."

"I love you too."

With that, we hang up the phone and I head back to the living room and take my seat again in front of the TV and wait.

For an hour, I sit there not taking my eyes or ears off of what is happening on the screen. I intently watch everything that is going on inside that ballroom in Vegas.

The second that the rep for San Francisco steps up to the podium, my back goes ramrod straight.

"This is it," Jonathan states and everyone in the room is in agreement. I stay silent.

This is it.

This is Hunter's big moment if what everyone is saying is correct. This could be the moment that he has worked all his life for. The first nine weren't for him, but this one has to be, I know it.

"With the tenth pick in the 2022 NFL draft, the San Francisco Gold selects Hunter Jacobi."

Excitement fills the room.

Pride fills my heart.

There are tears running down my face and a smile so big that it's hurting my cheeks.

He did it.

The arrogant, asshole jock that sat next to me and who has been showing me I'm worthy of love is one step closer to achieving his dream.

And if everything goes according to plan, I will be right next to him. Cheering him on, even if I don't know a thing about football.

But for him, I will.

EPILOGUE
HUNTER

THE GROUND under my feet vibrates like it hasn't before. In all of my life, I've only felt something like this once before, during the bowl game all those years ago.

Now, after so many years, I'm feeling it again, only this time, the feeling is beyond comprehension. What I felt at the bowl game was nothing compared to this. This is a different level, a different life, and I'm going to grab it for as long as I can, because who knows if I will ever feel it again.

You will.

Even in my mind, I'm a cocky bastard, but I'm not going to jinx anything, not even with my thoughts, not now.

Not when I'm playing the biggest game of my career. I will leave the cockiness for after the game and the clear winner is declared.

I look at the score hanging over the fans one more time. It was motivation and dedication that got us here.

Twenty-one games and now we are in one of the biggest sporting events in the country.

With forty seconds left on the clock, anything can

happen, the whole trajectory of the game could change. We have to stay focused so we can finish this game on top.

"Okay, listen up! We have forty seconds left. A lot can happen. We're ahead by three. Either we keep it that way or we add to it, there is no in-between. We run the play just like we did at practice. We know where their weaknesses are, so let's use them and get that fucking win. Understood?"

I look around at the men surrounding me. The men that in the last five years have become like a second family to me. Men that have my back and are gunning to win this title just as much as I am, if not more.

Head nods and grunts get thrown at me and soon we are breaking and retaking our positions on the field.

There's a silence right before I call the play. It's as if everyone in the stadium is holding their breaths, just waiting to see what happens next.

I start to count down in my head.

I call the play, everyone gets into position. The only sound I hear is my heart beating in my ears.

"Hike!" I say and within seconds, the ball is in my hands and the internal countdown continues.

One second, then two.

The offensive line is doing their job and my wide receivers are starting to get in position.

Five seconds.

My eyes search for the right target and once I find it, I swing my arm back and throw. The feel of the laces sliding against my fingers as it's released.

Fifteen seconds.

I watch as the ball is caught by the best wide receiver our team has.

Twenty seconds.

He grabs the ball and starts to run. I feel like no oxygen is going into my lungs as I watch him move. He dodges opponents and continues to run, the ball never leaving his grip.

Thirty seconds. I see it before I hear the crowd. He touches the end zone and the oxygen finally fills my lungs.

Celebration ensues, cheers fill the stadium. The clock continues to countdown.

Forty seconds and the whistle blows.

We did it. The San Francisco Gold just won their first Super Bowl in five years, and I was at the helm.

We're world fucking champions.

The number of bodies on the field doubles and soon I'm getting hugged and pulled by random people and getting hats and shirts thrown at me. Sports reporters pop out of nowhere and stuff a mic in my face.

All the questions are the same. How do I feel? What do I think about the play during the third that put us in the lead? And what am I going to do now that the season is over?

That last question brings a smile to my face. I give each reporter a generic answer because what I really want to do is standing a few feet away from me wearing my jersey with my name on her back.

Her smile is big and contagious, and even from where I'm standing, I can feel her excitement.

Never has a sight looked so damn good.

"Well, Hunter, that was an amazing game and a title well earned. Congratulations," the reporter, whose name I forgot, says.

"Thank you," I say, looking for the beauty making her way to me.

Within seconds, she's in my arms and this win feels ten times better.

"I'm so fucking proud of you." Selena's voice is like music to my ears and the second her feet land back on the ground, my lips find hers.

Even though I still have my pads on, I bring her as close to me as I possibly can.

It's been four years since we've graduated from Cal U, four years since I got drafted.

Selena and I have been through a lot these last couple of years. Everything from living separate lives while I was in San Francisco and she was in Seaside, to finally moving in together last year.

For the last few years, she's been working at a psychiatric clinic that specializes in sports psychology for young kids. Lennie loved every second of it but when the opportunity came to start a sports psychology graduate program at Berkeley, she took it and transferred to the San Francisco Clinic. So we moved in together.

She's still working on herself and her insecurities, but I'm there to help her every step of the way. I always try to remind her that she is the most gorgeous woman I have ever laid eyes on and that her body is something to drool over, not hide. Though I'm happy to say that her body is for me and me only.

As for me, I'm living my best life with my girl and my sport. I see my mom and siblings at least once a month and as for my dad, his obsession with having a star athlete for a child has gotten even more crazy. Blake just got drafted to play hockey for the Chicago Dark Knights and Dad is loving every single minute of it. My brother though, not so much. If he could live without our dad's interference, he would.

Putting thoughts of my brother and father out of my head, I concentrate on the woman that's currently in my arms.

"I love you," I say against her lips, holding on to her body tightly.

"I love you too." One more kiss comes my way before she pulls away a big grin taking over her whole face. "Baby, you just won the Super Bowl!"

I love that even though she doesn't care about the sport, she's still my biggest supporter.

"I know." I slide my arm around her waist and lift her up so that we are eye to eye. "And you know what I want to do?"

"What?" It's a simple word but it still sounds breathless.

"First, I want to fuck this body of yours until I get rid of all the adrenaline that is flowing through mine."

Her grin turns into a smirk. "I think that I can arrange that. Is there a second thing?"

"Yeah, there is." I lean my forehead against hers and take in the cucumber and mint scent I love so much.

"Oh, yeah? What is it?"

I place her on the ground yet again and reach for the box that was conspicuously handed to me during my first interview after the win.

As I pull it out, I hear Selena gasp and the gasps ring around us as I get down on one knee.

Opening the box, I look up to face Selena and see that she has tears in her eyes. A little ways behind her, I see her family and mine, standing by and watching it all go down.

"What are you doing?" Selena says through the shock.

I ignore her question. "Len, I knew you were my dream woman even before I saw your face, or even knew who you were. Then I got to know you and that was just confirmation of what I already knew. From early on, I knew I wanted to spend the rest of my life with you. That I wanted to kiss you every morning and night and be there when things got tough. I knew that no matter what you were going through, I wanted to be there for you. And I know now that I want to do that forever. Selena Montez, Lennie, will you marry me and make this Super Bowl win a whole lot better?"

Selena looks down at me, with a hand over her mouth and tears in her eyes.

Those better be happy tears, because no way am I getting rejected for millions of people to see.

I watch as she drops her hand and then drops to her knees in front of me and takes my face between her hands.

"Yes."

"Yes?"

Selena nods. "Yes, Hunter Jacobi. I will marry you."

Our lips meet and soon there are people cheering all around us and we are on the grass not having a care in the world.

She said yes.

Lennie said yes.

Len is going to marry Chase. The woman that commented on my nude picture, telling me that she has seen better, is going to marry me.

Never in my wildest dreams did I think that when I replied to that comment that I would be here. With my perfect woman in my arms. Forever.

Fuck, she's going to be mine forever.

And to the fuckers that said that a guy like me would never go for a girl like Selena, they are fucking dipshits.

This woman deserves to be cherished and is worthy of everything she ever wishes.

And I'm going to spend the rest of my life doing just that.

Because she is fucking worth it and more.

THE END.

WANT TO READ MORE OF HUNTER AND SELENA? DO NOT WORRY, THIS ISN'T THE LAST WE SEE OF THEM.

PLAYLIST

MAKE UP SEX BY SoMo
SATURDAY BY JAIME LORENTE
TE DESEO LO MEJOR BY BAD BUNNY
MUJERIEGIO BY RYAN CASTRO
PUT YOUR HEAD ON MY SHOULDER BY
PAUL ANKA
AMOR PROHIBIDO BY SELENA
MAL DE AMORES BY SOFIA REYES, BECKY G
CALL ME LOVER BY SAM FENDER
I AM WOMAN BY EMMY MELI
HAPPIER THAN EVER BY BILLIE EILLISH
MAKE ME WANNA BY BABEHEAVEN, NAVY BLUE
MY LOVE - MAYE
FUE MEJOR BY KALI UCHIS, SZA
CLOUD 9 BY PATY B

ACKNOWLEDGMENTS

Hunter and Selena are finally out in the world. Never did I think that the day would come when I would be able to say those words.

Originally, these two were supposed to see the world in 2021 but things happened and I pushed it back. I had the cover, I had the pre-order up and I canceled it and moved everything to this year. And I'm glad that I did. Their story needed time to come to life and come to life it did.

The idea for this story came about two years ago, when I was exploring a side of the internet that I didn't know existed. At first it was supposed to be a whole different story, but of course like every other one of my books that didn't happen.

This story was an unexpected one but I love everything about it. It was fun and heartbreaking all at the same time. There are aspects of this story that connect to me, like the family importance to Selena, the city that Cal U is located in. There is in fact a Seaside, California, I just took fictional liberties with it.

This story deals with some very heavy elements and I really hope that I did it justice. It was hard writing something so tragic but I wanted it to be real and have Selena be a character that you root for.

Like I said on the last page, this isn't the last time you see these two. They will be back.

Now to the thank yous.

To Shanoff Desings, thank you for making this amazing pre-made, I absolutely loved it the first time I saw it and love it even more now.

To Books and Moods PR, thank you for the beautifully done alternative cover. It was a one-shot thing and I love it!

To Ellie, thank you for not firing me when I told you to and for helping me with this manuscript even when it included the word waffle in a nonsense place.

To Rosa, for proofreading and catching the small mistakes that I didn't notice the five time I read it through.

To Shauna and the Wildfire team, for helping promote this book and for all the hard work that you do.

And lastly to the readers, thank you for continuing to take a chance on my words. Its your support that keeps me going and I don't know where I would be without your kind words, your excitement and your amazing posts. You all truly mean a lot to me.

Thank you all for your love and support and now we move to the next one!

BOOKS BY JOCELYNE SOTO

One Series

One Life

One Love

One Day

One Chance

One for Me

One Marriage

Flor De Muertos Series

Vicious Union

Violent Attraction

Vindictive Blood

Standalones

Beautifully Broken

Worth Every Second

Powerful Deception

Fake Love

Salutis Meae

ABOUT THE AUTHOR

Jocelyne Soto is a writer born and raised in California. She started her writing journey in 2015 and in 2019, she published her first book. She is an independent author who loves discovering new authors on Goodreads and Amazon. She comes from a big Mexican family, and with it comes a love for all things family and food.

Jocelyne has a love for her mom's coffee and writing. In her free time, she can be found reading a romance novel off her iPad or somewhere in the black hole of YouTube.

Follow her website and on social media!
www.jocelynesoto.com

JOIN MY READER GROUP

Join my ever-growing Facebook Group.

https://www.facebook.com/groups/jocelynesotobooks

NEWSLETTER

Sign up for my newsletter!
You will get notified when there are new
releases to look out for, giveaways and more!

https://www.
subscribepage.com/authorjocelynesotonewsletter

Printed in Great Britain
by Amazon

28347103R00202